"NORIE, I HAVE NEVER BEEN SO HAPPY TO SEE A PERSON!"

It was Deborah, coming to a skid at my elbow, blueberry eyes popping with terror. You would have thought we were about to be attacked by aliens.

"We are in a world of hurt!" she said.

"I know. Pavella found me. He's looking for you."

"It isn't going to do him any good to find me. I don't have the key!"

I looked at her sharply. "Why not?"

"Because I didn't find out until the end of first period. I didn't have time to get it."

"Bummer," I said dryly. I was actually relieved. At least now I didn't have to make a decision. My father's little edict the night before would have made it pretty hard to turn down a free answer key. I was ashamed to admit it to myself, but it was the truth.

"It doesn't have to be a bummer," Deborah said.

She was leaning in close and speaking in a murmur out of the side of her mouth. I didn't look at her.

"What do you mean?" I said.

"You could help."

"I haven't even said I was in on this," I said. My palms started to sweat.

Dear Parent,

Thank you for considering Nancy Rue's book for your teen. We are pleased to publish her *Raise the Flag* series and believe these books are different than most you will find for teens.

Tragically, some of the things our teens face today are not easy to discuss. Nancy has created stories and characters that depict real kids, facing real-life issues with real faith. Our desire is to help you equip your children to act in a God-pleasing way no matter what they face.

Nancy has beautifully woven scriptural truth and direction into the choices and actions of her characters. She has worked hard to depict the issues in a sensitive way. However, I would recommend that you scan the book to determine if the subject matter is appropriate for your teen.

Sincerely,

Dan Rich
Publisher

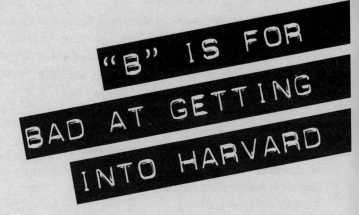

Nancy Rue

WaterBrook
PRESS
Colorado Springs

Y
F
Rue

"B" Is For Bad At Getting Into Harvard
PUBLISHED BY WATERBROOK PRESS
5446 North Academy Boulevard, Suite 200,
Colorado Springs, Colorado 80918
A division of Random House, Inc.

The characters and events in this book are fictional, and
any resemblance to actual persons or events is coincidental.

Scriptures are taken from
The Holy Bible, New International Version (NIV)
© 1973, 1978, 1984 by International Bible Society,
used by permission of Zondervan Publishing House.

ISBN 1-57856-033-0

Copyright © 1998 by Nancy Rue

Published in association with the literary agency of
Alive Communications, Inc., 1465 Kelly Johnson Blvd.
Suite 320, Colorado Springs, Colorado 80920.
All rights reserved. No part of this book may be reproduced
or transmitted in any form or by any means, electronic
or mechanical, including photocopying, recording,
or by any information storage and retrieval system,
without permission in writing from the publisher.

Printed in the United States of America
1999—First Edition

3 5 7 9 10 8 6 4 2

*For Saralinda Seibert Kiser,
a sister in growing and believing*

PROLOGUE

"WAIT, YOU GUYS!" CHEYENNE CAME HAULING TOWARD us across the school theater lobby, hair straggling out in all directions, voice shrieking.

"Stop making a spectacle of yourself, Cheyenne," I said. "Just sit down, shut up, and start praying."

She did the first one, but, of course, she didn't shut up. She never shut up, which was one of the things I really loved about the kid.

"Hi, Norie," she said to me, and then started around the circle. "Hi, Tobey, hi, Marissa, hi, Shannon—"

"Girl," Brianna said, "there is no need to give each of us an individual greeting. One 'hi' oughta do it."

But Cheyenne kept grinning with those wonderful, big lips that everybody was craving. I'd seen girls actually coloring in bigger lips on themselves in the bathrooms. I didn't even bother to put lipstick on the lips I did have. When Cheyenne grew into hers, she was going to be a knockout. Right now she was a freshman—need I say more?—and at five-foot-five she still only tipped the scales at about ninety pounds. The long, straggly dark hair could use some work. Even I could see that. But she was our baby so who was worried about it?

"What are we praying for?" she said.

"Nothing yet," Tobey said. "Not until I eat some of my lunch. I'm starving."

"You look like you never eat a thing," Shannon said.

Tobey dipped her chin at Shannon. "You should talk, honey. Gandhi eats more than you do."

They both looked like they had just been released from Dachau as far as I was concerned, but then I'm the boxy type—cubish face, square chin, stocky body with angles instead of curves. I always figured, Why fight it? So I had a short, boxy haircut to go with the rest of me.

I had Shannon pegged for an anorexic anyway. Of course, maybe that was because with the ivory skin, the corn-silky hair to her shoulders, the blue eyes a shade paler than a pair of robin's eggs, she looked translucent in every department.

Not so Tobey. She was like this golden girl: strawberry blonde hair; high, shiny forehead; signature combat boots with her willowy outfit.

"But what are we praying for once we finish lunch?" Cheyenne said, stuffing a cheese sandwich into her mouth with, honestly, two hands.

We all looked at each other. Brianna started to grin.

"You called the meeting," Tobey said to her. "Do you need prayer?"

Brianna tossed her head, although nothing on it moved. She wore her velvety brown frizz cut as close to her head as she could get it, and she pulled it off. You can only do that when you have enormous golden eyes like hers and an interesting nose and a mouth that neither gives nor takes any stuff off of any-body. All of that on an oval face. She could have shaved her head completely and out-Whitneyed Whitney Houston.

"I don't need prayer," Brianna said. "I just wanted an excuse to see you all."

"You are psycho," Tobey said, grinning back at her. "You made it sound like there was this big emergency or something."

"We need the world to be comin' to an end 'fore we have lunch together?" Brianna said. She gave her head that jerk that only she and her Afro-American sisters can do and really make it work. I loved it when she did that. I tried it once and nearly had to go see a chiropractor.

"I love it that you called a meeting," a soft voice said.

We all looked at Marissa Martinez. And she actually looked back. There was a time when she had seemed afraid of all of us—especially me, which is understandable since I tend to come on a little strong. She was another drop-dead gorgeous thing. Hispanic. Dark, thick hair, sort of chopped off at the chin as if to say, I can cut my hair with the gardening shears, and I still look like something off the cover of *YM*. Her skin was the color of a latte—I should know since I'm a coffee fiend—and when she finally did get around to looking up, all you could see were these fudge-colored eyes in perfect ovals.

Except for me, you would have thought looks were a requirement for being a Flagpole Girl.

"All I want to know," Brianna was saying, "is what's goin' down with you all. I just want to keep tabs, you know?"

"Life is cool," Tobey said immediately.

"Of course you'd say that," I told her. "When you go through the principal and seven-eighths of the student body condemning you, everything else looks like heaven."

"True," Tobey answered, unruffled by the reminder of what we called her "fight for right" after she discovered someone was being sexually abused.

"I'm okay, too," Marissa said. She gave an exaggerated sigh. "I don't have a date for this weekend, but I'm all right."

"You want a date, honey?" Brianna said. "I'll fix you up."

"No, thanks," Marissa said. Then she got all red and started to fan her face like if she had a date, she would be too embarrassed to even go on it.

"Man, if that were my worst problem," I said, "I'd be kissing the ground."

"You have a date for this weekend?" Cheyenne asked.

"No," I said. "But I don't expect to. I never even think about it."

"So what's your worst problem, Nor?" Tobey said. She crossed her legs Indian style and rested her elbows on her knees. She was all into it.

I wasn't. If there were any group I could have told it to, this was the one. Group of for-real Christians, actually living their faith like it meant something. Not just going to Sunday school and preaching to everybody and then going out and partying on Saturday night like youth exempted them from morality or something.

Actually, that was the reason I couldn't tell them what was duking it out inside me. They had it all together spiritually. After two whole months of hanging together—practically since See You at the Pole in September—they would probably expect me to be way beyond where I was. And I was just competitive enough not to let them know I wasn't. What was I supposed to say: Guys, I want prayer because, even after all we've been through together, especially with Tobey, I still basically feel like a cold, empty shell?

Sure, in those two months I'd done things, said things, and started to believe things I'd never thought would even drive by Norie Vandenberger's life much less come in and park there. But it had all come through Tobey, Marissa, Cheyenne, Shannon, and Brianna. How come it wasn't coming through me?

I felt a nudge in my side. "Are you going to sit there and daydream?" Tobey said. "Or are you going to tell us what your biggest problem is?"

"I hate chemistry," I said. It was the truth. Just not the whole truth.

"So drop," Brianna said. She snapped her fingers. "Next?"

"I hate school, period," Cheyenne said. "Except hanging out with you guys, of course."

"Of course," Tobey said. She stretched out to her full five-foot-ten length and flashed that incredible smile at Shannon. "What about you, Shan? You need any prayer?"

Shannon suddenly looked as if we had called her in from the back forty acres. She blinked at us for a minute and then said, "I'm okay."

"Liar," Brianna said.

Shannon's cheeks pinked, and she shrugged.

"I'm sorry," Brianna said. "I guess I thought we could just dump it all out here, when it's us."

"We can," Shannon said. She gave a flustered sigh. "I just can't talk about it. My parents . . . you know, it's a family thing."

"I hate parents, too," Cheyenne said. "Except for Tassie. She is so cool."

"So you've told us," Tobey said. She squeezed Cheyenne's leg. "Brianna?" she said.

"I'm still fightin' the racial thing," she said. "Do you know I can't walk down the hall without some white boy sayin' somethin' rude to me? If one more dude asks me if it would taste like chocolate if he kissed me, I might have to make it so he'll never kiss again."

"A guy who says something that hateful has probably never kissed," I said. "Jackals."

"Do we need a Plan of Action?" Tobey asked, sitting up straight.

But Brianna shook her head. "I have it handled so far. You all prayin', that helps a lot. I don't feel like a minority when I'm sittin' here."

"Well," I said, eyeing the two taggers who were wandering through the lobby in their eight-sizes-too-big jeans and giving us the there-are-the-Jesus-freaks looks, "when you think about it, we are a minority. What are we, six girls out of fourteen hundred students who showed up at the flagpole?"

"Ooh, but we make a big noise when we need to, don't we?" Tobey said. Her eyes were sparkling.

I wished mine would. Being around them, most of them so happy or at least together, made me feel emptier than ever. Maybe if I could just spill it to them—

"So let's pray," Cheyenne said, "before we run out of time."

So we did, circling up like usual and holding hands and putting it out there. I was right in there, except for my own stuff. That I kind of murmured in the depths of my mind. I was jolted by the bell ringing, which irritated the hackles right up on my neck.

"It's so absurd that they make that bell sound like a signal in a department store," I said.

"Why is that absurd?" Brianna asked.

"They're trying to make it palatable," I said. "But they might as well give it up. It's still a school!"

They all laughed as we straggled off to our fifth-period classes. A little jabbing like that usually made me feel better, but not now. The whole thing—the whole where-is-God-in-my-life thing—was dragging at me like a bad dream you can't forget.

I guess it was amazing that I was even thinking about it, to tell you the truth. And even more amazing that I ended up a Flagpole Girl.

I was about the last person anybody would have expected to show up at a religious gathering. The last person other than some tagger out there spray-painting the city, that is, or one of those girls in the French-cut leotards running cocktails in a Reno casino.

I would at least have been on most people's list of those least likely to convene at the school flagpole before school to *pray* of all things. Anybody at King High School who knew me would probably testify that I might appear at 7:00 A.M. for a conference on feminism or congregate at any hour for a chance at a hot story for the *King's Herald,* the school newspaper for which I was coeditor.

But get out of bed to pray? Not. I'd have paid somebody to go to church in my place so I could sleep in. I had a better grip on the twenty-six amendments to the Constitution than I did on the Ten Commandments.

But the reason was simple: I'd prayed for something, and I got it. First time I ever prayed in my whole life, that August, and bingo, I got it. I saw a flier that said Christian kids all over America were going to gather at their respective school flagpoles on a given date and pray for whatever needed to be prayed for. I had the feeling this was the kind of group I needed so I put on my T-shirt that said "God loves you—why not return the favor?" that Angel Boy gave me, and I showed up.

The result? I'd gone to church all my life—the most prestigious church in Reno, mind you—with my parents on the Sundays they didn't decide to sleep in. But being with those girls for two months had turned out to do more for me spiritually than a whole lifetime of sermons and communion.

Okay, okay, so I've made progress, I said to myself as I spun the lock on my locker. *But I still feel like I'm drowning, like I'm reaching for something to hold on to—*

I shook that thought off. *Let's not go there right now, Vandenberger. Let's not go there.*

But as it turned out, there was nowhere else to go.

CHAPTER ONE

"SO, I MEAN, WHY CAN'T WE DO A FEATURE ON, LIKE, how to be a babe magnet? I have some great material for it, like when I went up to Seattle to see my sister. Every time I took my niece to the park it was like, chicks flocking to me. Girls love babies, right? So—"

"Pavella," I said, "you are so clueless it's embarrassing, okay? Anybody else have any ideas?"

Jerry Pavella gaped at me out of his very cute but completely unintelligent blue eyes and let his lower lip go slack like he was short several chromosomes. How the guy stayed on the honor roll was always beyond me.

"What was wrong with that idea?" he said.

"Don't get her started," Deborah Zorn said. "You start talking about how to snag chicks and you're asking for an 'Exploitation of Women' lecture, all right?" She shook her long hair the color of acorns back over her bony shoulders. "I say we go with 'What Are You Thankful For?' This issue comes out right before Thanksgiving."

That's original, I thought.

Next to her, Mark Chester rolled his eyes.

"What?" she said, her own eyes popping at him. They always reminded me of blueberries, those eyes. They gave her this wholesome farmgirl look, although I was sure Deb had never gotten within a hundred yards of a cow.

"If you want to go around asking people what they're grateful for, go ahead," Mark said. "I'm not doing it."

Deborah slid down on her tailbone and crossed her long, lanky arms over her chest. "You come up with something then, Clark Kent. I'm tired of throwing out ideas so you all can use them for target practice. Every time we have one of these meetings, it's like, 'All right, guys, break out the hunting rifles. Deborah's got some clay pigeons for us.'"

"Okay, who has another thought?" I said quickly. Once Deborah got on a roll, it was hard to stop her. And the way her voice went up at the end of every thought jangled my nerves after about two and a half thoughts.

"What about a survey on what people actually do during that moment of silence we're supposed to observe after the pledge every morning?"

I looked at the kid who had just given the only decent input we had had in half an hour. Wyatt Fox was his name. New this semester, and until now pretty quiet.

"I like that," I said.

"You're going to get lame answers," Mark said, giving the customary eye roll. "I can just hear it: 'I pick out my navel lint.' 'I fantasize about the babe at the next desk.' 'I scratch my—'"

"Must you reduce everything to something vile?" Deborah said.

"No, that's Pavella who does that," Mark said.

"What do I do?" Pavella said.

"Tell me some more, Wyatt," I gave them all my best syringe-poised-above-the-vein look, and the sparring faded to an out-of-the-side-of-the-mouth muttering.

Wyatt adjusted his glasses. "I've been looking around during that time," he said.

"Oh," Mark said, "now we know what you do during the moment of silence!"

"Bag it, Mark." I nodded to Wyatt.

"And I've just noticed all the different stuff that goes on."

"Like what?" Pavella grinned stupidly at Mark. "Guys scratching their—"

"Like some people staring out the window, some people actually closing their eyes, some people messing around."

"So what's to survey?" Mark said. "You already have your answers." He slanted back in the chair and ran a hand over his basically shaved head as if he had just settled the whole thing.

I watched Wyatt. He gave a light shrug and looked back at me. I mean, really looked at me. Not like Pavella who always checked to see if I'd grown a bigger chest during the night. Not like Mark who usually rolled his eyes and then looked at the ceiling like he was hoping I'd disappear. Wyatt connected his twinkly blue eyes with mine. Then he just grinned. He didn't toss his ponytail, which was sandy brown and shiny, I noted. He didn't look smug or try to check me out. He just grinned. It was a very cool moment, filled with intelligence.

"I think we should go with Wyatt's idea," I said.

"Man," Pavella whined, "first idea he has, and you're all over it."

"You come up with something that doesn't reek of female exploitation, and I'll be all over it, too," I said.

"Told you," Deborah said to him.

"Don't you need to check it out with Rhonda?" Mark said. "She's your coeditor."

"Is she, Mark?" I said. "Why am I always the last to know these things?"

He wanted to call me something foul, I know. Only because our adviser, Mrs. Abbey, came out of her office did he refrain. I don't think she would have heard him though. Her recently permed reddish hair spazzing out and her eyes blinking behind her contacts told me she was in another world that had nothing to do with ours. Probably something to do with money. When you put out two issues of a high school paper a month, you're always worrying about money.

"How's it going, gang?" she said.

"Great," I said. "We just came up with our last column." I looked significantly at Mark. "And as soon as I check it out with Rhonda, we'll be done."

"Where did you say Rhonda was?" Mrs. Abbey said vaguely.

"She had a mandatory band rehearsal," I told her for the third time.

Mrs. Abbey started to blink even faster. Her eye movements were always directly proportional to the amount of stress she was under. "She's overcommitted," she said.

"Who isn't?" I said. I didn't add, "You included."

Mrs. Abbey was sharp, but they had her doing so many things at King, some days she didn't stop batting her eyes from the minute she walked in the door.

"This place is like a smorgasbord," she said. "There are so many wonderful opportunities for you kids to choose from, you all end up stuffing yourselves."

"Then I'm about to throw up," I said. "I have Academic Olympics tonight plus a ton of homework. I'm glad I got that English sheet done, or I'd be totally stressing."

"What English sheet?" Deborah said. She sat up straight in the chair and grabbed the back of her hair with both hands—big stress sign for Deborah. "Do we have an English sheet due to-morrow?" she said.

Mark hummed the theme from *The Twilight Zone*. Pavella joined him on backup.

"I hate to run you off, gang," Mrs. Abbey said, "but if you're finished, I need to get out of here. I have a meeting tonight, and if I don't make it to the grocery store sometime soon, my kids are going to call the authorities and tell them I'm starving them to death."

"Is this the future we have to look forward to?" Mark said, making no move to gather his stuff together.

"Future?" I said. "It's the present for me. If I had a minute to breathe, I'd probably use it to kiss the ground."

Pavella snickered. "That'll be the only thing she'll ever get to kiss," I heard him mutter to Mark.

I blew it off. Guys are always making comments like that about me. "It's not your looks," my friend Lance once told me. "I mean, you're not drop-dead gorgeous, but you aren't a dog. It's just the women's lib thing. They're afraid if they touch you, you'll slug them."

"I probably would," I told him.

So, aware that Mark and Pavella were doing a whole under-their-breath routine about my lack of make-out potential, I blithely stuffed my notebook in my backpack.

"Norie," a voice whispered above me.

It was Deborah, white-faced, with eyes bulging. She squatted down beside me.

"Can I borrow your English sheet?" she hissed. "I totally forgot about it, and there's no way I'll get it done by tomorrow. I haven't even written up my chem lab or started my book review for history."

I hesitated, hand curled around the strap of my backpack.

This was a common occurrence among the overachievers at King High. None of us could do everything that was expected of its brightest and best. Not a day went by that somebody wasn't bumming a solution to a trig problem or borrowing the notes they didn't take during history class because they were cramming for their French test. I was right in there with them, scrambling to get the A's they were always telling us we had to earn to be worthwhile human beings—or at least to be better than each other.

But it had been a while since anybody had out and out asked me if they could copy a whole assignment. And it had been a while since I'd done stuff like that without giving it half a thought. At least since the Flagpole Girls.

"It's not like I've just been sitting around doing my nails and talking on the phone," Deborah assured me in a desperate whisper. "I practically built the entire junior float for Homecoming by myself, and we just had that huge debate tournament in Sparks—"

"Tell me about it," I said. "I'm totally overwhelmed."

She nodded gratefully and then looked from my backpack to me and back again.

"So, can I borrow it?" she said.

"I can't give it to you, Deb," I said. "I don't have it with me."

Her face sagged like I'd told her she had only two months to live. I think that would have been better news.

"Get it from Mark," I said. "Or Pavella."

"I want a good grade," she said. "I can count on about an A– from either one of them."

"Sorry," I said.

And then her blueberry eyes lit up. "Can I get it from you at the Olympics practice tonight? We're meeting at your house, right?"

Curses. Foiled again. Trying to do the right thing wasn't as easy as they told you in those Christian magazines Tobey had been lending me.

"Remind me," I said.

I watched her hurry out and slung my backpack up over my shoulder—with the finished English sheet tucked safely inside.

It was all I could think about as I went to my locker and headed for the Jeep. Why had I done that? And what was it that bugged me more: that I hadn't wanted to let Deborah cheat off me like I'd probably done a thousand times before, or that I hadn't told her the truth?

Sometimes things were a lot simpler when I didn't have a conscience, I mused as I dumped the offending backpack into the backseat of the Wrangler.

If it hadn't been for what happened at camp last summer—and then meeting the whole Flagpole crowd—I probably wouldn't have this problem.

What problem, Bovine Brain? I asked myself as I pulled out of the parking lot and headed down King Drive. *You don't cheat anymore. It's wrong, period. That doesn't constitute a problem.*

Clear as that sounded, my head was still as murky as the gray November sky that was already gathering into darkness over the mountains. If we didn't hedge here and there, we National-Honor-Society types who were headed for success in the dog-eat-dog world the administration was always warning us about, how were we supposed to beat each other to the early acceptances at the Ivy League schools, and the scholarships, and the valedictorian position?

This is sick, I thought as I turned onto Roberts Street. I was grateful for the distraction of a kid striding jauntily down the sidewalk on my right.

I like the way that guy walks, I thought as I passed him and checked him out in my rearview mirror. Then I realized with a start that it was Wyatt Fox.

I pulled over at the next side street and blew my horn. He broke into a trot and leaned into the window I unzipped for him.

"Need a ride?" I said.

"I don't mind walking," he said.

"You're nuts," I said. "Get in. It's cold out there."

He grinned and slid into the passenger seat of Iggy. I'd recently named him that because Tobey had told me all cars had to have names. We decided since the Jeep was green and I was kind of don't-touch-me like an iguana, that fit. Iggy was his nickname.

"Nice vehicle," he said as I pulled back out into traffic.

"My father wouldn't let me be seen in something that didn't look like it cost him at least the price of a double bypass."

"You lost me," Wyatt said.

"He's a thoracic surgeon."

"I'm impressed," he said.

I was a little disappointed. I was working on not being impressed by things like money and prestige.

"Do you drive?" I said.

"I have my license, if that's what you mean. My mother wouldn't let me be seen in something I didn't pay for myself." He grinned again, that smile I liked. I noticed at the same time the little wisps of hair that curled out around his forehead. He probably hated them. I thought they were kind of charming.

"So where do you live, Caughlin Ranch or something?" he said.

Ooh, bingo—right on the nose. It was hard to get away from money and prestige when you lived in a section of town where houses reeked of CEOs and orthodontists.

"Yes," I said. "Do you have a problem with that?"

"No," he said. "Do you?"

"Only when I tell people that and they say, 'Ooh, your old man must be rich!' And then start wondering why I dress like a bag lady."

"I don't think you got those Doc Martens out of somebody's trash."

He was still grinning. I grinned back.

"So are you going to tell me where you live, or do I have to guess from the brand of tennis shoes you're wearing?" I said.

"Give it a guess," he said.

I glanced at his feet. "Reebok Cross Trainers. Foothills?"

"Nah. Got 'em on sale. Condos off of Seventh Street."

"I love those!" I said. "I had a friend in middle school who lived there. We used to swim in the pool at the end of that one street."

"Great," he said. "I was afraid you wouldn't want to be seen with me if I wasn't at least homeless."

"Stop," I said. "I'm just trying to get away from the whole you're-so-rich-you've-got-it-made thing."

"My impression of you hasn't been the little princess," he said. "I mean, for what it's worth."

I cut a glance at him as we took the corner onto Seventh Street. "What has your impression been?" I said.

I caught a glimpse of his little blue eyes sparkling behind his glasses. "That you weren't the type to care what anybody's impression was," he said.

I snorted. "Touché. So you got me—what was it?"

He took a minute to think about that, which was a new experience for me. Most of my friends pride themselves on always having the next glib, ironically twisted retort right on their tongues. They fall all over each other trying to be the first one to get it out.

"It's changed since I first moved here in October," he said finally. "You were a lot more driven then, I thought. It was like, don't get in her way when she wants something, or you'll end up with her tire treads on your back. Maybe it's just because I didn't know you before, but it seems like you've done this metamorphosis since then."

There was a time when I would have said, *Wow, a guy who uses five-syllable words. What a concept.* But I didn't want to interrupt him. I was entranced.

"From what to what?" I said.

"You want me to be blunt, or should I coat it a little?"

"Be blunt."

"From dragon lady to human being."

I caught my own expression in the rearview mirror. There is no other word for it—I looked astonished.

"Give me an example," I said.

"That's easy," Wyatt said. "Just today, when Deborah asked you if she could borrow your homework to copy and you told her you didn't have it."

"Who are you, Ethan Hawke? You were spying on us?"

"I usually know what's going on," he said.

"So why is that an example?"

He gave that light shrug. I had it pegged now as "This is what I think, but let's not make a federal case out of it." I wondered what gesture he used when he did want to make an issue out of something.

"I think back in October you would either have said, 'You can use it, but what's in it for me?' or you'd have said, 'Who am I, your mother? Do your own homework!'" He pointed to a street for me to turn. "Today, you just kind of wiggled out of it so you didn't have to make her feel like a reject."

"What makes you think I wiggled out of it?" I said. "What if that was the truth: I didn't have it with me."

"Was it?" he said.

I don't know why, but I had to say it. "No." I said.

"So you've changed, am I right?"

He gave a poke toward a driveway, and I pulled in. "How did you know I was lying to her?" I said.

"The look on your face," Wyatt said. "I bet you stink at poker."

"Seriously?" I said. This was blowing me away. When we had read the story "The Great Stone Face" in seventh grade, everybody in my English class had decided it was about me.

"Besides," Wyatt said as he extricated his backpack from the floor of the Jeep, "Deborah said you were lying. At least that's what I heard her tell Jerry and Mark in the hall. She said you're so competitive you won't even help anybody else." He shook his head. "I don't buy that part."

"Oh, I'm competitive," I said. "It's probably a good thing I don't do sports, or I'd be in a body cast most of the time. But that's not why I didn't want to loan Deborah my homework."

I looked at him. He was looking me full in the face again, and when our eyes connected, he didn't grin. He smiled. It was softer.

"I knew that," he said. "Thanks for the ride. You want gas money?"

"No!" I said.

"Okay, then I'll buy you lunch or something."

It wasn't a question; it was a statement. At the end of it he snapped the Jeep door shut and jauntily walked toward his front door. I found myself describing his walk in my head all the way home.

CHAPTER TWO

WYATT AND HIS WALK WERE ELBOWED OUT OF MY brain, however, when I got home. A caterer's truck was pulling out of the driveway as I pulled in, and my mind started to pulsate with evil thoughts. About my mother.

"Mo-om!" I yelled before I was even out of the laundry room that separated the garage from the rest of Pretentious Estate. That's what I called our four-thousand-square-foot house when I vented about it in my head. "Why was a caterer's truck here?"

My mother answered something, but the kitchen was about a half-mile away.

"It isn't for tonight, is it?" I said.

"Yes," I heard her say. "You kids have to have something to eat. Teenagers are always hungry."

I groaned as I dumped my backpack inside my room and went for the kitchen. "Why did you have to have it catered?" I said. "Why couldn't you just open a couple of bags of chips and a jar of salsa?"

She looked up from the assortment of trays that smothered the kitchen counters. "You don't think they'll like cold cuts and cheese?"

If it had been just bologna and Velveeta, that would have been one thing. But we were talking the best cuts of meat and gourmet cheeses with unpronounceable names. Not to mention four kinds of salad, five-grain breads, and enough made-with-Ghirardelli-chocolate brownies to feed a large Somalian family for a year.

"Mom, this is out of control," I said.

"Why?" She lifted a cover off yet another tray, this one glistening with organically grown grapes in every color. They were as shiny and perfect as my mother's nails and rings. The whole thing was blinding.

"Because it looks as if we're trying to impress somebody," I said. "It's just embarrassing."

"Teenagers are always embarrassed by their parents," she said. She put her perfect hands to the temples of her dark, sleek haircut and critically surveyed the spread. Like there could be anything missing.

There was no use trying to talk her into taking about half of that down to the Center Street Mission. I went into the family room and groaned again.

"Who's this giant fruit basket for?" I said.

"You and your friends," she sang out. "I know teenagers don't eat fruit, but then again, those boys will eat anything."

I ignored that. I was checking out the tag hanging from the basket. "Napa-Sonoma," it read. Pricey little food boutique at Franktown Corners. This was getting worse by the minute—although I shouldn't have been surprised. I didn't even have to lift the lid to know that the cooler in the corner was bulging with everything from Clearly Canadian to Perrier water. I'd have killed at that moment to see some generic cola from Safeway. The only thing that was going to save me from mortification was—

"Is Dad going to be home for this?" I called out to my mother.

"You know he wouldn't miss it unless he has somebody on the operating table," she said, from right behind me.

She set a basket of fastidiously folded cloth napkins on the bar, while I stifled the biggest groan yet. The kids might overlook the one-hundred-dollar-a plate repast, but they wouldn't get past my father. Dr. Quinton Vandenberger was a presence, an I'm-here-to-make-sure-you-people-know-your-stuff presence. I started to pray for some poor Reno resident to rupture a spleen in the next half-hour.

Too late. I heard the garage door opening. At the bar, Yolanda Vandenberger automatically ran her hands over her not-a-hair-out-of-place 'do and let them slide down her body as if she were checking to be sure she hadn't gained an ounce since her husband had left that morning. She did have a disgustingly great figure, gleaned from good genes and a two-hour workout every day at the Caughlin Club. I knew both my parents were disappointed I had the Vandenberger fire-hydrant body. That was probably why they were so determined that I be Miss Academic Everything. I sure wasn't going to be Number One Beauty Queen like my mother.

I could feel rather than hear my father come into the room. Even the white couches tensed up, and the cherry paneling came to attention.

"Hi," Mom said breathlessly. It always seemed to me she was halfway afraid of him. I resented them both for that.

"I thought there was supposed to be a meeting here tonight," he said. His eyes had a puffy not-enough-sleep look, but they were as sharp as always.

"Not until six-thirty," I said. I wanted to add, *Mom's getting everything ready now so she can slip into a haute couture gown before the guests arrive.* I didn't say it. According to Wyatt, two months before, I would have.

Dad glanced at his Rolex as if the entire Academic Olympics team should have shown up an hour early, just to get a jump on things. I tried to escape to my room and made it past the upstairs open hallway that overlooked everything below before he called up to me, "How was that chemistry test?"

"Fine, Dad," I said.

"Define 'fine.' A? A-?"

"I don't know. Mr. Uhles doesn't sit there and grade them on the spot. I just think I did okay."

" 'Okay' better mean at least a 98 percent," he said.

I gazed down at the top of my father's head, bald and as shiny as my mother's fingernails, rings, and grapes. Oddly enough, I remembered at that moment that I used to wonder when I was a little kid how his head could be so free of hair when his chin and chest were covered with it—kind of like an ape. Had it all just slipped off his scalp and gotten hung up below? I used to ask myself. It was a whimsical thought I hadn't had in a long time.

I haven't had any whimsical thoughts in a long time, I realized. *Thanks to you, Dad.*

I did the only thing I could to disentangle myself from the conversation. "I want to do my homework before they get here," I said.

Once again my father consulted his watch. "You're going to get all your homework finished in fifty-five minutes? Those Advanced Placement teachers aren't working you hard enough."

Dear God, I prayed silently as I went into my room, *please let me turn eighteen and get out of here before I commit patricide.*

Our Academic Olympics meeting started out being its typical battle of one-upmanship. And upwomanship. Deborah, Rhonda, and I were as cutthroat as Lance, Gabe, and Mark.

As usual, Mr. Uhles sat in a chair in front of us and called out questions. At my house, we lined up on the miles of white couches and tried to kill each other giving the correct answers first. We had to be able to get them out almost before Mr. Uhles could finish asking them if we were going to keep the school's first-place title, especially competing against the schools in Vegas.

And at my house, my father stood behind Mr. Uhles with his arms folded across his chest, looking like some kind of hairy, carnivorous bird. Every time somebody else beat me to an answer, he pecked at me with his beaklike eyes. It behooved me to "be sharp" as he always put it.

That night, it turned particularly venomous. Mr. Uhles was quizzing us on nineteenth-century literature and theater. Being a chemistry teacher, he was pulling the questions out of a book, and we were answering them faster than he could scan the page.

"Three plays by Ibsen," he said.

I was on that one. *"Hedda Gabler. The Master Builder. The Wild Duck."*

"Shaw."

"*Mrs. Warren's Profession—*"

"*Arms and the Man. Candida!*" Lance shouted over me.

I glared at him, making sure to focus on the scruffy, wannabe goatee he was attempting to grow. He groped at it self-consciously.

"Three Dostoevsky novels."

I ogled Lance's goatee. He stuttered.

"*Brothers Karamazov,*" I spat out. "*Crime and Punishment—*"

"*House of Death!*" Mark yelped it while knocking over an empty Clearly Canadian bottle on the marble coffee table.

"I had it!" I said.

"You paused."

"I was taking a breath! I guess I could have keeled over for the cause."

"It's a moot point," Mr. Uhles said dryly. "It's *House of the Dead.*"

"I thought that was by Stephen King," Rhonda said, fiddling with the barrette that kept her enormous head of naturally curly blond hair from taking one of us out. "I think I saw the movie."

"Go back to sleep, Rhonda," Lance said, reaching over to squeeze her knee. If there was a girl in the room, he had to touch her—unless it was me, of course. I don't think he saw me as a girl.

Dad's beeper went off. He gave Rhonda a contemptuous look she didn't see and left the room.

Rhonda crossed her legs peevishly. "I would answer more questions, if you guys weren't so agro about it."

"What the heck is 'agro'?" Gabe said. He flipped his ponytail, clumsily, as usual. I commented to myself that it wasn't as cool looking as Wyatt's—and then smacked myself mentally for not focusing.

"Going ballistic," Rhonda said. "You act like it's the end of the world if we don't win."

"If you don't think it is, then you shouldn't be on the team," Lance said. He glanced at Mr. Uhles, just to be sure he was impressed.

"Do you actually think we're talking Armageddon if we lose?" Deborah said. The blueberry eyes were ripe.

Lance looked at Gabe and Mark. They nodded in unison.

"We don't think we're going to, like, fall over dead," Gabe said.

"But you have to have the attitude that you might," Mark finished for him.

Lance leaned philosophically against the back of the couch. "It's like playing football. You don't really want to kill the guys on the other team, but you have to think like you do." He exchanged a veiled smirk with Mark. "'Course, women wouldn't know about that."

"Oh, and you would?" Deborah said. "When was the last time you tossed the old pigskin around? Sixth grade? Just before you stopped growing?"

"Time out," Mr. Uhles said. He put fingertips to palm in a T, the way athletes do. It seemed perfectly natural for him. Although prematurely gray, Mr. Uhles looked young and fit, and I'd seen him running after school. He had legs like Michael Jordan. Unlike Lance, Mark, or Gabe, he might actually have come into contact with a ball of some kind in his life.

Right now he stroked his neatly trimmed mustache and surveyed us all. "Have you ever read *Crime and Punishment*?" he said.

"No," Mark said. "We'll read *Brothers Karamazov* in senior English. I heard it was boring."

"Ever seen an Ibsen play?" he said. "Or a Shaw?"

"I've read some plays," Deborah said. "Not those guys, but Shakespeare. Let's see, we did *Merchant of Venice* freshman year, *Julius Caesar* sophomore year—"

"I think it's all right for me to say this," Lance said, "I mean, you're cool and all, Mr. Uhles, but I read the *Cliff Notes*. I still got an A."

"Did you tell Mr. Ellison or Mrs. Trice that you didn't read the material?" Mr. Uhles said.

Lance's Adam's apple did a pushup. "No," he said. "But, I

mean, they have to know we don't have time to sit there and figure out what every 'withal' and 'forsooth' means."

"So how do you know all this information we ask you for
AO?" Mr. Uhles asked.

"Same way we know everything else," Mark said. "Memorize
it."

Mr. Uhles continued to stroke his mustache. "So tell me
something," he said, "what have you actually learned in high
school? Not memorized or picked up from *Cliff Notes* but really
internalized?"

"Are you going to quote us on this?" Lance said. His mouth
was smiling, but his eyes weren't. I had to hand it to Lance. He
always made the attempt to look like he was being respectful.

"No," Mr. Uhles said. "It stays right here in this room."

I believed him. He was one of the few teachers who treated
us as if we were actually people, as opposed to College Material.

"How to keep a dozen balls in the air," Rhonda said. "You
know, skip a newspaper meeting to go to band rehearsal—borrow somebody's history book review from last year and change
a word here and there and turn it in because I have three other
papers to write the same week, and I have to sleep sometime. I
look at my parents, and I figure this is a pretty valuable life
skill."

"So why do you do so much?" Mr. Uhles said.

"Because if I don't, my college applications will look like I
was a slacker," she said.

The entire room nodded.

"What about the rest of you?" Mr. Uhles said. "What are you
learning? This is fascinating to me."

Deborah giggled. "How to pass notes without getting
caught."

"You haven't learned that," Mr. Uhles said. "I see every note
you and Rhonda slip to each other. It looks like the Pony
Express in my class."

"Are the notes about us?" Gabe said, ponytail and green eyes
on Babe Alert. He had nowhere near Lance's finesse.

"Get over yourself," Deborah said.

"What about you guys?" Mr. Uhles said.

Mark ran his hand over his shaved head. "I don't know. I've learned how to get the busywork done so I can do what I want."

"Shortcuts," Lance put in.

"Such as?"

The three of them looked at each other, shrugging and nodding like a bunch of roosters.

"I get my mom to edit my papers on the computer," Gabe said. "She thinks she's just correcting my spelling, but every time she does, she adds a sentence here, a paragraph there. I'm acing English."

"I write really well," Mark said.

You do? I thought. *Couldn't prove it by the articles you turn in to me.*

"But math is what messes up my GPA," he went on. "This year I sit next to Kim-Anh what's-her-name, the Asian chick, in trig. I get her talking, and then while she's jacking her jaws, I get most of the solutions from her. Enough of it sticks with me that I can squeeze out an A- on the tests."

"I'm listening to all this," Gabe said, "and you know what I think I've learned in high school?"

"Tell," Mr. Uhles said.

"How to read teachers."

"Oh, get over it," Deborah said.

"No, I'm so serious," Gabe said. He flipped the ponytail five or six times for emphasis. "Like, for Mr. Lowe, you have to do all this flowery stuff when you write and pretend you think Robert Frost is totally deep. Mr. Dixon, in math, asks at least one question every class period, and he thinks you're all into it and gives you these class participation points if you answer the question. You get enough of those points, and you can skip the homework about once a week. American History, she wants the binder to look like something out of the Library of Congress. Other than that, you can basically slide."

"How do you read me?" Mr. Uhles said. His almost-black eyes were interested.

"You're one teacher I can't read," Lance said smoothly.

"Brown-noser," Mark said.

"No, I'm so serious. Mr. Uhles, you are like total teacher, man. You want everything—you give really hard tests, you want these complete lab reports, you expect all the homework, class participation. I don't play games with you, honest."

"Uh-huh," Mr. Uhles said. As I was thinking he didn't look the least bit convinced, he turned to me. "So, Norie, you've been unusually quiet."

I was really glad my father had left the room. By this time he would be rocking back and forth on his toes and heels and jingling the change in his pocket. He only did that when he was about to fire a nurse or tell me I was a bleeding-heart liberal. Even though he was out in the hall, talking on the phone, I trod carefully. I was about as safe saying what I really wanted to say as I would have been leaping from a 747 without a parachute.

"I've definitely learned how to achieve under pressure," I said carefully. "You can't let it get to you or you're history."

Mr. Uhles nodded a what-else? nod. I swallowed hard.

"Anybody interested in dessert?" My mother sailed in with the tray of brownies gourmand. I hadn't been that glad to see her since I was lost in the Kmart at age three.

"Good idea," my father said, following her in. He rubbed his hands together. "Then we can get back to work. Coffee, Chuck?"

Mr. Uhles nodded and followed him and my mother out to the kitchen. I fled to the bathroom where I sat on the toilet and wondered why I was the only person in that room who had seemed the least bit ashamed by our conversation.

How can we sit there and say the most valuable things we've learned in high school are how to take shortcuts, get other people to do our work for us, and manipulate teachers, lie to them even?

I'd heard Lance say two days before that all you had to do in Mr. Uhles's class was look like you tried on the tests, and he would cut you slack.

How can we say all that and not even blush, not even show the tiniest bit of remorse? I thought miserably. *We're actually proud that we're a bunch of finagling little grade mongers out to look like something we're not.*

I glanced in the mirror while I washed my hands. My cheeks were blotchy red, and I could barely meet my own eyes. My normally steely gaze was definitely not tonight.

"That's what I've learned in high school, Mr. Uhles," I said to my reflection. "Now will you please excuse me while I go puke?"

I dragged myself back to the family room, hoping they were already back to the AO questions so we wouldn't have to continue the discussion. But only Deborah, Lance, and Gabe were in there. They all looked up when I came in, guilty-faced as a trio of shoplifters.

"What did you guys do, rip off my mother's silver?" I said.

"What do I want with silver?" Lance said. "Now, your Dad's Jaguar—that I'd steal."

"It's a Porsche, idiot," Gabe said.

"No, really," I said. "What were you guys talking about? You look like you've been planning a holdup or something."

Gabe leaned back and interlocked his fingers behind his ponytail. "Nah, I'm more into white-collar crime, myself."

Lance whacked him on the side of the head, and Deborah bulged her eyes at him. Reactions way too big for a lame comment like that. I had the distinct feeling I was standing on the outside of a closed circle.

"Where is everybody?" Deborah said. "I have to go home and do homework." She looked at me. "By the way, Norie, I got the English from Rhonda so you don't have to bother."

"Cool," I said. "I'll get Rhonda and Mark."

"Way to go, Gabe," I heard Lance hiss as I left the room. "Why didn't you just come right out and tell her?"

Tell me what? I wanted to say to him. But I really didn't want to know.

CHAPTER THREE

WHEN EVERYBODY LEFT THAT NIGHT, I TRIED TO REACH my room before my father got to me.

Dream on.

He stopped me before I even got to the bottom step. Marching right into a conversation, he expected me to fall into step. "Those are some sharp kids."

"They really are," Mom said, breezing past us with the last of the ravaged cold-cut trays. "That Gabe is a cutie, isn't he? I've never seen such green eyes—"

She floated into the kitchen with my father glaring at her from behind as if she had interrupted his agenda. *Oh, he's a real cutie, all right,* I thought. *He was a total sweetheart to Tobey last fall. Tried to get her booted off the judicial board.*

"I was a little annoyed with Uhles when he went off on that tangent," Dad said. "You kids have a lot of territory to cover. You can't be wasting time doing warm fuzzies."

"You heard what everyone said?" I gulped and tried to remember what words I might have leaked. But I decided to keep going and say what I really thought. "I wouldn't exactly call that conversation 'warm,' Dad. I thought it was disgusting."

"I'm glad to hear that." He pointed a finger at me for emphasis, a gesture I'd been seeing since the first time my baby hand had reached for something off-limits on the coffee table. "You keep your focus."

I refrained from doing a Mark-thing and rolling my eyes.

Dad had missed my point. I started up the stairs, but he wasn't ready to adjourn the meeting.

"I'm glad to see you're sticking with this group," he said. "This is going to do a lot more for you than that other crowd you started to hang around with."

I froze midstep and snapped my head over my shoulder. "What 'other crowd'?" I said.

"That group of girls you had over here that night when the Mexican girl—"

"You mean my Christian friends?" I said.

My voice was testy, and he honed in on it with his eyes. "Whatever you want to call them," he said. "I see a bunch of little busybodies trying to solve everybody's problems. They're not even in your league. You don't have time for that."

"I don't have time to be a decent human being?" I said. My hackles were way up.

"Don't get on your soapbox, Noreen," he said. "That isn't what I mean, and you know it. If you're going to get into ethical discussions with people, you're going to have to learn to keep your emotions out of it. Don't you have more homework?"

End of conversation. Dismissed.

You're right, they are out of my "league," I wanted to say as I stomped up the stairs. *I'd give my right ear to be in their league.*

But I didn't say it. The reply just stuck in my throat, and it was still there the next day when I met the Flagpole Girls for lunch.

We used to meet only on Fridays. Now we had lunch together a couple of times a week. It was too cold to sit outside anymore, but we had found a corner in the big lobby between the theater and the gym where we could sit in a circle on the floor tiles. Nobody bothered us. It helped that it was on Ms. Race's beat. She was Mr. Holden, the principal's, secretary, and he had her patrol that area during lunch for little miscreants out to unhallow the halls of King High School.

She was also our mentor. I couldn't even tell you how that came about, but suddenly it just seemed like she was there with us whenever important decisions had to be made. I'd been skeptical about her at first. Who could work for an administrator and still be trusted? I should have known by the way she didn't dress like the other secretaries. She chose cool, ethnic-influence garb as opposed to the heels-hose-Casual-Corner-off-the-rack outfits. And she never said, "You people had better move on" to kids in the halls. I should have known she potentially could be one of us.

But she proved it to me soon enough in the incident with Tobey. I kind of wanted to get to know Ms. Race better, but it was one of those things that, as my father would have said, I "didn't have time for."

"How's everybody doing?" she said to us that day as we settled in with our assortment of lunch containers.

"Fine," Shannon said. She would have said 'fine' if her house had been bombed and she was homeless on the street, but she probably was fine. She appeared to have the most unruffled life of anybody I'd ever met.

"I'm not fine," Cheyenne said dolefully.

Ms. Race cocked her gorgeous head of auburn hair, pulled back into a French braid with tiny curls stubbornly wisping out around her ears. "You look fine. What's going on?"

"I'm flunking English."

"I'm sorry," Marissa said. She was our mother figure. Took everybody's problems on her shoulders. My father would have straightened her out right away.

"You all right, girl?" Brianna said. "I've never known you to worry about your grades before. Somebody feel her forehead."

"I bet none of you guys are failing anything," Cheyenne said.

Shannon, of course, shook her head. It was kind of a ridiculous question to ask Tobey or me—recent National Honor Society inductees that we were. Brianna gave me a sardonic smile.

"You would probably call my grades failing," she said. "I only have a 3.0."

Marissa just flung an arm around Cheyenne's shoulders. "At least you're worrying about it. That's a start."

"Yeah, join the rest of us stress queens," I said. "You, too, can have an ulcer and insomnia."

I felt a hand on my shoulder. Ms. Race gave it a squeeze. "You work so hard, Norie. I don't see how you get it all done."

"It just looks that way," I said. "It's all done with mirrors."

"Cheyenne needs some of those," Marissa said. "I'd help her, but I'm not that smart."

"You are, too," Shannon said to her.

"She's a genius," I said. "But why don't you let me do it? I'll tutor you in English, Cheyenne."

"Do you have time?" Tobey said.

"No," I said. "I don't have time to work out or do my nails, either, and I'd rather do this." I opened my datebook and ran a finger down the jumble of assignments and reminders. "What about breakfast before school tomorrow?" I said to Cheyenne. "I'll pick you up. What's your address?"

She whispered it to me as Brianna said, "All right, girls, let's get those heads down. We have to pray for Cheyenne—and Norie."

We laid down our half-eaten sandwiches and bowed our heads. Ms. Race squatted down with us as we prayed. The warning bell coincided with our "amen."

"That was awfully nice of you to offer to tutor Cheyenne," Ms. Race said to me.

I wriggled into my backpack and edged off. No matter how much clout a person had, you didn't show up late to Mr. Uhles's class. "It's okay," I said. "I don't add that much spiritually to the group. I might as well do what I can—and I can always make the grades."

She cocked her head, a sure sign that she wanted to delve deeper into that. I didn't have time.

"I have to go to class," I said.

"Let's talk sometime," she said. "You have my number."

"Yeah . . . somewhere," I said. We all did. Ms. Race had made sure of that during the Tobey crisis.

"Feel free to use it," she said.

Fabulous, I thought as I made my way through the now

jammed halls. *She thinks I'm a basket case.* I grunted to myself. *She's probably right. I'm stressed academically, stalled emotionally, stunted socially—*

"Whoa!"

The shout came on top of a major push from behind, which knocked me forward into a couple making out against their locker. My backpack was shoved up the back of my head, and the corner of my fifty-pound chemistry book that was sticking out stabbed me in the ear.

"I am so sorry," said a voice behind me. "That whole mess of football players shoved me right into you. Are you all right?"

It was Wyatt. I looked past him at the broad-shouldered huddle that was continuing its way down the hall without so much as a glance backward to see who they had just plowed over.

"Where's the flag?" I yelled at them.

The couple I'd disturbed curled their lips at me and moved on. Wyatt was now on his knees, picking up the stuff that had popped out of my unbuckled backpack pocket on impact.

"I'll get that," I said.

"I have it." Wyatt stood up and straightened the stack of newspaper ad forms. I grabbed for them, but he pulled them away and kept tidying.

"They're fine," I said tightly.

"Are you? I hit you pretty hard. I'm really sorry."

"Would you stop?" I said. "I'm fine. I'm not delicate, okay?"

Wyatt grinned. "I know that, but I think you're probably breakable. I just want to be sure you're okay."

He was starting to get on my nerves. I snatched the obsessively straightened pile of papers from him and tried to elbow my way past.

"I'll take that as a yes," he said.

"Look," I said. I blew at my bangs and sent them sprawling across my forehead. "I don't need pampering and coddling just because I'm a female. I deal with those animals every day, the same as you do. Does somebody come to your rescue every time you take a chemistry book in the face?"

I waited for the eye rolling, followed by two hands held up in surrender and the backing away while muttering some uncomplimentary female term under the breath. That's what usually happened—not that I'd ever had a guy try to rescue me in the hall the way Sir Lance-a-Wyatt, late of the Round Table, had just done. But whenever I informed some guy that I wasn't into the whole men-are-stronger-than-women-and-therefore-superior thing, they usually got away as fast as they could, with as much what's-your-problem body language as they could exhibit.

Wyatt, however, just grinned and connected his eyes with mine. "So, Norie, tell me how you really feel."

I tried not to stutter. "I just did," I said.

"You must be a trip to go out with," he said.

I had to clench my teeth together to keep my mouth from falling open. Only through sheer will power was I able to say, "That's something you're never going to find out."

He did his happy little shrug thing. "Well," he said, "if you change your mind, just let me know. I think it would be a blast."

He walked away—jauntily—and I stood there fuming, a tardy in chemistry looming unheeded on my horizon. I absolutely hated it when anybody—especially a guy—refused to take me seriously. And to think for about ten minutes the day before I had thought I'd actually met a male with a mind that wasn't in some gender-oriented gutter.

I realized about then that I was still watching him walk away. I whirled on one heel—and ran smack into Jerry Pavella. He was panting like a Great Dane.

"Norie," he said, "have you got the key?"

"Key to what?" I said. I narrowed my eyes suspiciously. "I've told you, Pavella, I don't lend out my Jeep."

"No!" Pavella wagged his cute-but-dumb head. "Not that key!"

"Pavella—yoo-hoo—Popcorn-for-Brains!" That came from Deborah, who sallied up beside us and linked her arm through his.

"There you are!" Pavella said. "I've been looking all over for you."

"I'm here," she said. Her voice, as always, was going up at the end of every phrase, but it had more of a singsong tone than was even normal for her. She may have looked guilty the night before, but now she sounded like she was Death Row material.

"What the Sam Hill is going on with you people?" I said.

"We're going to have detention for the rest of our lives if we're late for chemistry again," she said, giving me a strobe-light smile. Then she dragged Pavella off down the hall, whispering feverishly into his ear.

"What is up with them?" I muttered to myself as I did my own hundred-yard dash for the chem room.

I didn't have time to think about it for more than about seven seconds. Written on the board was the message: *Surprise quiz today. You have five minutes to refresh your memories.*

The room went into a chorus of moans. I scrambled for my notes on chemical equations, but it did me five points worth of good. The quiz was worth ten.

"I'm going to be doing extra credit until I die," I told Lance as we were leaving class at the end of the period.

"Why?" he said.

"Because I just blew that quiz."

"Oh," he said. He stroked his untidy little goatee and gave me a superior smile as he turned the corner to his locker.

I followed him. "You didn't think it was hard?" I said. "You knew all that stuff?"

"I got a ten, if that's what you mean," he said. He deftly twirled his lock and pulled open the door. Then he pulled it to him as if I'd just surprised him in his boxer shorts.

"What?" I said.

"What?"

"What are you hiding in your locker? What is going on? You and Gabe and Deborah are all acting like you have a cocaine ring going or something."

"Look, Vandenberger," he said, "we're not all possible subjects for your newspaper articles, okay? Maybe we want some
privacy once in a while."

"Don't give me that," I said. "I know when you're lying."

Lance slammed his locker and looked down at me, hands
planted in points on his negligible hips. "What—you have some
kind of mystic powers that only women have?"

"No," I said. "I've just seen you do it often enough."

"To who?"

"To every girl you ever dated, for openers. And every teacher
we ever had. I've seen you lie your way out of taking a final
exam, for Pete's sake. Gabe sticks out like a donkey in the girls'
locker room, but you—you've got it down to a science."

"So you're jealous," he said. He jerked back his head and
slitted his eyes, both of which were the same colorless color, and
rehoisted his backpack. "I have to go," he said. "If you need any
lessons in prevarication, let me know."

I didn't comment, as I normally would have, that I was surprised he even knew what that meant. I think I was too stunned
at just having been blown off.

Blown off by three, no four, counting Pavella, kids I'd been
competing, sparring, and fighting with through honors classes
since we had all first darkened the doors of this place. There
wasn't one of them I hadn't run right over on the PSAT. I had a
GPA at least three hundredths of a point above any one of them.
None of them could even touch me when it came to number of
activities. Yet here they were doing their own little clandestine
thing right under my nose and practically throwing it in my
face.

I was hashing that over in my head for about the fourteenth
time on the way home that afternoon. I had a Jars of Clay tape
in, something Tobey had given me and which, in spite of my
usual taste for grunge, I actually liked. But I was shouting over
it, "Why don't they just stick out their tongues at me and say,
'We know something you don't know. Nah, nah, nah, nah, nah,
nah!'"

Which was why I almost missed Shannon D'Angelo walking down the sidewalk in weather with a windchill factor of thirty-five degrees. I pulled over ahead of her and waited for her to catch up. She opened the passenger door and peeked in.

"Don't you want a ride?" I said. "You're going to freeze your buns off."

She nodded gratefully and climbed in. I watched her shut the door and arrange her book bag on the floor. She was the only person I knew who could look cleaner and less wrinkled on the way home from school than most of us did on the way to. She smiled at me from within the stand-up collar of her white ski jacket. White, mind you.

"Where to?" I said.

"I was going to Rancho San Rafael," she said apologetically. "Is that too far for you to drive?"

"The park?" I said. "No, I can take you. What are you doing over there?"

"Walking," she said. Then she laughed. It was surprisingly husky.

"I'm driving you someplace so you can walk," I said. "That makes sense."

I thought she was going to offer to get out, but I shook my head at her. "Don't mind me. I've had the worst day in life."

"Bummer," she said.

I wanted to ask her if she had ever experienced a bad day, a bad hour. But I restrained myself and said instead, "So, you're just going to walk around the park?"

"Yeah," she said. "It's beautiful. But I'm sure you've been there."

"I went to the balloon races there once," I said. "That's about it. What's over there?"

"Gorgeous gardens," she said. "All kinds of neat places to sit. I like to go there to think."

I snorted before I could stop myself. "I'm not making fun of you," I said quickly. "I was just thinking how it must be nice to have time to sit around and think. I haven't done that since . . . well, I don't think I've ever done that!"

She didn't seem to know what to say, which was fine, and not surprising. Of all the Flagpole Girls, Shannon was definitely the one I related to least. We had about as much in common as Martha Stewart and me. But she was one of us. The least I could do was be nice to her.

"So, what do you think about while you're . . . thinking?" I said.

She cleared her throat, folded and refolded her transparent little hands, ran her teeth back and forth over her lip. I was beginning to be sorry I asked.

"Just things," she finally said—profoundly. "My family, mostly. Stuff we talk about at Flagpole. I'm going to pray for Cheyenne."

"Don't worry about Cheyenne," I said. "She seems pretty bright. I'll fix her up."

"That would be neat," Shannon said. "You can just pull over right here."

I stopped the Jeep at the entrance to the park and waited while she climbed out.

"Thanks," she said.

"No problem."

I put the car in gear, but she hesitated shutting the door.

"You really ought to come here sometime and just walk around," she said.

Then, as if she thought she had stomped on my toes, she shut the door, gave an embarrassed wave, and hurried off.

"I'll do that, Shannon," I murmured as I pulled away. "When my life gets as uncomplicated as yours."

And that, it seemed, wasn't going to happen anytime soon. When I got home, a message was on my answering machine from Deborah.

"Nor? Call me."

I did. She talked as if she were out of breath. "I guess Pavella told you what's up with us," she said. And then, before she gave me a chance to answer, she plowed on. "I was going to tell you, Norie, really, but Lance wasn't sure you would be with us since you wouldn't lend me your English homework."

My mind was starting to knot. "What's your point?" I said.

"Bottom line?" she said.

"Yeah."

"Do you want the answer key to the next chemistry test?" she said.

CHAPTER FOUR

DEBORAH WENT ON AS IF WE WERE DISCUSSING WHO was taking whom to the Homecoming dance. "Like I said, we would have given you the key to the quiz we had today—"

"How did you even know we were having it?" I said. "It was a pop quiz."

"I'm Mr. Uhles's aide first period," she said.

Like that explained everything—and made it perfectly acceptable.

"So, now that we've gotten past that whole thing with the English sheet," Deborah said, "I thought we should invite you in."

I sank slowly down onto the futon in my study area. I could feel myself going cold. *You mean, now that Pavella has spilled the beans to me, you'll invite me in. It has nothing to do with your getting over anything.*

"And don't tell Mark or Rhonda. Mark can't keep his mouth shut, and Rhonda's too high-strung. They aren't in on it." She hesitated. "You're not mad, are you, Nor?"

"Huh? No," I said. "I'm just . . . thinking."

"Oh."

There was a funky silence on the line. My mind was racing. I was sure hers was stumped.

"I don't know what there is to think about," she said finally. "But take your time, I guess. The test isn't until Wednesday."

"Thanks," I said. "I have to go."

"Yeah, me, too. I have to get on-line and find some

information for that English paper we have to do. Hey, are you going to Gabe's party tomorrow night? You can tell one of us then."

"Who are 'us'?" I said.

"Gabe, Lance, Pavella, and me."

"Cozy," I said.

"Yeah, well, come to the party."

*You can go directly from admitting you're part of a major cheat-
ing ring to talking about a party—in the same breath?* I thought as
we hung up. I picked up a dirty T-shirt I'd left lying around and
stuffed it over my face.

That wasn't the half of it. There was a time when I would
have jumped at the chance for information like an answer key.
That would give me all that time to study something else, or
write a piece for the *Herald,* or organize a Teens Against Gender
Discrimination rally or something.

Now that I thought about it, I'd done my share of cheating
before—though not on this scale. I'd taken a glance across the
aisle at Gabe or Lance or Rhonda's paper to validate one of my
answers, and I'd borrowed geometry proofs several times sophomore year when I'd gotten bogged down doing a world-history
project. I'd even seen people blatantly passing answers during
tests and never thought much about it.

But now it seemed clearly wrong to me. Not just you're-only-
hurting-yourself kind of stupid but wrong, like rubbing-
sunburn-with-sandpaper, against-my-principles wrong.

Whoa. That was a jolt.

I sat up on the futon and studied the T-shirt. *So if I have these
high moral standards now, how come I didn't just tell Deborah no?*

It wasn't like me to be afraid of hurting somebody's feelings,
that was for sure. And I'd never hesitated before to tell people I
thought they were behaving like idiots and they ought to get lives.

I'm going soft, I thought. *Yikes.*

I studied some that night, but I couldn't keep my eyes open
past ten-thirty. In fact, I conked out on the futon with my
chemistry book flattened open on my chest. That might have ac-
counted for the recurrence of the drowning dream.

I was at camp—again—floundering around in the lake out

by the raft. I had all these clothes on—a letter jacket, basketball shoes, and a prom dress. It was all dragging me down, and the water was coming up in these fifteen-foot swells as a storm raged out over the lake. The waves would lift me up and leave me teetering on top of one of them. Then they would drop out from under me, and I'd go crashing toward the raft—over and over and over again. I never hit it, but every time it got more ter-rifying because I couldn't see it. Everything was dark. Until the lightning finally cracked open the sky, and in my mind I knew I should be able to see everything. But I couldn't.

I woke up breathing like a locomotive and sat straight up. The chemistry book tumbled onto the floor with a thud. It was a full two minutes before I could sort out the reality from the nightmare. Even as I flopped, clearheaded again, back onto the futon, I wasn't so sure that reality itself wasn't a nightmare.

I was dragging when I drove to Cheyenne's house the next morning at six. An icy drizzle misted Iggy's windshield, and I checked out the Sierras in my rearview. It was snowing up there. People at school would be freaking out about going skiing. I hadn't been since I had started high school. The one sport I was decent at, and it fell at my most stressed-out time of year—November to March.

I shrugged that off and concentrated on finding Cheyenne's. It was on a side street off Seventh, in that neighborhood that had probably been pretty decent when it was built twenty years ago, but by the time I came along, it had been taken over mostly by people who worked the graveyard shifts at the casinos and slept all day. Some of the places looked like somebody gave a hang whether the occasional tree grew. Others had old cars and rusted-out barbecue grills in the backyards.

The house Cheyenne had directed me to was surprisingly neat for the block it was on. It was painted white and had black shutters and a big wooden tub of gourds and Indian corn on the front porch. Somebody had actually raked the leaves from un-der the lone oak.

When I rang the doorbell, a woman with very white hair that seemed too old for her face opened the door. She had one of those bodies that was all chest, and she wore two things you don't see much anymore: an apron and a smile with a front tooth missing.

"You must be Norie," she said.

"Right."

"I'm Tassie. Cheyenne's almost ready. Come on in out of the cold."

I did, into a small but incredibly cheerful living room. A fire was crackling in the minuscule fireplace, and three bright red corduroy love seats were pulled up to it. *What a great place to snuggle in with a good book,* I thought.

"Do you want to sit down?" Tassie said. "Have some hot chocolate?"

She pointed to the kitchen, which opened up onto the living room. There was a round table in there, and even if I'd wanted to sit down at it I couldn't have. All six seats were taken by teenagers.

One I recognized as Diesel, the Incredible Hulk look-alike who had helped us out when Tobey was in trouble. We nodded to each other.

The other four besides Cheyenne I'd seen around school—while they were sitting outside the discipline office, waiting to be seen. Two guys in skater-style flannels and jeans, and two girls, one with too much makeup and the other with not enough—and you didn't dare call her on it or she'd punch you out. She probably could have taken on Diesel.

"This is our family," Tassie said. "Everybody introduce yourselves."

I groaned inwardly, but they didn't look as if they thought this was cheesy at all. They threw out their names to me, all of them grinning and poking each other.

"Diesel."

"Avery."

"Brendan."

"Ellie."

"Felise."

The last one was the chick who looked like a heavyweight-boxing champion. I'd have laughed at the irony of the name if I hadn't been afraid she would clip me with a hard left.

"You done with that juice, Cheyenne?" Tassie said.

"Yes, but I told you Norie was taking me to breakfast."

"At McDonald's," Tassie said. "If you got a single vitamin in that place it would be the biggest miracle since the loaves and fishes."

Cheyenne took her glass to the sink, washed it, dried it, and put it in a cabinet. I looked around for a dishwasher and didn't find one. My eyes snagged on a pile of thick sandwiches on the counter. Cheyenne dropped one into a brown bag and grinned at me.

"Ready?" she said.

Actually, I was more ready to sit in the chair she had just vacated and eat one of those blueberry muffins in the basket in the middle of the table.

"You have money for breakfast?" Tassie said to her.

"Oh, no, this is my treat," I said. "Don't worry about it."

Tassie surveyed me with a critical eye. "All right," she said. "Then you come here for breakfast one morning. That'll keep everything even."

"Okay," I said as I eyed the basket. "As long as we have those."

"These are trash compared to the banana nut ones," said the smaller kid in the bigger flannel shirt whose name, I think, was Avery. It was a surprising comment coming out of a guy who looked as if he would just as soon shove a banana nut muffin down your throat as share one with you.

"Tassie liked you," Cheyenne said as we climbed into Iggy.

"How can you tell?" I said. "I was there like two minutes."

"She doesn't invite people to eat with us unless she likes them."

"She seems cool," I said.

"I tell her I think she saved my life," Cheyenne said.

I tried to stay neutral faced.

"She tells me she saved it; now it's up to me to hold on to it." Cheyenne gave a big sigh. "That's why I have to raise my grades. If I don't make it through high school, I might as well hang it up. I'll end up like my mother."

"And how was that?" I said.

Cheyenne spread out her fingers and started to count on them. "Alcoholic. Jail record. In rehab. And without me."

"Oh," I said. "So is Tassie, like, a relative?"

"She's my foster mother," Cheyenne said. "The best one I ever had. I hope I get to stay with her for a while."

That started about a thousand questions popping up in my mind. How many others had she had, for Pete's sake? And why would they move her on if she was doing fine here?

But I controlled myself and said instead, "So do you still have room for McDonald's?"

We ordered a sack of stuff that couldn't even come close to what Tassie had been serving and took over a booth to get on with Cheyenne's English. We were only about two bites into our Egg McMuffins when I realized that explaining the theory of relativity would be easier than bringing up Cheyenne's grade.

She barely read on a fifth-grade level, as far as I could see. And her spelling was, shall we say, creative.

"What's the next thing you have to turn in?" I said, after she had struggled through reading the first paragraph of "The Lottery" to me aloud.

"We have a vocabulary test today," she said.

"Do you have a list?" I said.

She shook her head. "I lost it," she said.

"So you haven't studied?"

"I remember some of the words though," she said.

I groaned inwardly. And prayed. I was going to need all the help I could get.

"Do you think I can pass?" she said when we had basically sounded out the five words she could remember: fabricate, fervent, facetious, fanatic, and facade, which she pronounced "fa-kaid."

I groped for tact, never my strong suit. "Um, could be tough this time, Chey," I said. "I'm thinking we're going to need like a whole Sunday afternoon to get this thing rolling, you know?"

Cheyenne looked as if I'd just invited her on a trip to Hawaii. "This Sunday?" she said.

"Sure."

"It would have to be after church. Maybe you could come for Sunday dinner. Tassie always makes us sit down for chicken or a ham or something and then we can do whatever we want. Well, not whatever we want, but, how does she say it, within reason—"

"Okay," I said quickly. If I listened to this entire monologue it would be fourth period. It was already 7:15.

In fact, we tore into the school just as the first warning bell was ringing. Cheyenne was still talking nonstop at my elbow and followed me all the way to my locker.

Deborah was waiting for me there. She didn't even seem to see Cheyenne. Her eyes were aimed only at me.

"It's about time you got here," she said.

"Nice to see you, too, Deb," I said.

She blinked at me for a second. "Yeah, well, I needed to tell you this, okay?"

My suspicion antennae went up, but I tried to look non-committal as I opened my locker. Cheyenne was still at my elbow, but she had stopped talking.

"What?" I said.

"Look, on that thing I was talking to you about last night—" she said.

For some reason, that rankled. "You mean the cheating thing?" I said.

Her eyes popped, and she glanced over her shoulder. "Could you have said that any louder?"

"I just wanted to make sure we were talking about the same thing. Go on; what about it?"

"When I called you, I was sure you'd want to be in on it," she said. "But when you didn't say yes right away—that's making Lance and Gabe nervous."

"What about Pavella?" I said.

"Pavella thought you already knew, remember? We just give him the keys; we don't expect him to help figure out the logistics."

"That would make sense," I said dryly. "So Lance and Gabe are nervous. I always like them best that way. Especially Gabe. He falls all over himself."

"I don't," Deborah said. "They drive me nuts. Just reassure me that you're not going to tell about this, whether you decide to join us or not, okay?"

I stared at her. Her voice had started to shake, and the skin around her lips was slightly blue. She was upset about this. They were in deeper than I'd thought—and it left me cold.

I pretended to concentrate on pulling my American history book out of my locker. This was getting weird. Every time I talked to one of them, I felt farther and farther outside their little circle—the circle I'd practically built myself. The whole thing felt criminal to me, and the only thing they were worried about was getting caught.

But the feeling of being a stranger in unfamiliar territory was just as strong. I needed to find some secure footing. "It would sure be a bummer if somebody found out," I said carefully. "It'd be curtains for all of us, you know."

Deborah pulled on her hair with both hands. "That's what I'm saying."

I watched her try to hide that she was stressed out beyond her normal limits.

"You don't have to worry about me," I said.

She broke into a grin and even wrapped her fingers around my wrist for a second. "Thank you," she said. "I told Lance and Gabe we could count on you. I'll have the key to you by Monday." She backed away. "I have to get in there." Then she turned and disappeared through the crowd.

"I better go to my locker," said a voice at my elbow.

I jumped about six inches. I'd forgotten Cheyenne was there—and I was sure Deborah had never even noticed her. Why would she think Cheyenne was with me anyway? She wasn't in our "league."

"Yeah," I said to Cheyenne. "Don't be late. You need all the points you can get."

"I'm going to be fine," Cheyenne said. She stood on tiptoes and hugged me. "Thanks," she said.

For what? I thought. *I'm sure turning out to be some role model.* Ha. I didn't know the half of it.

CHAPTER FIVE

I AVOIDED ALL OF THEM FOR MOST OF THE MORN-
ing—not a simple task when we were generally tripping over
each other in honors and AP classes. I just didn't want to get
into another discussion until I had a chance to sort out what I
was thinking.

It was easiest to keep my distance in fourth-period journalism. Editors were doing consults with staff writers about their
articles, and my first one was with Wyatt.

If the memory of our little tête-à-tête in the hall the day before was bothering him, he wasn't showing it. He did his jaunty
little walk up to my desk and presented me with his plan for the
piece on the moment of silence as if I hadn't told him where to
get off twenty-four hours ago. I, on the other hand, was feeling
unexplainably sheepish.

Which is probably why I went at his proposal with my red
pen poised. It never hit the page.

"I asked a couple of people the questions already, just to field
test them," Wyatt said as I perused his ideas for the third time,
trying to find something to critique. "I hope that's okay."

"Fine," I said crisply.

"Any changes you want me to make, I'm willing. I don't
think every word of mine is sacred or anything."

"Uh-huh."

"I'd also appreciate your suggestions. I really respect you as
a writer. Your stuff is good."

I glanced up at him sharply, but his little blue eyes were

sincere behind the glasses. "Thanks," I said. Then I tapped his sheets of paper together until the sides evened up and smoothed them out on the desk. "This is good," I said. "Really good. Insightfully thought out, intelligently written, thoroughly researched."

"Wow," he said.

"What wow?" I said. I went back to looking for a spelling error, a typo, a misplaced comma—anything.

"You just didn't strike me as the type of editor who would hand out a lot of praise."

"I don't," I said. "If it were trash I would tell you."

"Oh, I bet you would."

"So why wouldn't I be just as likely to tell you if it was good?" I said.

" 'Were' good," he said.

"What?"

"You would want to use the subjunctive in this case. 'If it were good.' "

"Thank you, Amy Vanderbilt of Grammar," I said.

"Hey, no problem." He grinned.

I didn't.

"Did I say something wrong?" he said.

"I don't know," I said. My hackles were prickling up for no reason I could put my finger on. "I'm not even sure what you said. Go ahead with the piece. It should work really well."

I stuck my pen over my ear and looked around for Pavella, who was supposed to bring me an outline for a feature.

"I was just kind of messing around," Wyatt said. "I thought you'd appreciate the humor."

I peeled my eyes away from Pavella, who was at the copy machine flirting with a sophomore, and glanced at Wyatt. "What humor?" I said. "You're critiquing my syntax, and I'm supposed to think it's funny?"

The grin faded. So did something inside me.

"Sorry," he said. "I guess I'm a little confused."

"Yeah, well, you're male," I said. "You're supposed to be confused."

"No, it isn't me," he said. "It's you. You keep changing your rules."

I looked Wyatt full in the face. He was calm eyed and still sitting jauntily—if anybody can sit jauntily—and there was no trace of the sarcasm or the I-am-so-sick-of-you-feminazis sneer I often get from guys. He really did look mildly bewildered.

"What rules?" I said. "I don't have any rules."

"Sure you do. Everybody has rules. It's like the set of things a person has to learn about another person to get along with her."

"Do you have rules?" I said. I was interested in spite of myself.

"Sure."

I pushed back my bangs and eyed him suspiciously. "What are they?"

"Hey, Vandenberger," Pavella called from the copy machine. The sophomore had obviously not been fascinated. "When are you getting to my piece?"

"Now," I said, still looking at Wyatt.

Wyatt gave his signature shrug. "I still say we should go out sometime. We could talk about all this stuff."

"Come on, Pavella," I said. "Bring your outline over here."

Wyatt walked—buoyantly—over to a computer and started to type. I focused on Pavella's proposal for a feature on people's study habits. It was awful, but I wasn't as hard on him as I normally would have been. I was having trouble concentrating.

All thoughts of Wyatt were eradicated in fifth-period chemistry, after lunch. We were working at our desks on some equations, and I was still trying to avoid interaction with the Fraudulent Four, when Mr. Uhles called me into his little office just off the classroom. He had his grade book out, and he asked me to sit down. Not a good sign.

"How's it going, Norie?" he said.

"You mean, in general, or in chemistry?"

"Chemistry."

"Maybe you should tell me."

I craned my neck toward the grade book. Mr. Uhles fiddled

with his neat mustache. "By anybody else's standards you're doing fine," he said. "The last test and yesterday's quiz . . . " He
cocked an eyebrow at me. "They both brought you down to
a B."

"Seriously?"

He nodded. "Like I said, there are people who would give
a lot to be making a B at this point. But you aren't those
people—and those people don't have your father."

"My father?" I said. I stifled the groan that sprang to my
chest.

"He took me aside at your house the other night and told me
he wants you to be valedictorian. Plus, he said you're going for
Harvard."

"I know, you have to walk on water to get in there," I said.

"You still have a couple of months till the end of the semester, which is why I'm telling you now. You can bring this up if
you really think you need to."

"Extra credit?" I said. "I can write a report on—"

"You have to have the test scores," he said. "I have to be sure
you know the basic material."

"I'm trying," I said. "You wouldn't believe how much I
study."

"I think I would." Mr. Uhles leaned back in his chair and
stroked its arms, opening himself out like he was inviting con-
fidence. "What do you plan to study when you go to college?"

"Journalism," I said. "I've known that since freshman year."

"I'm wondering if a journalist needs to make an A in chemistry."

I glanced over my shoulder with mock concern. "Don't let
them hear you say that, Mr. Uhles. We honors students are supposed to make A's in everything."

He gave the same mock-concern glance. "That's hogwash,
and we both know it. I expect you honors students to do the
best you can in everything. I could care less about the
grades—to a certain extent, of course. I'd be perfectly happy
with a B for you. In the first place, your numerical scores would

normally put you in the A- range, but the curve is high this semester. We have some people with a real aptitude for the subject in here. You're not a scientist, and this is an advanced course. I'd be downright impressed if you pulled a strong B."

"My father wouldn't."

"Would you?"

"When it comes to grades, my father and I have to be one and the same," I said. I stopped at that, because my hackles were starting to rise on the back of my neck. I clutched the seat of my chair and twitched a foot.

"I didn't mean to get into unsafe territory here," Mr. Uhles said. "I just wanted to let you know where things stood. You like to have all the information."

"Thanks," I said. "I plan to study extra hard before Wednesday."

He surveyed me carefully out of his almost-black eyes, and then he smiled and reached over to touch me lightly on the shoulder. "You take care now," he said.

I'm going to have to take more than "care," I thought. *I'm going to have to take tranquilizers for this anxiety attack.*

It wasn't just the chemistry. I'd been having the same kind of struggle in trig. For the first time in my life, things like math and science were starting to feel foreign to me. It wasn't just a matter of paying attention in class and studying for the tests anymore. I was lost about half the time—I mean, really lost.

I had trig last period, and I hustled through the halls to get in there before anybody else did. Mr. Dixon was writing something that looked like Greek on the board.

"Mr. D?" I said. "Is this a good time to talk about my grade?"

"B," he said, without missing a chalk stroke.

"You know, just like that?"

"I keep them up to date on the computer," he said. "I know yours because I think you can do better." He looked at me sideways, which was difficult to do considering the Brillo pad of a beard he had. "If you're going to be a women's libber, you can't use 'women aren't good at math' as an excuse."

"I don't think that is an excuse," I said.

"Talk to Deborah Zorn," he said, as if I hadn't even spoken. "She's driving the curve right through the ceiling."

"I'll do that," I said. I walked away before I had a chance to say something really insolent. Mr. Dixon was known for having a low threshold for adolescent impudence.

I met Tobey in the library that afternoon after school, supposedly to work on an English project. But all I could do was moan about the state of my GPA. "I don't think I can work any harder, L'Orange," I said. "I barely get any sleep as it is."

"I'm sorry," she said.

"And it doesn't seem to be doing me that much good studying for those two classes. I'm stuck at B level."

"Bummer."

"My father's going to kill me. I'm going to end up fifth in the class or something. So much for Harvard or Yale or Princeton. I can kiss the entire Ivy League good-bye."

Tobey shook her head sadly.

"What is that, L'Orange?" I said. "Why don't you tell me how to fix this?"

She gave me an incredulous look. "You're the one who told all of us we shouldn't try to fix each other. We should tell our own story and let the person figure it out for herself—her and God, of course."

"Forget I said that," I said. I flung my head down on my arms. "Tell me what to do."

"I can't," she said. "But I'll tell you my story."

I grunted.

"I'm sick of this whole pressure thing," she said. "When you mentioned it in September—when we first met at the flagpole, remember?—I thought, 'What's she talking about?' But you were right. They expect us to be excellent in everything, and I'm not buying it anymore. I do my best, and that has to be good enough. I mean, I figure it's good enough for God."

"God isn't my father," I said.

She raised both eyebrows. I put up a hand before she could open her mouth.

"That didn't come out right," I said. "I know God is my Father, but my earthly father has a whole lot more to say about this, you know what I mean?"

"I don't know. I think God says a lot."

"What are you saying? God talks to you?" I said.

"Kind of. I mean, I hear this—what do they call it?—'still, small voice.'"

I sat up slowly. "What . . . like when you're doing your homework or taking a shower or something?"

"No, I definitely have to get really quiet and listen. But I know it's God—and that's what I listen to."

She ended up shrugging. There was a lot of that going around. I still wanted to grill her about it further, but the library door burst open, causing both after-school librarians to look up with their shhh fingers poised, and Cheyenne came flying in. She was moving so fast her hair was standing straight out like wings, and her mouth was going, baby-bird style.

"Norie!" she squawked, heedless of the pistol eyes the librarians were shooting at her. "Look at this!" She was waving a paper she was obviously determined to show me. She made a dive across a kid squatting at the magazine rack and nearly mowed down somebody else who was crossing to the checkout counter with a stack of books—just trying to get to me.

"What the heck, dude?" Tobey muttered to me, brown eyes dancing.

Cheyenne arrived at our table out of breath and still clutching the paper, which she smashed down onto the tabletop and finally let go of with a flourish. A large red B- stared me in the face.

"What's this?" I said.

"My vocabulary test!" she said.

Cheyenne could get pretty far up there on the hysteria scale, but I'd never seen her look quite that jazzed. Her eyes were out of control, and her cheeks were like a pair of ripe tomatoes. All the shushing in the world wasn't going to bring down her voice one decibel. She basically was shrieking.

"The one you took today?" I said.

Yes!"

"You got a B-?"

"Yes!"

Tobey was examining the sheet. "What's F-A-K-A-I-D?" she said. "It's one of the ones you missed."

"We went over that!" I said.

"Doesn't matter," Cheyenne said. We hadn't dimmed the neon grin by a single watt. "Look at all the ones I got right."

"I'm impressed," Tobey said.

"And amazed," I said. "We only studied for, like, fifteen minutes."

"It was a piece of cake," Cheyenne said. She started to whip the sheet away but I grabbed at it and studied it myself. She was right. She had gotten a large percentage of them correct. Even "facetious."

"She called out the definitions, and you had to know the right word?" I said.

"Yes!" Cheyenne's voice was getting impatient.

Tobey put a hand on her arm. "That's way cool, Cheyenne," she said. "I think this calls for a Flagpole Girls' celebration. We haven't had one in a while."

Cheyenne's voice wound up again. "That would be rad!"

"Hurry up and plan it before she goes into orbit," I said.

"Pneumatic Diner," Tobey said. "I'll call Shannon and Marissa. Cheyenne, you get ahold of Brianna."

"What time?" I said.

"Let's do it early so everybody can go off and do whatever else they had planned," Tobey said. "Since it's Friday and all."

"Six o'clock," Cheyenne said. "I have a nine o'clock curfew until my grades come up." She snatched the paper and kissed it—actually kissed it.

I snorted. "What is that, like your parole paper?" I said.

I could have immediately bitten off my lip. But Cheyenne didn't make any connection between that comment and her incarcerated mother. She stuffed the paper happily into her backpack and backed off, still grinning. "See you at six," she said.

"Perfect," Tobey said. She slapped her literature book closed.

"I can still make it to our youth group thing after. What are you doing tonight?"

I stopped midway through trying to jam my binder in between my chemistry and trig books. "I was invited to a party at Gabe's."

Tobey gave me a look.

"I know, there's no love lost between you two after everything that went down last fall. I wasn't planning on going."

Especially not now that he's into Grand Theft Chemistry Exams, I added in my head.

I hadn't thought about the cheating thing for hours. Suddenly, with Tobey there, I wanted to talk about it. L'Orange would know what to do about that, and I'd make her give me advice this time.

But Tobey was already standing up and looking at her watch. Maybe later, while we were eating or something. Then she would go off to her youth group thing, and I'd—do what?—go home to study trig and chemistry?

Not.

When I got home from school, I lugged my backpack up to my room and threw it into the back of my closet. It was Friday night, dad-gum it. There had to be something halfway entertaining I could do.

For reasons I cannot to this day explain, I got a phrase in my head: *You must be a trip to go out with.*

Wyatt.

If you change your mind, just let me know.

No way!

I hurled myself toward the phone and started to dial Deb's number. She was always up for seeing a movie—Then I hung up. Deb was going to Gabe's party. So were Lance and Pavella. Probably Rhonda, too.

The sensation of being outside a circle was suddenly overwhelming. They were my best friends—at least, that's what I'd always called them in my mind. Now it was like I'd been dropped off the list—shoved out of the ring—and I didn't even know what rule I'd broken—

Everybody has rules.

"Enough with Wyatt, already!" I said aloud.

You keep changing yours.

I snatched up the phone with a snort. "All right," I said as I pawed through a bunch of debris on my desk for my journalism phone list. "I'm not spending a whole evening with you in my head. Let's get this conversation over with."

"Hello," he said—cheerfully, of course.

"Wyatt? This is Norie Vanden—"

"Hey! Blow me away, why don't you?"

"—berger."

"This is cool. What's up?"

I didn't have an immediate answer for him, unbelievable as that may sound. I was still reeling from the enthusiastic reception. Few people greeted me like that—especially not guys. Rule number one—never let a girl know you're really interested. Not that they ever were—

"I called about the rules," I blurted out.

"Great. You want to go out tonight and talk about them?"

"Look—"

"I'm free tonight."

This kid had a mind like a steel trap. He might have been the only kid I'd ever met who was as aggressive as I was. "I'm free, too," I said. "Around eight. But not for a date. Just for a—"

"A go-out-and-talk thing."

"Yeah. And only if I pay my own way."

"You're going to have to drive, too, because I don't have a car."

"No problem," I said.

When we hung up, I couldn't have explained why I'd agreed to all that if my GPA and SAT scores combined had depended on it. Nor could I explain why the evening ahead suddenly looked a lot brighter.

Until just as I was going out the door to head for the Pneumatic Diner, Mom hailed me from the kitchen. "Did you get your mail?" she said. "On the table in the hall?"

There was actually a letter for me in the silver dish—with a

Harvard return address. I ripped it open and took it to the bottom step to sit down. My heart was pounding loud in my ears—ridiculously. All I'd done was inquire about early application. It wasn't like this was going to be an acceptance letter or anything.

"Dear Ms. Vandenberger," it read. "Thank you for your inquiry, blah, blah, blah." I scanned the page. Ah, there it was—the list of requirements.

"SAT scores of 1300 or better. We assume you will be taking those in December. Four written recommendations. Score of 4 or better on at least two Advanced Placement examinations."

And then I gasped.

"A GPA of 3.9 is required for the early acceptance program. The majority of our entering freshmen are in the top one percent of their high school class—"

I felt as if I'd been stabbed. I didn't have to have my father there to remind me. *Two Bs for the semester, Norie? Are you out of your mind? You get that, and you can forget the Ivy League. You can forget everything we've been preparing you for since you were three years old. You, Norie, can forget your dreams.*

CHAPTER SIX

THE PNEUMATIC DINER WAS AN OBSCURE LITTLE restaurant upstairs behind the Truckee River Lodge on, of course, the Truckee River. It consisted of about six tables that surrounded an island of a kitchen where a bunch of young guys—the kind who ride their bicycles everywhere, attend Earth Day functions, and sneer at you if you wear leather—made these incredible concoctions like Potato Bayard and Apricot Dyna-Flows. New art was always on the walls, and a dance class was going on in the studio next door, which you could see through the two-way mirror.

It was the perfect turf for the Flagpole Girls. Nobody else from King High was likely to come in there on a Friday night and whisper to each other about us being the Jesus Freaks. The clientele of the Pneumatic was pretty much people on their way home from a Nevada Festival Ballet rehearsal or a poetry reading at UNR. Considering that we were in Reno, the place didn't have to be very big.

The diner felt cozy when I came in out of the biting early November wind off the river. Everybody was sitting around already except for Cheyenne and Brianna. They trailed in as I was gathering up a few more chairs from nearby tables. John, the owner, never minded how much we moved the furniture, as long as we were willing to joke around with him when he came to take our order.

"So let's see it, Cheyenne," Marissa said.

Cheyenne pawed around in her jacket pocket.

"You actually brought your vocabulary test with you?" I said, snorting.

She produced it, now wrinkled and greasy, probably from being passed around in Tassie's kitchen.

"That's beautiful," Shannon said. "Congratulations."

Brianna nudged me. "And you, too. When are you going to start tutorin' me?"

"I didn't have anything to do with it," I said. "We worked on it for all of about ten or fifteen minutes."

"Tassie was so impressed, she un-grounded me for the weekend," Cheyenne said. "Oh, and Norie, she said you could come for Sunday dinner. We always dress up."

"I'll break out my mink," I said.

John glared at me from the counter.

"You going to wash your hands before then, girl?" Brianna said to Cheyenne. "Or is that some kind of fashion statement?"

"What?" Tobey said.

All necks stretched toward Cheyenne, who thrust her hands into her lap.

"She has writing on her hands," Brianna said. "Looks like she has tattoos or somethin'."

"It's a freshman thing," Marissa said. "No offense, Cheyenne. We did that when I was a freshman."

Tobey grinned. "Last year."

"You grow up a lot between freshman and sophomore years," Shannon said.

"I never wrote on my own hands," Tobey said. "Guys liked to do it to me though. They thought they were so clever if they could get something gross on you that wouldn't wash off, and then you'd have to walk around with it on there all day."

"I never had that problem," I said dryly. "No guy ever wanted to hold my hand long enough to write on it."

"When are you going to stop puttin' yourself down, girl?" Brianna pulled her perfectly tweezed eyebrows together. "You talk like you're some kind of canine or somethin'."

"To hear men tell it, I am," I said.

"Don't worry about it, Nor," Tobey said. "I think they just hate it when a girl is smarter than they are."

"I'll never have that problem!" Cheyenne said.

"You might if you keep this up." Brianna tapped her nails on the vocabulary test, which was still displayed in the middle of the table. "But no boy is going to want to hold your hand with that ink all over it."

"I'm not holding hands with any guys tonight," Cheyenne said. "Me and Ellie and Felise are going to the movies. Anybody want to come?"

She looked at me so hopefully, I think I felt my heart split a crack. "I already have plans," I said. "Or I would. Felise looks like she would be a kick."

"What are you doing tonight?" Tobey said. "I was going to invite you to our youth group, and then we got off the subject."

"I'm going out," I said. I tried to make it abrupt enough so they would switch to another person. No such luck, not with this group. They zeroed in like I was sending off some kind of signal: Ask me more! Ask me more!

"That sounds interesting," Brianna said. She hovered over her strawberry fizz, fingering the straw. "Going out with who?"

"You probably don't know him," I said.

Antennae went up all around the table. It looked like a car with five CB radios.

"Him?" Tobey said.

"Do we know him?" Marissa said.

"Or are we being too personal?" Shannon said. "Aren't we prying?"

"Sure we are," Brianna said. "I want to know who the dude is."

"What's he look like?" Cheyenne said.

"How come you haven't told us about this before?" Tobey said.

"Because I just asked him an hour ago."

Brianna's eyebrows shot up. "You asked him?"

"No, he asked me first, and then I called him up and said yes. Only it's not a date. We're just going to go out and talk."

"Sounds like a date to me," Brianna said. She surveyed the table with her eyes. Four heads nodded.

"I'm so glad we all agree," I said, voice dripping sarcasm. "I'd hate to go out without everybody's approval."

"I haven't approved yet," Tobey said, grinning. "Who's the guy?"

"Wyatt Fox," I said.

"Well, if he's a fox," Cheyenne said, "it's okay with me!"

She giggled until Brianna poked her, and then she plastered her hands over her mouth. She was such a freshman.

"I know him," Tobey said. "He's in my American history class." She cocked her head over folded hands. "He's perfect for you. Mrs. Bowman loves him. He'll discuss anything. The rest of us sit there like warts on a toad."

"'Warts on a toad'?" Brianna said. "How attractive."

"That's what she calls us. She calls Wyatt the next Bertrand Russell."

"Who's Bertrand Russell?" Shannon said.

"A great philosopher," I said.

Tobey grinned around the table. "See what I mean?"

"Okay, you guys, enough with the Cupid thing, all right?" I said. "Wyatt works on the paper, and we've had like two conversations. We're just going out for a Coke so we can talk and not be interrupted by a bell or something."

"Talk about what?" Cheyenne said.

"I don't know . . . just stuff."

"Let's guess," Tobey said. She was grinning earlobe to earlobe, and her eyes were about to dance out of their sockets. There was no point in trying to stop her. She was too far gone.

"I think you two are going to discuss . . . politics," she said.

"No, girl, she's blushin' way too much for that," Brianna said. "I'll put my money on their favorite poets."

"I don't have a favorite poet," I said.

"You better get you one," Brianna said. She nodded to Cheyenne, who nodded back and then went into another fit of giggling.

"I think they're going to talk about the newspaper—at first," Marissa said. She was fighting a smile; I think she was still a little afraid of me at that point.

"Then what?" Tobey said.

"Then what movies they like."

"Something at the Keystone, no doubt."

"And then their favorite music—"

"Which will lead to sitting in the car listening to tapes," Brianna said. "And who knows what all after that?"

"You guys, I think we should stop. We're embarrassing Norie."

I was as surprised as anybody else to hear that coming out of Shannon. I think she even surprised herself, because she turned three successive shades of red and rolled her eyes all over the ceiling. She was probably as relieved as I was that John chose that moment to start sliding plates onto our table.

"Yes!" I said, with too much enthusiasm. "This looks incredible. I'm starving."

"Ooh, let me have a bite of yours, Norie," Cheyenne said before I could even get my fork into the melted cheese that was drizzled all over the top of my potatoes. She stuck out her hand across the table at me, opening and closing her fingers like a four-year-old begging for change for the ice cream man.

"Chill," I said. "I'll cut you off a hunk."

I did and dodged the platter John was giving Marissa before I handed Cheyenne my fork. She grabbed it, palm open.

That gave me a brief, if crinkled, shot of the "tattoo" Brianna had been talking about. I thought I saw something that started with an F. Part of me wanted to grab her wrist and say, "Hey, is that something obscene?" Another part of me, a surprising part of me, wanted her to get her hand back into her lap before anybody else saw it.

What is the matter with me? I thought as John continued to feed the chaos with still more steaming plates of food. *I should be smacking that kid up the side of the head!*

Maybe I would have, seriously, if the last order of burritos hadn't found its way to the right eater and if we hadn't automatically joined hands and bowed our heads to pray. The minute we opened our eyes, Cheyenne looked at all of us with tears glimmering like little crystals on her eyelashes and said, "I really love you guys. Nobody's ever made me feel this special before."

Even I, Ms. Tell It Like It Is, couldn't burst into that.

Once we started digging in, the conversation turned to safer subjects, like where Brianna and Ira were going for the evening, what Tobey's youth group was doing, and what movie Cheyenne and company, which now included Marissa, were going to see. We already had polished off the giant piece of carrot cake, served with six forks, before I thought about Wyatt again.

The minute he was back in my mind, I forgot to ask Tobey about the cheating thing. I wouldn't admit it to myself, but I was starting to freak out about picking this guy up and spending a whole evening with him. I could tell myself whatever I wanted, but this was the closest I'd ever come to a date in my sixteen years. By the time I climbed into the driver's seat of the Jeep, my hands were so sweaty they were sliding off the steering wheel.

Come on, knock it off, Vandenberger, I scolded myself as I drove through town. *You're the one who's always saying guys aren't this big mysterious entity. He's just a person—no better than you—so quit stressing.*

That worked. When I reached his driveway and found him hanging out by the mailbox, I was ready with my first sarcastic retort.

"Hi," he said as he slid in. "I thought you might feel weird coming up to the door."

"What are you hiding in there, Fox?" I said. "Is your mother a lady wrestler or something?"

His face saddened in the headlights of a passing car. "You're close," he said. "She's a bouncer down at JJ's."

"Really?" I said.

He grinned. "No, I'm just messing around."

"Get out," I said. But I pulled the car on out and took off up the street. At the corner, I said, "Where are we going?"

"Bowling?" he said.

I snorted. "Bowling? You actually bowl?"

"I average 120 a game."

"Is that good?"

He grinned again. "Okay, forget bowling. You pick."

"Movie?"

He shook his head. "We can't talk at a movie. I mean, we could, but we would probably get thrown out."

"I've been shushed by a few ushers in my time," I said.

"If we did see a movie, what would you pick?"

This was coming dangerously close to Marissa's prediction. "There's nothing decent playing right now anyway," I said. I eyed him sideways. "So you wanted to talk?"

"Yeah, but I can see it all now."

"What?"

"We go down to the Emerald City or Walden's or something, sit down face to face at the table, and neither one of us will be able to think of anything to say."

"That's never been a problem for me," I said ruefully. "I can usually talk longer than people can listen to me."

"Yeah, well, I have a better idea."

"Which is? You'd better hurry up; the light's going to change any minute, and I have to pick right or left."

"Left," he said. "Remember how I said you would be a kick to go out with?"

" 'Trip' was the exact word you used," I said.

"I want to prove it."

"You're going to prove to yourself that I'm a trip. Is this supposed to be fun for me?"

"I say we challenge each other to a scavenger hunt."

I all but groaned aloud. Terrific. The old sixth-grade standby for birthday parties. Everybody go out and knock on doors and request an out-of-date Burger King coupon and a purple button.

"You make out a list for me, I make one out for you, and then we compete."

I felt my interest quiver. "Compete? You against me?" I said.

"Yeah, only there are rules."

"Of course. You love rules."

"We have half an hour, and we have to do it all within a one-block radius of downtown."

"We have to be off the streets by nine down there," I said. "It's a totally stupid law, but—"

"Okay, so are you up for it?"

I glanced at him. His face was shimmering with the anticipation of it all, and he was already coming up with a list in his mind. I could tell from the way his eyes were sparking behind his glasses.

Well, if there was one thing I was good at, it was competing. And if I had to go my own way for half an hour, maybe I could get calmed down again. I was beyond sweaty palms; my armpits were starting to leak.

"You're on," I said.

"Dude. Park in the El Dorado Parking Garage, and we can do our lists in there. Do you have paper and pencil?"

"Do I have paper and pencil? What do you want, lined, unlined, recycled?"

Beyond the garage, neon signs chased themselves in squares and horns blew and early partyers whooped as Wyatt and I scratched out five items each. I came up with the most impossible things I could think of: napkin from the Silver Legacy signed by a waitress, canceled valet ticket from the parking garage, that kind of thing.

He chuckled when he looked at it.

"What's so funny?" I said.

"You'll see," he said. "Okay, remember you have to stay within a block, because there are lights and lots of people. It can be rough down here if you get away from the crowd."

"I've lived in Reno all my life," I said. "I can handle it."

"Okay. Meet back here as soon as you're done. First one back with all the items—"

"Yeah, yeah. I know the rules."

He shrugged, naturally, and jogged off across the garage. I took off for the elevator as I unfolded my list. I about tripped when I read it.

A two-line poem written by somebody looking for a handout.

A piece of a real plant.

A drink straw formed into the shape of an animal.

Something Native American.

Proof that someone in Reno has an artistic bone in their body.

"What the Sam Hill is this?" I said.

The couple next to me in the elevator stared at me curiously.

"Lost?" the guy said. "We live here. Can we help?"

"Not unless you have an artistic bone in your body," I said. I shook my head. "Never mind. I'm on a scavenger hunt—it's—never mind."

"You need something artistic?" the woman said. She nudged the man. "Draw something for her, honey. He's really good," she assured me.

"I don't want to bother you."

"No problem. Do you have a piece of paper?"

I, of course, did. We all got off the elevator in the lobby of the El Dorado, and the guy took my spiral notebook and pencil and started to draw. I felt like an idiot.

"He's so talented," the woman said. "I wish somebody would discover him."

"I'll do my best," I said dryly. I gave the guy a nervous glance. He was licking the end of the pencil to get some kind of special effect. "It doesn't have to be like a Picasso or anything," I said. "Just any little sketch."

"How about this?" he said.

He presented the notebook with a flourish. There was a perfect replica of Gumby trotting across the page.

"Incredible," I said. "Thanks so much."

"Bob," he said, pumping my free hand.

"And Barbie," the woman said.

"Hey, good luck in your career," I said. And then I bounded off, muttering, "Fox, I'm going to smack you."

I hurried for the nearest door, since minors aren't supposed to be in casinos unaccompanied by an adult. I did take the time to pick up a drink straw that was lying on the floor.

"Gross," I muttered. "No telling where this has been."

I wiped it on my jeans, stuck the notebook under my arm, and walked down the sidewalk while trying to form it into a cat. *Leave it to a guy to make this so hard I can't possibly beat him,* I thought. *Where am I going to find a plant growing in the middle of Reno?*

I dodged the guy in full warpath regalia who was standing in front of Harrah's with some kind of sign and craned my neck toward the planters that faced the sidewalk. Silk and rubber, all of them. How tacky.

I consulted the list again and screeched to a halt in the middle of the sidewalk. Native American. What about a nice feather plucked from a fake Indian in rented headdress?

There was one floating by even then. I leaned over to pick it up, spotted a blade of a weed struggling to get its head up through the sidewalk crack, and was simultaneously mowed down by something hard and heavy.

I sprawled out on the sidewalk like a five-year-old falling off a bike, still clutching the spiral notebook, the part-cat-part-drink-straw, a feather, and a now mutilated piece of a weed.

Hands curled around one arm and then the other, and I was suddenly on my feet. I shook free and glared upward. A guy with a shaved head and a gold tooth looked down at me.

"Excuse you," he said.

"Sorry," I said.

I'd have given him something more flippant, probably more caustic. But the sight of this guy gave me the creeps. I'd seen gang wannabe's and the occasional tough type at school, but I'd never come face to face with anything quite this hard before. His eyes were glinty. His mouth was sour. His pectorals under the skin tight T-shirt had the visual consistency of bricks.

I just nodded and moved away.

"Hey," said the guy who had been on my other side. "You're not going to pay us?"

"For what?" I said.

"We just saved your life," Shaved Head said. He glanced at his cohort, who glanced back at him, so he could glance back in some kind of eyeball secret code. I forgot for a second to be scared. I hated it when guys acted like you were stupid because you didn't know what one blink and two eye rolls meant.

"You just knocked me down," I said. "I figure we're even."

One of them swore. The other one spit on the sidewalk. I had a scathingly brilliant idea. "Okay, look," I said. "I'll give you two dollars if you'll make up two lines that rhyme."

They did another exchange of codified gazes.

"Five bucks," I said. "You two aren't going to get a better offer."

Shaved Head took a step toward me, but the other guy, the one with all the ear and nose rings, said, "Roses are red, violets are blue."

"Uh-huh," I said, still eyeing Shaved Head. He was giving me a power stare.

"Give us five bucks or we're going to mug you."

I believed him. As hard as his eyes were, he probably had all that piercing done at one time, with no Novocaine.

"Here," I said, digging into the envelope-sized purse I wore draped by its strap over my chest. "Take ten dollars. I don't have any change." I tightened my hold on the spiral notebook. Wyatt was just going to have to take my word for it. Asking these two to write out their poem would be pushing it.

"Thanks, guys. It's been real," I said. "Let's do lunch sometime, okay?"

They didn't see the humor. While they were once more giving each other optical Morse code, I took off and lost myself in the crowd. Once I left them behind, I started to feel pretty smug.

Eat your heart out, Wyatt Fox, I thought as I waited for the light to change so I could cross the street back to the parking garage. *I am going to be back with my booty so far ahead of you, you're going to feel like a lightweight.*

He hadn't known who he was dealing with, that was obvious. The light changed, and I hot-footed it out into the intersection. About halfway across, I had another incredible thought. If I went the back way, through the alley, I could get to the Jeep without Wyatt even seeing me and add the element of surprise to my having beaten the pants off of him.

I crammed my loot safely inside the notebook, hugged it to my chest, and took off around the corner.

So it's outside the official one-block radius. Who made up that rule anyway?

The rules—now that was something I wanted to talk about with him. That whole thing about everybody having rules you had to know about to get along with them. I was dying of thirst.

Maybe we could go to like Denny's or something, have a milk shake, and get to the bottom of that.

I chuckled to myself as I skittered into the alley that led straight to the block where the parking garage's entrance was. Wyatt had probably been right. An hour before it would have been a really stupid conversation with both of us feeling about as awkward as middle schoolers. Now I actually couldn't wait to see him when he showed up at the Jeep, grinning. Of course he'd be grinning—

"We meet again."

"How 'bout that."

I came to a startled halt. A hulking shadow moved in front of me and planted itself in my path. In silhouette, I could see it was Shaved Head. No doubt that was Mr. Pierce-All breathing down my neck. My every pore smarted in fear.

"Let me pass," I said. I tried to sound slightly bored, maybe exasperated. I'm sure I wasn't successful. They didn't budge.

"Give us the rest of what's in that purse, Rich Witch," Pierce-All said.

"Fine, take it," I said. "Take the whole thing."

I fumbled with the strap and managed to get it wrapped around my neck as I tried to pull it over my head. Shaved Head grabbed it and pulled. I screamed, just before I started to choke.

"Freeze! Police!" The voice echoed through the alley like it was coming out of Andre the Giant. Pierce-All took a second to squint over my head. But Shaved Head dropped the purse and took off at a run, down the alley ahead of me.

"Come on!" he screamed over his shoulder to his accomplice.

Pierce-All gave the alley behind me one more glance before he, too, took off. I could hear footsteps in the gravel from both directions. I put my hands to the sides of my face so I wouldn't scream and waited for gunshots. After the footsteps faded, there was nothing. Except a voice at my side saying, "Norie, are you okay?"

CHAPTER SEVEN

IT WAS WYATT, PASTY FACED AND AS TREMBLY AS I WAS.
I clawed at the sleeve of his jacket and looked frantically over
his shoulder.

"Where are the police?" I said.

"I don't know. I wish they would show up."

"Then who was that yelling? You?"

"Yeah. Let's get out of here before those two baboons figure
it out."

Wyatt grabbed my hand and hauled me out of the alley the
way I'd come in. We had been so close to the light and laughter
of Virginia Street; yet I'd felt so far away from everything in
those few terrifying moments. I wanted to hang on to Wyatt's
hand for dear life, a thought which was terrifying in itself. I
yanked my hand away and double-timed it down the sidewalk.

Wyatt matched me step for step. "What were you doing going down that alley anyway?" he hissed at me.

"Going to the car."

"What, were you trying to get jumped?"

"Yes, it's my hobby." I shot him a dirty look as I shoved open
the door to the El Dorado. My face probably looked like a
crumpled paper bag at that point, but I was keeping up the
attempt at sarcasm. I was too embarrassed to do anything else,
and I was becoming more so the farther away we got from
Shaved Head and the Piercer.

"It was pretty stupid, Norie," Wyatt whispered as we
boarded the escalator.

"So you've said. Okay. Drop it."

"Are you all right?"

"Yes."

'You're shaking like a leaf."

"I am not."

"Yes, you are. You should see your lips."

"All right. I'm a mess," I said. "Are you satisfied?" I charged off the escalator at the top and whipped past the hoards of people waiting to get into the restaurants. The parking garage was about a hundred yards away, and I planned to take them at a sprint.

But Wyatt snatched at my hand again and pulled me against his side. I tried to pry myself away, but he was stronger than he looked. Solid was the right word. I had to fight the urge to melt right into him.

"Let go," I said through my teeth.

"Not if you're going to tear off like a squirrel," he said. "You're in shock."

"Get over yourself. I'm fine." I wrenched myself away from him, but I didn't take off. My insides were turning into a Jell-O salad, and it was about all I could do to stay two steps ahead of him.

When we reached the Jeep, I fumbled for my purse. Just holding it in my hand sent a wave of terror over me. I sagged against the car and willed myself not to shake. I felt Wyatt's arm go around my shoulder.

"Don't," I said.

"You're coming unglued. Who wouldn't?"

"I'm not!" I wriggled away and clawed in my purse for the keys. They jangled to the floor, and Wyatt got to them first.

"Let me have them," I said.

"Why don't you let me drive?" he said. "You're so shook up."

"I don't need you to tell me what I am, and I don't need you to protect me, and I don't need—"

"What do you need then?" he said. "This?"

He put both his arms around me and scooped me into a hug—that turned into a kiss. I don't know how long I stayed in it before I squirmed away. He let go easily, and he looked like he wanted to go through the garage floor.

"I'm sorry," he said. "Don't be mad. Norie—"

"Just get in," I said. "I'll take you home."

I don't know which of us felt more like a total idiot. Neither one said a word all the way to his house. I was sure he was thinking I was the stupidest, most wigged out, ungrateful wench he had ever come across. I didn't have a clue to what I was thinking, except that if I didn't get off by myself in the next ten seconds I was going to burst into tears. And that really would make me mad.

When I pulled into his driveway, I was on the verge. Wyatt sat there for a second; I could feel him looking at the side of my face.

"Well, thanks," I said.

"It's okay. I'm glad it worked out."

I waited for him to exit. He started to, and then he stopped with his hand on the door handle. "You know, you don't have to be this brick wall," he said. "I was scared, too."

"I really need to go," I said. I was holding back a whole throatful of tears, and I didn't know how much longer I could do it.

"Okay," he said. Once more he went for the door handle, and once more he stopped himself. "I think you won," he said.

"What?"

"I was still trying to get a blue free drink ticket when I saw you go down the alley so I didn't get everything on the list. I bet you did."

All I could do was nod.

"I knew it," he said. He tried to grin, and then he said, "See you."

That time he did get out of the Jeep, and not a moment too soon. I was crying before I reached the stop sign at the end of his street.

There was nothing I hated more than to cry. Must have been all those years of my father telling me to stop being a baby and "think this thing through." "You can handle anything if you just think it through," he had said to me a hundred times.

But "think" was about the last thing I wanted to do. My

parents were out when I got home. I shut myself up in my room and put a pillow over my head to close everything out. It didn't work. The thoughts just grew louder, shouting at each other in a verbal war.

What is up with this? Are you such a winning-weenie you'll go darting through dark alleys just to come out on top?

Why wouldn't you just say thank you to Wyatt when he saved your tail?

Why did he have to go and kiss me?

Why did I let him?

Why did I stop letting him?

"This is stupid," I said aloud. I paced the room, pillow jammed against my stomach. "Just go back and think about it. It wasn't that bad."

It wasn't. Two thugs had followed me into an alley because they knew I had money. I'd made that abundantly clear out on the sidewalk.

So they had grabbed my purse. Granted, it was wrapped around my neck, and I thought I was choking to death. But nobody had hurt me. The whole thing had lasted all of about thirty seconds. And now I was fine.

Thanks to Wyatt.

My breathing started to race again, and I hugged the pillow harder. This was too weird. Here I was, Norie Vandenberger, coldest chick in the junior class. I had an answer for everything. I was focused and driven and that was all that had ever counted. It had been convenient that boys were usually jerks, and I honestly didn't want to get involved with them.

Now here comes this almost-too-short-for-me, unassuming guy with glasses and a ponytail, and suddenly I'm as confused as Cheyenne, as tongue-tied as Shannon. And acting as hard-nosed as Brianna.

The thing was, I didn't want to act that way.

Miserably, I eyed the phone. *Maybe I should call him and apologize.*

I got as far as my hand on the receiver. No way. All I could do right now was cry. He would really think I was a psycho.

Not that it matters, I told myself.

But it did matter. And I hated that I just couldn't let it be okay to fall apart over a horrible experience, over a guy, over the dreams that seemed to suddenly be slipping away no matter how hard I worked.

That was part of it, too. I knew in a chunk of realization that also included Deborah, Lance, Gabe, Pavella, and the cheating thing.

I sank down onto my bed and let the pillow go.

"Dear God," I said out loud, "everything I've always held on to is falling apart. And I don't know how to stop it. Please help me. I don't know the rules anymore. I don't know the rules!"

If I'd thought I was crying hard before, I hadn't seen anything. I buried my head in the rest of my mound of pillows and sobbed. I sobbed until my throat was squeezed shut and my stomach felt like it was in a vise. Sometime after the tears ran out and the hiccups kicked in, I must have fallen asleep.

The dream started the minute I hit REM. It went on and on, over and over. My swimming out to the raft with the waves splashing into the side of my face. My laughing at them. My clinging to the raft, still laughing, until the thunder rolled across the water like a bowling ball and rocked the lake into breakers. In huge walls they crashed into me, then picked me up and hurled me back down.

I'm going to hit the raft, I wanted to scream but couldn't. *I'm going to hit the raft. I can't see it!*

Then the lightning came, cracking open the sky, blinding me with light. I should have been able to see everything then. But I couldn't. I couldn't see anything. I just kept crashing toward my certain death, over and over again. And I couldn't stop it.

I didn't wake up until ten the next morning. It wasn't surprising that I felt like I hadn't slept at all, though I was pretty shocked when I stumbled to the bathroom and squinted at myself in the mirror. I was still in my jeans and sweater from the night before, which made me look like a wino hauling myself up from the gutter. That image was accentuated by the red, swollen-into-slits eyes and the black bags under them. I leaned in to check for morning moss on my teeth, and I gasped.

One side of my neck had a bright red, angry-looking stripe that tortured itself into my skin. It took me a minute to realize it must have been from my purse strap, when Shaved Head was yanking on it. I grabbed for a washcloth to put on the burn, and I saw my own hand, shaking like a junkie's.

This is out of control, I thought. *I'm really losing it here.*

Holding the washcloth on my neck, I staggered back to my room and leaned against the window. *Please, God, I am so confused.*

Outside, a spectacular Nevada November morning was on display. Cloudless sky, blue to the ends of the earth. Leaves in outrageous oranges and golds sizzling against it like a painting. A clear sun sparkling crisply through the cold. You would barely need a sweater out there today.

Tobey said she gets quiet and listens, I thought.

Below, I could hear my mother rattling something in the kitchen, probably a waffle iron or a soufflé pan. My father's jazz was improvising its way out of the stereo speakers, and he was barking orders over it at my mother.

So much for listening. I looked angrily out at the day. I could also hear my backpack calling to me from the closet: *You have B's in chemistry and trig. You better get cracking.*

I think I'd have let that voice have the last word, if I hadn't heard another one, softer but surprisingly husky. *You really ought to come here sometime and just walk around,* it said.

I washed my face and threw on a different sweater, one that didn't bear the smells of downtown Reno.

"Where are you off to this morning?" Mom said as I passed through the kitchen and grabbed a bagel.

"Rancho San Rafael," I said.

"You should stop by the Doctors' Wives Craft Fair at Washoe Med," she said. "I'll be there all day. Your dad's on call so he'll be at the hospital or his office."

So I'm on my own, I thought as I climbed into my Jeep.

That was exactly what I wanted.

For all the good it did me. Just as Shannon said, Rancho San Rafael was perfect: quiet, unfolding from one incredible garden into another, all dotted with benches and gazebos for sitting and thinking.

The trouble was, every time I sat down, so much noise was in my head, I couldn't listen to any part of it.

Has it always been like this? I thought. *Or am I just going nuts now?*

I couldn't even pray. I hadn't been doing it all that long, mind you. Only since August really, except for the Now-I-Lay-Me-Down-to-Sleep thing when I was little. But until today, I'd at least been able to say, "So, God, how about a little help with this chem test?" or "Would you mind checking in on Tobey? She's about wrecked at this point."

But that day, with all the conditions perfect and pristine, I couldn't pray a thing. I became so anxious I couldn't even sit still. I stuffed my hands in my jeans pockets and walked, hard and fast, head down.

Which is probably why I didn't see Shannon until I nearly tripped over her.

"Norie?" she said. "Are you okay?"

I lifted my face to see her standing at the edge of the path near a fluffy knoll of chrysanthemums. It was too late to erase the pain that was obviously smeared all over me. It registered immediately in her pale eyes. She put a translucent hand on my arm.

"What's wrong?" she said. "You look awful."

I tried to snort. "Well, at least that confirms what I thought when I looked in the mirror this morning."

She bit down on her lip. I shook my head. "I'm sorry," I said. "I'm just more obnoxious than usual today."

She nodded. Standing there, blonde hair blowing thinly in the wind, wispy little body looking vulnerable against the chill, sympathy sitting softly on every surface of her face, she looked so peaceful, so serene, so everything I wanted to be.

I caved. "I came here to listen to God, like you said." My voice came out weak and wobbly. "But I can't hear anything. I feel so messed up."

Shannon squeezed my hand. "I'm really sorry," she said. "I feel bad for you."

"Thanks," I said. I didn't add that that didn't help me a whole lot. I was already sorry enough for both of us.

"You know what I do when I feel like that?" Shannon said.

I refrained from saying, "You? No way!" I just shook my head.

"I go see Ms. Race. She's wonderful."

I shrugged.

"Really, I went over to her house one Saturday. It was one of those days when I could hardly stand to be in my own skin, you know?"

I did. The hard-to-believe thing was that she did.

"Just call her," Shannon said. "She has a way."

"I don't know," I said. "There's so much going on with me. I don't think you—"

"Is your entire family falling apart?" Shannon said.

"No, but—"

"Do you ever wish one of your siblings would just drop dead?"

"Uh, no, but I'm an only child—"

"Do you ever think about running away from home?"

This time I just shook my head. There was a vulnerable looking pink spot in the center of each of Shannon's cheeks. She was as wrecked as I was.

"She helped you with that kind of stuff?" I said.

"Yeah. I don't know what I'd do without her."

"Wow," I said.

I felt about half an inch tall as Shannon gave my hand a last squeeze and went on, hands slipped into the pockets of her sweats, face up to the wind. I almost felt like I owed it to her to phone Ms. Race.

I had the number in my calendar book in the car. I also had the cell phone in my car. There was no excuse, and I had no idea what else to do.

"Hi," I said when she answered. "This is Norie."

"How bizarre," she said. "I was just thinking about you."

"Oh," I said.

"Norie, what's wrong?" she said. "You sound wretched."

"That seems to be the consensus," I said. "Do you think we could get together sometime?"

"Sometime? How about now?"

"Really?" I said.

"I'll brew up some coffee. How about a mocha?"

"Okay. You live on Plumas?"

"Big white house with columns. I'm on the second floor. You hang tough till you get here, okay?"

"Okay," I said.

I hadn't known how close I was to tears again until I hung up and saw the two streams trailing down my sweater.

Her apartment was actually the whole second floor of a big old 1920s vintage house on a shady section of Plumas. Even as hard as I was bawling, the decor of the living room registered with me when she opened the door. The walls were covered with gold-green-and-orange-striped fabric that matched the inviting collection of pillows on the couch. There was a plethora of bamboo and jungle prints and plants that leaned toward the sunny alcove of windows. If Ms. Race hadn't pulled me in, the room would have.

"Bless your heart," she said. "Sit down. Let me get you a mocha. Take your shoes off if you want and warm your tootsies by the fire."

"I don't even know why I'm crying," I said. "It's so stupid. I feel like a baby."

She stopped in the doorway, steaming pedestal mug in hand, and shook her head at me. "Let's get something straight right off the bat, Norie," she said. "Babies aren't the only ones who get to cry." She pulled up a cushioned footstool beside me and pressed the hot mocha into my hand. "Crying may be the first healthy thing I've ever seen you do."

I held the mug between my palms and cried some more. She sat there patiently beside me until I caught my breath.

"Why don't you start at the beginning?" she said.

I took a sip and let the amazing warm blend of coffee and chocolate ease into my chest. Then I told her about summer camp.

CHAPTER
EIGHT

THE BROCHURE DESCRIBED IT AS A CAMP FOR "EXCEP-
tionally gifted students." The two weeks I was there were set
aside for "talented young journalists."

"If this wasn't tailor-made for you, I don't know what is,"
Mrs. Abbey said when she showed it to me at the end of sophomore year. "You'll have to jump through some hoops to get
in—"

When it's something I want, I can do hoops of any size. I
wrote the required pieces and put together a portfolio—like I'm
so published!—and hustled up a bunch of letters of recommen-
dation. As a result, I ended up at the beginning of August on
Lake Calumet, somewhere near Chicago with fifty other high
school juniors who thought they were the next Woodward or
Bernstein just like I did.

The lake was this glassy pool that mirrored more trees than
we had in the whole state of Nevada. The oaks were thick and
running into each other and rustling their leaves in the occasional breeze that rippled across the water.

But I didn't take too much time to relish all of that. The competition was what turned me on. Gabe, Lance, Deborah—they
were pacifists compared to the kids who went to this camp. At
the supper table the first night, I was the only kid who had
never had anything published in her city's newspaper, and these
people were from like Jacksonville, Atlanta, and Dallas—not
podunk towns. Three-fourths of the girls in my cabin had
their sights set on Harvard, Stanford, or Vassar, and all of us

confessed in one of those midnight, while-the-counselor-is-out sessions that we would do just about anything to keep our 4.0s. One chick said she had even offered a teacher a bribe to give her the half a point she needed for an A.

They had these incredible workshops, a lot of them taught by magazine and newspaper editors, and all of us had access to students from the School of Journalism at Northwestern, who were also our counselors. That's only probably the best journalism school in the United States. Those people were sharp. I finagled a seat next to one of them at every meal and basically picked their brains dry.

It wasn't just being with competitive people that had me jazzed. It was the competition they set up among us while we were there. In addition to all the stuff we did in our workshops, we were also required to contribute to this huge newspaper that was going to be compiled at the end of the camp, just out of our writing. The big contest was to see whose work was going on the front page. You could do features and sports pieces and all that, but nobody was going for those. We were all scratching and clawing to write the Big Story that would be plastered right there under the masthead.

The catch was that everything we wrote had to be gleaned right there at camp. No fair dipping into your file of *Time* and *Newsweek,* which 90 percent of us had brought with us. You had to collect your facts and write your piece about something that was going on on that twenty-acre plot of land.

People were scrambling. One guy staged a panty raid just so he would have something to write about. Another girl faked food poisoning so she could do an exposé on the conditions in the kitchen. My personal favorite was the kid who was bent on proving that the camp director was actually an FBI agent sent there to investigate the possibility that the camp was a front for a money-laundering operation. Go figure.

I was, of course, determined to get that front-page center spot, and with something I didn't have to fabricate. We were close to the deadline, and I hadn't come up with a thing. I pretended I had the whole assignment pretty much wrapped up, but two nights before we were supposed to turn our stuff in, I was lying in bed staring up at the ceiling and hoping for inspiration while everybody else slept.

Which is why I heard Carolee, our counselor, sneak out of the cabin.

I got up on my elbow and watched through the screen as she padded barefoot down the path. From out of the shadows, another figure joined her, and then another. They barely made a sound as they disappeared toward the lake.

My nose-for-news was twitching as I slid out of bed and jammed my feet into a pair of sandals. Come to think of it, Carolee was out of the cabin a lot at night. We were all so busy out-GPAing each other, we hadn't put anything together.

I was feeling incredibly smug as I slipped soundlessly out the screen door and trailed the group of what looked like six counselors down to the lakeside. By the time I got there and hid myself sufficiently in the shadows, they were swimming out to the middle of the lake toward a stationary wooden raft that during the day provided a place for diving and sunbathing, when we weren't out snooping into other people's business and concocting stories for the front page.

There was no moon that night, so the counselors' figures melted into the darkness when they got to the raft and climbed aboard. I must have had my neck stretched out there for an hour, but I couldn't tell what they were doing.

It was definitely quiet out there, and they weren't moving around much. I could detect that they were sitting in a circle.

I sniffed the air. Marijuana, maybe?

I really didn't smell anything, but I decided that was a distinct possibility. That or some kind of make-out session. My imagination was cranking out options like a copy machine spits out copies. If I could come up with the right one and prove it, I was a shoo-in for that coveted front-page position.

My byline was dancing before my eyes as I crept back to the cabin and devised a plan. My only chance was to get out there to the raft and observe what was going on. And the only way to do that was to get out there the next night and hide, maybe in the water on the other side of the raft, and wait for them to show up.

I don't know how I got through the next day without bursting an intestine or something. I hadn't been that excited since Christmas Eve when I was about seven. The only way I stayed calm was by going over the plan repeatedly in my head.

While everybody else was brushing their teeth and putting in their retainers and all that before bed, I nonchalantly arranged my pillows and sleeping bag so it would look like I was in the bed. Just before lights out, I went into the bathroom and stayed there.

It took an eternity for it to get quiet. Carolee told them to shut up about eight times until they finally settled in. I waited, standing up on the toilet in a closed stall and feeling deliciously like Lois Lane. I was rewarded by the creaking of the screen door.

I exited after Carolee, crept around to the back of the cabin, and ran like a chased mental patient through an uncleared thicket, tearing off my pajamas and revealing my bathing suit as I went. I dumped the pj's behind a bush just before I emerged out onto the lake shore.

Nobody was there yet, and from the sound of it, I was farther ahead of them than I had thought I would be. All I could hear was the whistling of the wind, no counselor's voices coming down the path.

At first when I stuck my toe into the water it was chilly, but I smacked myself inwardly. *You've swum in Lake Tahoe, for Pete's sake, Vandenberger. Get a grip.*

Walking backward so I could keep an eye on the shore, I got into the lake and reached the place where it was deep enough to swim underwater. Taking a huge breath, I dove beneath the surface and swam for all I was worth.

I hadn't taken into account that I was no athlete. I ran out of air halfway to the raft and had to come up and try to gasp quietly. I made a mental note to start working out if I was actually going to become an investigative reporter.

But there was still no action on the shore, besides the kicking

up of the sand by the wind and a few branches skittering along
the shoreline like retreating rabbits. That same wind slapped
waves against the side of my face the next time I came up. I was
a little beyond the raft, so I figured it was safe to swim back to
it on top of the water. Easier thought than done. The lake had
turned into Big Sur, and I was hard put to swim against the
current.

But I was still feeling quite proud of myself as I latched on to
the back of the raft and peered cautiously over the top. The
beach was still empty. This was incredible. I had time to catch
my breath before they got there to do whatever it was they did
in the middle of the night.

Whatever it is, they've got to have stamina to do it, I thought.
By now the raft was rocking so hard I was having a tough time
holding on. I pressed my hand on the top to hitch myself up
higher onto it, but as I did, a two-foot swell hit and brought the
raft up with a lurch to meet my chin. I bit back a howl and sank
down into the water.

The impact had not only scraped my chin, but it had
smacked my jaws together so hard my teeth were aching.

Don't be a wimp, I told myself. *Just think about getting all the
dirt on these people, going back to the cabin, hiding in the bathroom
with the laptop, and having the winning article tomorrow.*

That kept me going, up and down with the now three-foot
waves that were colliding with the raft, until I heard a noise. It
wasn't Carolee and the others shouting from the shore. It was
the unmistakable roll of thunder, as if it were heading across the
water right toward me. For the first time—attuned to nature as
I am—I looked up at the sky. Even without a moon I could see
heavy, angry clouds tangling with each other right above me. As
I gazed, open mouthed, a fork of lightning stabbed into the
whole mess and lit up the night.

The stormy night.

No wonder nobody was coming out to the raft. I'd been so
engulfed in my plan, I hadn't even noticed that we were about
to have the storm of the summer, if not the century. And I didn't
know the half of it. In Nevada we get thunderstorms now and

then, most of which are far enough away that you can watch the whole thing without getting a drop of rain on you. This was like nothing I'd ever experienced before, certainly not from a raft smack in the middle of it.

With every new, violent roar of thunder the lake kicked up higher until the raft was pitching around like a windsock. There was no way I could hang on to it from where I was without smashing my face into it every ten seconds.

Scratching and clawing at the splintery wood, I managed to drag myself up on top of the raft and look around for something to hang on to. I thought I remembered some cleats or something that held the ropes it was weighted down with.

But it was too dark to see except when the lightning was ripping open the sky, and in those moments I squeezed my eyes shut and screamed. With every bolt I could picture myself being seized with electricity and fried to a piece of charcoal—one of the disadvantages of having an active imagination.

The lightning, it turned out, was the least of my worries. It started to rain, a hard, slanting downpour that felt as if it were going to tear off my flesh. With it came more wind, angrier than before—a wind that rolled me right off the edge of the raft.

I hit the water with a slap and lost myself in the swirling blackness. Thrashing wildly, I tried to grope for the surface, but in horror I realized I didn't know where the surface was. It was so dark I couldn't see a thing. I wasn't even sure I was there anymore.

A blessed flash of lightning burned the sky, and I reached for it. I felt the raft, dangerously close to my head, and I clawed it. It seemed to bite my fingers, but I held on, and I screamed. It was a nightmare I couldn't wake up from. Over and over, a wave would shove the raft sideways and lift it up until both of us were tossing above the lake like helpless toys. Then with a sickening drop we would be plunged back down again, and I would feel my head whipping back like it was determined to disconnect from my neck.

The most terrifying thing was that I couldn't see. Even when the lightning slashed across the black hole of the night, it was too blinding to illuminate anything. All I could do was hold on and scream, and with every new attack from the storm, I was losing the ability to do even that.

I don't know how long it was before I realized somebody else was there. At first, when I saw the rubber-boat thing, I wasn't even sure it was real. I was so crazed by then, I thought for a second that I'd already died.

But the arms that took hold of me were very real. They hauled me into the boat, and the voice attached to them told me to hang on to the rope that ran along the inside of the boat and not to let go for anything. I'd have chewed off a foot if he had told me to. I was shuddering and crying and basically beyond helping myself.

We were inside the boathouse before I even looked to see who had just saved me from being the biggest front-page story that camp had ever had. He was one of the counselors. Big, broad-shouldered dude with a square jaw and dimples and very plastered-with-rain blond hair. He was an angel as far as I was concerned. And because to this day I can't remember his name, I still refer to him in my mind as Angel Boy.

"I'm not even going to ask what you were doing out there," he said to me as he wrapped a towel around me and flung me over his shoulder like a fifty-pound sack of potatoes.

But that was the first thing the other five counselors asked me when Angel Boy dumped me on a couch in the lodge and told them where he had found me.

"What on earth?" Carolee said.

She, too, looked angelic. I wanted to hug her, not something I normally have the urge to do with people.

I spilled the story between hiccups and shivers and sips of the hot tea somebody put in my hand. I expected a torrent of reprimands accompanied by some eye rolling and is-this-girl-a-freak-or-what looks. But when I was done, they were all grinning and looking sheepish.

"If I closed my eyes, I would swear that was you talking, about four years ago," Angel Boy said to Carolee.

"That's odd," she said. "I was thinking the same thing about you."

There wasn't one of them in the room who didn't have a similar story of how they had pulled some stupid stunt to, as Angel Boy put it, "show everybody else what a mental stud I was."

I guess I was supposed to be comforted. I was only confused.

"But don't you have to be competitive to make it in journalism?" I said.

"That's what they would have you believe," said another guy, "especially at Northwestern. They tell you the first day you have to either be willing to go for the jugular or go become a starving poet."

"Isn't that true?" I insisted.

"I used to think so," one of them said.

"I bought into it until about a week and a half ago," another one responded.

Everybody in there was nodding, and the mood turned suddenly more serious, as if somebody had dimmed the lights and faded in the moment-of-truth music.

"I don't get it," I said.

They all looked at Carolee. "Basically," she said, "if you want to remain a human being with any kind of morals and peace of mind left intact, you have to have your own set of principles and you have to stick to them, no matter what."

"In our case, it's all about God," Angel Boy said.

"And about a group of people who think it's about God," somebody else said. "I mean, I feel like I have a pretty strong relationship with the Lord, but if I can't talk about it with somebody else, pray together, all that—I'm history."

"I'm not trying to preach at you or anything," Carolee said to me, "but if you're going to be in this field and you don't have your faith to keep you straight, you're going to become hard and messed up."

Angel Boy shook his big blond head. "And from what I saw out there at the raft—anybody who would do that—you're a prime candidate."

"For what?" I said.

"For being totally lost."

"Do you want prayer?" Angel Boy said. "That's why we go

out to the raft at night, by the way." He grinned the dimples into operation. "What did you think we were doing out there?"

"You don't want to know," I said.

They tossed out a few guesses, all of which were worse than what I'd dreamed up, which just goes to show how naive I really was in the midst of all my superior knowledge. Then they joined hands in a circle, me included, and they bowed their heads and started to talk. It took me a minute to realize they were talking to God. They were praying, and it washed over me like a warm bath. It was an incredible night, and it lasted until the next morning, when I woke up on the couch with Angel Boy sitting on the floor beside me, still praying.

"Did you write your article?" Ms. Race said.

I looked over my empty mocha cup at her. Her eyes were dewy, and her face had that soft look people get when they've just seen a great feel-good movie.

"I wrote one," I said. "Not the one I planned, of course. It was about six people finding each other in a drowning world and helping each other keep their faith and principles afloat."

"Sounds incredible."

I toyed with the rim of my mug. "I think it's the best thing I ever wrote."

"Did you win first page?"

I snorted. "Are you kidding? They stuck it on the second page of the Religion Section. And they gave it the headline: *Counselors Sneak Religion into Curriculum*. Everybody quit reading it after the second paragraph when they found out it wasn't about subliminal messages."

Ms. Race laughed a rich, genuine belly laugh I hadn't heard from her before. She sank back against the luxurious mountain of cushions on the bamboo-and-stripes couch and looked at me softly. "You still won though, you know," she said.

"How so?"

"I'm guessing that night with those counselors wouldn't leave you alone, even after you left camp. I think you've had a deep yearning for God and for other God-seekers ever since then. That's why you were drawn so strongly to See You at the

Pole." She pushed up her sweatshirt sleeves. "If I remember correctly, you were the one who was so bent on keeping the group together, making it the cohesive circle it is now."

I sighed, somewhere from the depths of myself. "That's true," I said. "But I'm so frustrated. I mean, I'm doing all this stuff, and it feels good and all, but I keep dreaming about being out there by the raft. I don't know, it's like it has something to do with the way I can't get close to God. Tobey says listen. Shannon says sit in the park. That isn't working for me, and I feel like I really need God because my whole life is coming apart at the seams that I sewed, you know what I'm saying?"

"I know exactly what you're saying," Ms. Race said. Her eyes lit up as she leaned forward and touched my hand. "And I think I have the perfect solution for you, Norie. This is going to fit you like it was made for you."

CHAPTER NINE

MS. RACE DISAPPEARED BEHIND A VERY COOL BATIK screen. I sat back against the cushions and felt, for the first time in days, maybe weeks, like possibly I wasn't going to freak out after all.

Her place was so comfortable, so alive with color and yet so soothing with all that softness and Ms. Race-ness. I picked up a wooden rhinoceros from the table and stroked its smooth surface. There was such a calm about the place.

"You can't look a rhino in the face and not believe that God has a sense of humor," Ms. Race said as she reappeared from the room beyond the screen carrying a stack of spiral-bound notebooks.

"You've actually looked a rhino in the face?" I said.

"One of the summers I was in Africa," she said. "They are so comical looking with that horn growing right out of the middle of their faces. I just think God must have had a blast thinking that up."

"What were you doing in Africa?"

"I was on a mission." Ms. Race set the notebooks on the table and cocked a questioning eyebrow at my empty mug.

"No thanks," I said. "What kind of mission?"

"I've made a commitment to spend every summer going to a Third-World country to do whatever needs to be done for struggling people."

"Are you, like, spreading the Good Word or something?"

"That happens as a result. But mainly I go to help build

houses, help give shots to little kids, maybe muck out a village that's been destroyed by an earthquake. My favorite was the work at the leper colony in India with Mother Teresa."

"No way."

"Way. That's why I picked school secretarial work as a career so I can get away every summer."

"Why not teach?"

"I've thought about it. But that isn't what I've heard from God through the years. I've heard I'm to do what I'm doing right now. That's enough for me."

I scooted to the edge of the couch, hackles slightly raised. "Okay, so God tells you stuff. You're about the third person who's said that to me, but nobody wants to explain to me how to hear it!"

"I'm about to," Ms. Race said. She tapped the pile of notebooks. "It's all right here."

"I don't get it."

Ms. Race sat on a striped footstool and picked up one of the spirals. The way she twitched her auburn French braid over her shoulder, I knew we were getting down to business.

"This is just what I do, mind you," she said. "It wouldn't work for, say, Cheyenne, I don't think. But for you I bet it's perfect." She opened the notebook and spread it on her lap. "I find a quiet place, someplace that's peaceful to me. It smells pleasing, it feels good to my body, the sounds are good, you know, all that."

I nodded, although at the moment I couldn't think of a single place I knew that was like that except this room.

"I get comfortable, then I get still, and then I listen."

"For what?"

"For something that isn't the usual noise that goes on in my head. It takes work at first. I had to learn to push aside the nagging things. Did I turn off the iron? Am I going to have enough gas to get to work tomorrow? Am I out of coffee? And then I had to learn how to just breathe right past the little voices that said, 'This is a waste of time. You could be balancing the checkbook, washing the car, cleaning the toilet.'" She smiled. "When I first started doing this about twelve years ago, I'd spend nine minutes sending all those annoying thoughts packing and about two actually listening for God."

"So what does he sound like?"

"Like none of the other voices in my head, that's all I can tell you," she said. "Once I clear out the nagging and the pushing and the ugliness, what's left is this easy flow of thoughts that I know isn't coming from me because I'd never think them in a thousand years."

"Like what?" I said. "Or is that too personal?"

"No, of course not. I'm happy to share." She looked down at the notebook. "Like just this morning, I was sitting in the window there. I listened for the usual ten minutes. Then I opened the notebook, like I always do, and I wrote down everything that came to me. And there was the thought that I needed to pray for you."

"Me?"

"It was so clear to me that you were hurting, and there weren't many people who would understand what you were going through. That it was going to be very hard for you to ask for help."

"And then I called you?" I said. "That is way too weird."

"It doesn't always happen that fast, believe me," Ms. Race said. "When I was still in Illinois last year, perfectly at ease with my teen girls' Sunday school class that I was teaching, my nice little Christian school where I was the secretary, my garden apartment where the roses were just starting to take hold—my life was pretty close to perfect. Certainly perfectly easy. Then I started to get these messages from God in my quiet time. 'You're too comfortable. You could be doing so much more for kids. They need you in a place where not everybody goes to church and has a prayer life like they do in this town.'"

She smiled wryly. "I fought moving to Reno every way I could think of. Who wants to live where they have slot machines in the drugstores, for heaven's sake?"

"So why did you come? Just because God said you should?"

"That's definitely the best reason I could think of. As it turns out, it isn't that much more of a jungle here than the Amazon."

I stared at the stack of notebooks. I have to admit I was dying to grab about three of them and take them home to read. As it was, I ran my hand across the top one.

"So let me get this straight," I said. "You get all comfy and quiet. You listen for ten minutes. Then you take out your notebook and write down what you heard."

"Right. Lately I've been listening longer. Sometimes God really gets on a roll."

"And you think that would work for me?"

"Why wouldn't it? Writing comes as naturally to you as breathing. And with your intelligence, it's going to be so easy for you to sort through the garbage thoughts and get to the gems. Your only problem, as I see it, is going to be having the patience to sit still that long."

"I don't know if it's so much patience as it is just having the time. Most days I can't afford to take ten minutes to just sit there."

Ms. Race hugged the notebook to her as she leaned forward to get her face closer to mine. "Norie," she said. "I don't think you can afford not to."

She said it the way I'm sure a doctor tells a cancer patient he has to quit smoking. It stunned me into stillness. She let me sit there and absorb that before she said, "I'm starving. How about an early supper?"

"What time is it?" I said.

"Four o'clock," she said.

She went behind the screen again, and I used the phone to leave a message in my empty house at Caughlin Ranch. Then I wandered into the kitchen and was once more swept into the arms of a friendly, welcoming room. Everything was painted this wonderful, calming green except the butcher block table in front of the windows where she at once had me chopping up red peppers for our sautéed veggies on brown rice. We started to talk again, and we didn't stop until I left at nine. By then, Enid

Race knew more about me than any other human being on the face of the earth, and I'd only begun to scratch the surface.

"I've loved this," she said to me as I was leaving. "You're an incredible young woman. I'm so glad I know you."

"Why?" I said.

"Oh, Norie," she said. She patted my arm. "I think you're about to find that out for yourself."

Our house was completely quiet when I got there. A note told me about a casserole in the refrigerator that I could stick in the microwave. But I patted my stomach full of the most amazing vegetables I'd ever put in my mouth and headed straight for my bedroom.

It took me ten minutes just to find a spiral notebook that wasn't full of chemical equations or bored, done-in-history-class doodles. The one I finally found under my bed didn't exactly look worthy of the words of God, but I vowed to buy a fresh one at Raley's tomorrow. Then I looked around for a place to get quiet.

The sight that greeted me was startling. It wasn't that my room—actually, my three-room suite made up of bathroom, study room, and bedroom—looked any different than it ever did. It was just that I'd never realized how barren it was.

The bed wasn't made. Clothes punctuated the floor at uneven intervals. My bookshelves were basically empty because most of the books were in stacks next to the chair, futons, and bed. The walls were bare except for a life-size poster of Gertrude Stein and a calendar with different buildings at Harvard on each page that my father had given me last Christmas. It was still on June.

"This place leaves me cold," I said to it. "It looks like a jail cell."

Not that my mother didn't encourage me to do something with it. She asked me on a weekly basis if I wanted to look at some decorating magazines to get ideas. But every time she came toward me with fabric swatches and wallpaper samples, I told her I had to write a term paper. That was basically true. If I had had time to do the interior-decorator thing, I'd probably have done something else with that time, like sleep for seventy-two hours straight.

With spiral notebook and ballpoint in hand, I cleared off a space on the carpet in front of the window with my foot and plopped down. Maybe if I faced out, I wouldn't think about the mess behind me. Tomorrow I might think about making the bed or something. For right now, I wanted to get started.

It took me a good twenty minutes—no kidding—to get comfortable and still. First my armpit itched. Then I was thirsty. Then I had to go to the bathroom. I even had to convince myself that I did not have to get up and get a bowl of ice cream or I was going to faint dead away.

Once I got the body quiet, the mind refused to settle in. I closed my eyes and saw the periodic table of elements. I shook that out, tried again, and up popped a graph packed with cosines and tangents. Everything went through there, from the writing on Cheyenne's hands to the look on Wyatt's face when I dropped him off at his house.

After who knows how long, when I'd wiped out every nagging, evil, clutter-up thought from my brain, I got silence. I saw a blankness that was honestly frightening. I couldn't even sit there with it.

I rolled over on my stomach, snatched up the pen, and held it over the empty notebook page.

What am I going to say here? I didn't get anything!

But I put the pen to the page. I started to move my hand. Words appeared. And where they came from, I had no idea.

Don't try so hard. Do what you can and wait. I will come.

I slapped the notebook closed. This was obviously another dead end. Norie Vandenberger was not going to try so hard? She was going to do what she could? She was going to let somebody else do it for her?

I went to bed depressed because there was no way I could follow that advice.

The next morning was one of those Sundays when my parents chose sleeping in over church. Dad always used the excuse when he was on call that it would be disrespectful to the church to have his pager go off during communion. Mom did whatever Dad did.

I hauled myself out of bed, dressed, and went to the 10:30 service by myself. It was a first. I was surprised the stained-glass windows didn't all shatter at the sight of me.

I wasn't at all sure why I was there. I told myself it was because I wanted something to do between the time I got up and the time I was due at Cheyenne's, other than study chemistry and trig. God seemed to have other ideas.

I was just sitting there before the service started, halfway listening to the organ prelude. Then I noticed people coming in, pulling out the kneelers, and getting down on their knees for a few minutes before they sat down and started to read the bulletin and look up the number for the first hymn. I wasn't sure why I'd never noticed people doing that before. It was probably because we were always arriving late, and everybody was already in the middle of the processional hymn.

For a few minutes, I wondered what they were praying about. Please provide the money to pay the mortgage, maybe. Please don't let me start my period while I'm sitting here in church? That was always a biggie for me.

Then my mind shifted. What if they weren't praying? What if they were just listening? Was God saying something to them—right then?

Of course. I'll talk to you, too. You just have to hear me.

I was glad when the organ cranked up for the first hymn. I knew I was losing it.

But it happened again during communion. I kneeled after I came back from the altar rail instead of doing my usual, which was to sit in the pew and watch people go down the aisle and wonder what they did for a living or where they had gone to college.

It was different being on my knees. I felt small. Dependent. Vulnerable. Things I seldom felt.

My first impulse was to get back on the seat. Search the bulletin for grammatical errors. Anything to fight off these unfamiliar, not-in-control feelings.

But I stayed there. I took deep breaths. I pushed aside the conviction that any second now somebody was going to shout, "That girl isn't Harvard material! Look at her—she's too weak."

And pretty soon my head got calm. And quiet. For about a whole minute.

I felt like I'd slept an hour.

"Look at you, all dressed up," Tassie greeted me at the door when I arrived at Cheyenne's.

I looked dubiously at my khakis, loafers, and baggy sweater. Most of the girls at King would have called my outfit "casual wear on the dull side." I'd once overheard a girl in a rest room, who didn't know I was in a stall, say, "If I had Norie Vandenberger's money, I would have the most incredible wardrobe. I sure wouldn't walk around looking like an Eddie Bauer ad—for guys."

"Thanks," I said to Tassie. "Cheyenne said you guys always dressed up for Sunday dinner."

"We do," she said, ushering me into the living room with a wooden spoon. "I always tell my kids, 'Put on the best you have for the Lord.'"

I understood why she thought I was decked out for the Inaugural Ball when I saw Felise, Cheyenne, and Ellie darting around the kitchen mashing potatoes and cooking chicken. 'The best they had' amounted to clean jeans and T-shirts with nothing printed on them. I found myself grinning. I liked it. I liked it a lot.

"Norie, honey, grab a potholder and check on those biscuits, would you?" Tassie said. "If I don't get after this gravy, I'm gonna have some ticked-off children on my hands."

"You got that right," Avery said from the table where he was dealing mismatched plates onto place mats.

I opened the oven to two dozen golden mounds of heaven and stood there breathing them in.

"I think they're done," I said. And planned to eat at least four.

There were a few moments of delicious chaos as Tassie and the girls put the food on the table and Avery, Diesel, and

Brendan finished stoking the fire in the fireplace and stood behind our chairs to seat us.

"I can really do it myself," I said to Diesel

"Not in my house you don't," Tassie said. "Ain't nothin' wrong with a boy learnin' to be a gentleman."

Except that he might get slapped, I thought. That would have been my average response to a guy trying to do the chivalry thing with me. It was so demeaning.

That opinion suddenly seemed lame as Diesel eased my chair, with me on it, under the table. Yikes.

I started to go for one of the biscuits, but Cheyenne groped for my hand on one side and Diesel grabbed my other one. Of course. We were asking the blessing. Tassie did the main thing. Then each of us had to say what we were thankful for.

"Being invited to this table," I said when it was my turn.

Cheyenne squeezed my hand. It occurred to me to look to see if she still had writing on her palms. They were clean today.

I didn't have time to think about that for long. Keeping up with the conversation at the table was like watching a tennis match, from inside the net.

Diesel talked about the engine parts he was going to buy for his truck next time he got some money. Brendan and Avery interrupted that monologue about five times to give Tassie the complete agenda for where they were going skateboarding that afternoon, who they were going with, and what time they were coming home. Felise was negotiating with Ellie: She would paint a poster for their room if Ellie would take her turn cleaning the room. Cheyenne bragged about me, to my complete embarrassment.

Through the whole thing, Tassie corrected everybody's manners and told them how wonderful they were. Cheyenne's B- was still receiving rave reviews, right up there with the intricate geometric design magnetted to the refrigerator door that Felise had done and the toaster that Diesel just that morning had rendered functional again.

The chicken was fried; my father would have been giving a full declamation about the horrors of putting anything cooked with Crisco in your arteries. The crockery was chipped; my mother would have been politely dropping hints about an upcoming china sale at Macy's. There wasn't a person at that table with a GPA over 2.5.

And it was the happiest bunch of people I'd ever been around. I had half a mind to ask if I could move in.

I was in that same kind of wistful, mushy mood when Cheyenne and I settled down at a card table in a little room off the back of the house that was the designated homework room. Cheyenne had explained to me that everybody had to put in at least an hour in this room every school night and complete all their assignments before they could turn on the TV, use the phone, or play backgammon with Tassie. Evidently that last one was a big deal. Ellie was the current champion.

"You are really lucky to have this kind of family, Cheyenne," I said to her.

"They're cool," Cheyenne said. "I just hope I get to stay here."

I opened her freshman literature book, but my mind was operating in a different direction. "Do you, like, talk to God about that?" I said.

"Yes," she said promptly. "I do prayers with Tassie most nights. Not everybody does. She doesn't push it on anybody. Mostly it's me and Diesel."

"So you pray aloud," I said. "Do you guys ever, like, listen for God?"

She considered that while chewing on the ends of her hair. "Sort of," she said. "I'm still getting used to that. I never even believed in God till I came here so I'm kind of slow."

"When did you come here?" I said.

"August."

That took me back about six feet. She was as green at this as I was. I suddenly felt kind of protective.

"Do you want to try something?" I said. "Something Ms. Race taught me?"

Ms. Race had said this probably wouldn't work for

Cheyenne. I didn't know why I was trying it. I didn't know why I was doing a lot of things lately.

"Sure," Cheyenne said. Her eyes were shining. She would probably have pulled out all her nose hairs with red hot tweezers if I'd asked her to, that was becoming apparent.

I filled her in on Ms. Race's method. She had her notebook open before I even finished.

"Let's do it right now!" she said. "It'll be kind of like a writing assignment or something."

Her enthusiasm was touching but contagious. While she dove for the tape deck and put in some kind of harp music Tassie had told them was "conductive" to studying, I pulled pillows off the halfway unstuffed sofa and arranged them on the floor.

It wasn't Ms. Race's open-armed apartment, but it was at least homier than my bedroom. Of course, what wasn't, aside from Alcatraz? But it was comfortable enough, safe enough. And apparently just what God was looking for.

It didn't take me as long to sweep out the dust-thoughts and get to the quiet. At first, I wanted to run from the silence again. And then a thought came. A thought that didn't sound like anything I would say, as Ms. Race would put it, "in a thousand years."

There is no competition, Norie.

I almost laughed aloud as I wrote it down. Right. That was easy for him to say. He didn't have to get into Harvard. He didn't have to compete with a high curve in chemistry or trig. He didn't have to deal with my father.

"Let's share," Cheyenne said.

I looked up at her as she beamed over the top of her ink-spattered notebook.

"You go first," I said.

She was more than willing. "This is what I heard," she said. "And I mean loud and clear, like an intercom was on in here or something—"

"Tell it," I said. I had a curfew, after all.

" 'Norie is my special gift to you,' " she read. " 'She's your role model. Follow her, and you'll be going in the right direction.' "

"Yikes," I said. "Are you sure that's what He told you?"

"I'm telling you," she said, "it was like an intercom, like that one they use on the football field."

My father, on the other hand, was not so enthusiastic about me when I got home. He actually looked up from the television while the 49ers had the ball and said, "Norie, come in here a minute."

He muted the TV and pierced me with a look. "You had company while you were gone."

"Who was it?" I said. An image of Wyatt flashed unbidden across my screen.

"Tobey and Shannon," he said.

"Oh, man! I'm sorry I missed them." I glanced quickly at his disapproving frown. "Were you trying to work or something when they came? Sorry about that."

"No. That isn't the point. I thought you weren't going to hang around with that group anymore."

My hackles grew instantly restless. "I never said that. I don't know where you got that idea."

"I thought we agreed on it."

"When was this?"

"Just the other night. I distinctly remember saying to you that you needed to spend more time with kids who are on the same path you're on."

"I didn't agree to that," I said.

"Obviously. Where were you today?"

"I was at Cheyenne's house, tutoring her."

"You were tutoring her? What about your own schoolwork?"

"Dad, when did I ever not get my homework done?"

"It isn't a matter of getting it done. It's a matter of getting it done right. Well."

"The best," I finished for him. "You've always made that clear, Dad."

"Don't get smart with me, Norie. I see you losing your focus, and I'm calling you on it. You need to be prepping for AO, studying for your classes, running that newspaper. You can't be wasting time tutoring and holding prayer meetings and whatever else you were doing all day yesterday."

He widened his eyes, like he expected an answer. I knew he wouldn't want to hear any of the things that were waiting on the end of my tongue.

"Are we through?" I said in as civil a voice as I could summon up.

"I think you ought to spend some time in your room thinking about this," he said.

"That's where I was headed," I said.

He nodded. Dismissed. Summarily.

I took the steps two at a time and flung myself into my room. I only stopped myself from slamming the door because that would have brought him running, and I'd have been in for another round.

I made my way around the room, picking up debris and trying to get my hackles to settle down. Not an easy task when my father had just told me that my real friends were a waste of time and my cheating, I'll-cut-your-heart-out-if-you-do-better-than-me friends were the best thing that had ever happened to me. Throwing helped. I was hurling all the pillows off my bed to make it when my mother tapped on the door.

"Hi," she said as she poked her head in. "You want some chocolate chip cookies while you study? I bought some at the bakery boutique they had yesterday. Some of the most scrumptious desserts you ever saw. I gained ten pounds just looking at them."

"Thanks, Mom," I said. I didn't look at her as I brutally pulled up the sheets and tucked them in. She crossed to the other side of the bed and tucked there.

"Now, to me, that Tobey seems like a bright girl, and so does little Shannon," she said.

I looked into the air to see where that had come from.

"Your father says they aren't college prep, but I—"

"They are," I said. "They're smart. They're nice. They're honest."

"I think if you just explained that to him—"

"Why should I have to, Mom?" I said. "Why can't I be trusted to pick my own friends? And why do they all have to be in the Top Ten? I can't even talk about it. Let's change the subject."

She swallowed back a reply and plumped up a pillow. "What possessed you to clean up your room?" she said.

I shrugged.

And then I looked at her. She was trying so hard to keep smiling, it almost hurt for some reason. I couldn't have been that delightful to be around at that moment. And what had she done? Nothing but try to avoid my father's wrath, which was no different from what I tried to do.

"I'm thinking about decorating it, actually," I said.

Mom's face turned on like a flashlight.

"I want to do it myself," I said hurriedly. "No wallpaper books and paint chips, okay?"

She nodded.

"But if I, like, decide what kind of curtains I want or something, will you help me get the stuff?"

"Of course!" she said. "Now, you're going to need a decorating budget, to start with—"

"Decorating budget? For what?"

Dad's form filled my doorway. His eyes were narrowed on my mother.

"We were just talking about doing up Norie's room," Mom said. Her hands went to her hair, as if smoothing it down were going to smooth him. No such luck.

"And she's going to do this when? Three o'clock in the morning?" he said. He looked at me, stormy eyed. "We just finished talking about how you don't have time for another thing, and then you come up here and start to plan a quilting bee with your mother."

"It isn't going to take up any of my precious study time, Dad," I said. I was doing everything but chew through the inside of my cheek to keep my voice even. "I'll probably study better if I have some order around me."

"Order and decor are two different things," Dad said. He nudged my now overflowing wastebasket with his toe. "You pick up the trash once in a while and then all you have to do is keep order in your head."

I raked a hand through my hair. If he didn't leave in the next five seconds, I wasn't going to be able to hold back any of the retorts that were wrestling to come out of me.

But he had no intention of leaving. His eye had caught on something in the trash can, and he leaned over and pulled it out. A storm—a hurricane—gathered on his face.

"What is this, Norie?" he said.

"I don't know. I can't see it," I said.

He turned it to face me. The huge red "5" on it flashed across the room.

"My last chemistry quiz," I said stiffly.

"This is failing," he said.

"It was just a pop quiz," I said. "It's only worth ten points. Mr. Uhles already told me I could bring it up before the end of the semester."

"End of the semester?" Dad said. "Tomorrow! Tonight!"

"I will," I said.

"You're darn right you will." Dad crunched the offending quiz into a ball in his fist, so hard it made both Mom and me wince. "You are not to spend time with any of those girls until I receive written certification from Uhles that this grade is up to an A."

"Dad, come on!" I said. "That is so unfair! We have a test Wednesday—"

"Then talk to me Wednesday night," he said crisply. "Until then, I see no reason to discuss this further."

He turned on his heel and left, slamming the door behind him. I stared at it in disbelief.

I wouldn't even have noticed my mother hurrying from the room after him, if she hadn't stopped at the door and looked back at me. Her glance was brief. I decided maybe I was imagining that she looked just a little angry. And it wasn't at me.

CHAPTER
TEN

MOM WASN'T THE ONLY ONE. I WAS STILL SO IRATE THE
next morning on the way to school I was blowing my horn at
people who even looked like they were going to change lanes in
front of me.

I made it a point not to talk to anyone the first two periods
because I was afraid I'd chomp somebody's head off. I was so
mad, in fact, that it didn't even occur to me that in the past I en-
joyed taking verbal bites out of people.

But I kept my mouth shut all the way until third period, and
then I was forced to talk. By Pavella.

He flew out from behind a trash can when I went to
my locker between second and third and physically turned
me around by the shoulder. I was in no mood to be man-
handled.

"Get your paws off me, Pavella," I said, "or I can't be responsible for what I might do to you."

"Have you got the key?"

I groaned aloud. "Haven't we had this conversation before?"
I said. "No, I don't have the key."

It was his turn to groan, as if he were going to vomit right
there into my locker. I started to close it, just to be on the safe
side, and then I turned to stare at him.

"Key to what?" I said. "We don't have a chem test until
Wednesday."

"We're having another pop quiz fifth period," he said.

"How do you know?"

"Lance just told me that Deborah told him. She found out at the end of first period."

My stomach turned to ice. This couldn't be. This just could not be.

"Have you seen her?" Pavella said. "I have to find her!"

I shook my head. He was gone before I could open my mouth. Although what I would have said was beyond me. There wasn't much to say about either situation—that I was in the middle of a cheating operation, or the certainty that I was about to plunge to a C in chemistry.

I hadn't cracked the book all weekend. I figured I had until Wednesday to study. And it seemed like all that other stuff I did Saturday and Sunday was more important.

That couldn't have been God's voice I heard, telling me there was no competition, I thought. That had to be Satan himself!

I grabbed my chemistry book, and my wheels started to turn. I could probably sneak a peek at some of the stuff during American history. I might get lucky.

"Norie, I have never been so happy to see a person!"

It was Deborah, coming to a skid at my elbow, blueberry eyes popping with terror. You would have thought we were about to be attacked by aliens.

"We are in a world of hurt!" she said.

"I know. Pavella found me. He's looking for you."

"It isn't going to do him any good to find me. I don't have the key!"

I looked at her sharply. "Why not?"

"Because I didn't find out until the end of first period. I didn't have time to get it."

"Bummer," I said dryly. I was actually relieved. At least now I didn't have to make a decision. My father's little edict the night before would have made it pretty hard to turn down a free answer key. I was ashamed to admit it to myself, but it was the truth.

"It doesn't have to be a bummer," Deborah said.

She was leaning in close and speaking in a murmur out of the side of her mouth. I didn't look at her.

"What do you mean?" I said.

"You could help."

"I haven't even said I was in on this," I said. My palms started to sweat.

"You don't have to use the answers if you don't want to, but you could get them for the rest of us."

I rolled my eyes, as my armpits went into gear. "How am I supposed to get them?"

"Piece of cake. I have it all figured out." Deborah moved in so close I thought she was going to climb into my locker and pull me in with her. As it was, I could barely hear her she was muttering so low.

"You have journalism fourth, right?" she said.

"Yeah, so do you."

"Not today. I have to make up a math test. That's why we need you. Now here's the deal. You can wander around all you want fourth period because the people on the paper are always out doing interviews and stuff. Nobody will notice you. Fourth is Mr. Uhles's prep, and I know he has a parent-teacher conference in the counseling office today. All you have to do is slip into his office, type some codes into the computer, and it'll spit the thing right out."

"What, you want me to sit there until the right codes come to me in a vision? I'm a genius, Deborah, not a prophet."

"Don't be a geek. I have the codes. Write these down."

"I didn't say—"

"Just write them down!"

She flipped open the notebook I was carrying on top and shoved a pen at me. "First it's 'JED,' that's his dog's name. Then it'll ask for another one and you type '8604.' Then you hit the pound sign. That's it."

Everything was swirling around me. I wrote the codes so she would go away and leave me to find my bearings before I got motion-sick.

"You know how to print and all that. It's almost like the computers in journalism. You'll figure it out." Deborah pushed the notebook closed and pressed her hand around my arm. "Like I said, you don't have to use it, but at least you can help the rest of us. I don't see why you wouldn't though. What's it going to hurt? Who's ever going to use chemistry anyway?"

She finished rationalizing and backed off toward the hall. "I'll meet you at lunch. You can give it to us then."

Without waiting for me to answer, she turned around and ran to the dinging of the department-store bell. It might as well have been a prison alarm, as far as I was concerned. I sagged against the locker and tried to breathe. I felt like somebody was strangling me.

By the time I got to journalism, I was feeling absolutely green. Mrs. Bowman had made us discuss the Boston Tea Party all third period. I tried to open my chemistry book once, and she caught me and gave me a five-minute lecture on time management. With articles to edit all fourth period and a Student Council meeting at lunch, there was no time to study. I didn't see how I had much choice but to get the answer key.

And use it.

But I had about as much savoir-faire at this sort of thing as one of the Three Stooges. I walked into journalism, dumped my backpack in my cubbyhole, and flopped down into a chair with my head in my hands. I had to figure out how I was going to get out of here, down to the math-science hall—

"Norie?"

I jumped like I was wearing a pair of defibrillator paddles. Wyatt was leaning over me. He cringed a little when I looked up.

"I know you're probably going to go for my throat or something," he said, attempting a grin. "But I just had to ask you—are you okay?"

I was too agonized to spar with him. I just nodded. "Yeah," I said. "Thanks for asking."

He looked at me for a minute, and then he shook his head. "You're about the worst liar in life," he said. He gave his shrug, only this one looked heavier than usual. "I guess I'll try to find a blank disk and get to work," he said.

In the split second it took him to turn around to walk away, I really wanted to blurt out everything and tell him to help me find a way out of this mess. But it passed with the arrival of an idea—a way to get out of here and down to math-science.

Mrs. Abbey was at her desk, surrounded by people with a thousand questions. I kept one eye on them as I walked casually across the room and picked up the last box of blank computer disks on the supply shelf. As Mrs. Abbey bent down behind her desk to dig in her bag for something, I slid the box of diskettes behind a row of dictionaries.

Heart beating like a trip-hammer, I crossed the room at a march and parted the crowd with my arms. "Mrs. A.," I said, "we're out of diskettes again. What do people do, eat them?"

"I just saw a box," Mark said.

"An empty box. I hate that," I said. "I have so much stuff to do—we all do. Why don't I go down to math-science and borrow some? They always have millions."

I didn't wait for an answer. Mrs. Abbey looked happy to let somebody else make a decision, and she turned back to Pavella, who was whining to her about something. I fled from the room with my stomach crawling up my esophagus.

Okay, okay, just slow down. Think it through. You can handle anything if you just think it through.

My father's voice was so clear in my head, I stepped around the corner and sank against the wall.

Is that what he would say to me in this situation? I thought. *Would he tell me to do whatever it took to get that A?*

The thought was so sickening, I found myself heading for the bathroom, just to get my head together. I was convinced my face was a dead giveaway to anybody who might see me going into Mr. Uhles's door.

I put my hand on the handle to the bathroom door, and it opened from inside. Shannon stepped out.

Thoughts whipped through my head like a tape on fast forward. Could she see how guilty I already looked? Was she going to expect me to stand there and talk to her when I didn't have much time? Was she going to ask me if I'd talked to Ms. Race—a thought that was suddenly very disturbing.

But all those possibilities disappeared the second I took a good look at Shannon's face. She bore the unmistakable signs of an entire morning, if not a whole night, spent sobbing. Her eyes were like road maps and almost swollen shut. She obviously had been gnawing on her lips because they were cracked and bleeding. And the poor kid's nose put Rudolph to shame.

"Shannon, yikes," I said. "What's wrong?"

She couldn't even talk. All she could do was shrug and look at the ceiling and act like she wanted to disappear.

"Hey," I said. I took her by the shoulders. "Seriously, are you all right? Do you need to go to the nurse or something?"

She shook her head. "Just stand here with me for a minute, would you?"

Her voice was barely audible, and what I could hear was unrecognizable. With my eyes closed, I'd have pegged her for a four-year-old.

"Sure," I said. "Come here."

I put my arms around her, clumsily I'll admit. I wasn't into hugging. It just seemed like the thing to do though. She would have fallen over, physically and emotionally, otherwise.

She shivered head to toe, but she didn't cry. I figured she had long since run out of tears.

"Do you need to talk about it?" I said.

She nodded and then shook her head in rapid succession. "I can't," she said. "I want to, but I'm not allowed to."

"Says who?" I said, hackles rising.

"My parents."

"Oh," I said. "I hear you."

She nodded, and then suddenly her arms tightened around me like I was saving her from drowning. I held on, too.

I don't know how long we would have stood there if I hadn't heard familiar footsteps coming down the hall. I didn't even have to look up to know it was Ms. Race.

I looked up and pointed silently to Shannon. Ms. Race nodded and put her hands on Shannon's hair.

"Hey, sweetie," she said. "What's up?"

Shannon turned from me and transplanted her arms from my neck to Ms. Race's. Ms. Race nodded her auburn head at me.

"You go on to class, Norie," she said. "I'll take care of our Shannon."

I stepped back from them, but I didn't know which way to go. I was going to walk away from these two good, beautiful people into a teacher's office and rip him off?

What am I going to do? I screamed at myself. *What the Sam Hill am I going to do?*

It looked like I was going down the math-science hall, just like I'd planned. That's the way my feet took me. On both sides of me, classroom doors hung open, and I could see kids lounging in their desks, gazing with glazed eyes at chalkboards and overhead projector screens. They could care less what kind of grades they got, as long as graduation came soon.

Why did I have to end up caring so much? I thought miserably. *Look at them—they don't have a care in the world. Look at Cheyenne—*

I did a double take. That was Cheyenne, slouched in the front row of her math class. She saw me at the same time, and I thought she was going to stand up and flag me down right there in the middle of a lecture on square roots.

As it was, I only got three more steps down the hall before she was on my heels like a cocker spaniel puppy, waving the bathroom pass in one hand and a sheet of notebook paper in the other.

"Norie," she said in a stage whisper, "look at this!"

I arranged my face before I turned around. "What?" I said, with ultra patience.

"This! My math test!"

She produced the paper. At the top was a big C+ and the words "much improved."

"When did you take this?" I said.

"Just now. We graded them in class. I'm usually really embarrassed when we trade papers to check them like that, but I did decent this time, didn't I?"

Simultaneously I nodded and looked at the hand she brought up to take the paper from me. My nod lurched to a halt.

She had writing on her hands again, and I could make it out clearly this time. Those little squiggles weren't obscenities. They were basic algebraic formulas if I ever saw them, and I'd seen plenty.

I studied Cheyenne's face. She made no attempt to hide her palms. Instead, she happily took the math test from me and linked her arm through mine. I felt like somebody had just dumped a huge load of something on my back, and it was clearly stenciled "Responsibility."

"Were you going to the bathroom to wash your hands?" I said.

"No. I came out to talk to you."

"Go wash them anyway. Get all that stuff off there." I took hold of her hands and held them palms up. "And don't do this again until we talk, do you hear?"

She looked vaguely confused, but she flung her arms around my neck and then skipped off to the bathroom. When she was gone, I didn't just sag against the wall, I leaned hard and slid all the way to the floor. I sat there with my eyes closed. I didn't have time to mess with shoving ugly thoughts out of the way. I needed a clear shot.

"Come on, God," I whispered. "Come on."

To this day, I don't know if was God's voice or my own common sense that spoke to me. I'm not so sure we don't mistake God for common sense most of the time anyway. But it was undeniable. I sat there and I heard it: *There is no competition, no competition in being human. You all have your own path.*

It was the most radical thought that had ever entered my head, and I'd had a few in my time. The thought almost didn't leave room for the rest of the message: the part about being Cheyenne's role model; the part about wanting to be in the same league as my Flagpole friends; the part about doing what I could and then waiting.

But I heard it all. I was sitting there, eyes closed, going over it again, when I sensed somebody standing above me. I opened one eye to see Wyatt.

"What are you doing?" he said.

"Sitting here," I said.

He pulled a box of diskettes out from behind his back. "I found these," he said.

"Good," I said. "The door to math-science was locked anyway."

He stuck his hand down to help me up, and I took it.

CHAPTER ELEVEN

FROM THERE ON IT WAS LIKE I'D DROPPED A ROCK IN A pool. The ripples from that one decision seemed to go on. And on. And on.

The first thing I did was call an emergency Flagpole meeting for lunch. It was amazing how fast we could get the word to each other when we needed us.

Two minutes after the lunch bell rang, we were in the corner in the theater lobby, Ms. Race included, heads bent over our sandwiches and our problem. Because that was the way it was with us. The minute I let it out, it wasn't just my problem anymore. It was all of ours. Ours and God's.

"I'm so glad you said no to that," Tobey said when I was done "spilling my guts," as Brianna put it. "I'm proud of you."

"For what? Refusing to do something I knew was wrong all along?"

"Girl, it just isn't that simple," Brianna said. "Cheating wouldn't be a temptation for me because I flat-out don't care that much about my grades. But if it came to something I was really into, like if it had something to do with Ira, there's probably a lot of sinning I'd be tempted to do."

"May I say something?" Ms. Race said.

"I wish you would," I said.

"You've been into one way of thinking for so long, you can't expect yourself to turn it off like a light switch. Was there a time when you would have done it without batting an eye?"

"Probably," I said.

"Then you've made progress. Let God forgive you and get on with it. What do you say?"

"I'm for that," Marissa said. And then she turned about the shade of watermelon. "Not that it's up to me. I just hate to see people stuck."

"'Stuck,'" I said. "Great word. Wretched concept. I do want to move on." I looked around at the group, feeling as close to helpless as I ever get. "But I don't know what to do now."

"What do you mean?" Tobey said.

"I guess I could just say I'm not going to cheat and let it go at that. But it doesn't feel right."

"You thinking of turning those people in?" Brianna said. "I'm not sayin' don't do it, but you can expect a major big thing if you do. Mmm-mmm."

"I don't know," Marissa said. "Do teachers get that upset when people cheat? I see it going on all the time in my classes, and I know the teachers aren't blind. They have to know it's happening, but they act as if they don't care."

"It isn't just for right now though."

We all looked at Shannon. It was the first thing she had said since we sat down. I felt a little guilty, because I'd forgotten she was crying earlier. She looked better now; at least she seemed to be tracking.

"What are you saying?" Tobey said.

"They care about it in college, big time. My sister—she goes to William and Mary. She said they had to read and sign an honor code when they started as freshmen. If somebody breaks the code, they're thrown out of school."

"Whoa," Marissa said.

"And aren't all these kids you're talking about going off to Yale or something?" Brianna said to me. "Mmm-mmm, they are gonna have some kind of awakenin' when they get there."

"Does that answer your question, Norie?" Ms. Race said.

"It tells me to do something. It doesn't tell me what."

"Then we need to pray," Tobey said. "It'll come, right?"

There was a consensus on that. When we joined hands, I

realized for the first time that Cheyenne was on my left. I felt another shot of guilt. There was definitely one thing I was going to have to do, and that was to get her out of the cheating habit. I had the ugly feeling that, somehow, I'd gotten her into it in the first place.

"Can we talk later?" I said to her when we were packing up for fifth period.

"Are you going to yell at me?" she said.

"What?" I said. "No, of course I'm not going to yell at you."

"You're yelling at me now."

I stopped with my mouth halfway open. This was going to take some time—more than I had right now.

"Look, I have to do layout for the paper after school," I said. "I'll call you tonight."

She hesitated.

"And I won't yell, I promise," I said.

She smiled, slung a hug around my neck, and took off.

"Nor, do you want me to go to fifth period with you?" Tobey said. "In case it gets vicious?"

"What are they going to do to me?" I said. "Deborah has pretty long fingernails, but the guys are harmless."

"You're so cool," she said.

I snorted. I knew I wasn't fooling either of us a bit. The fact was, I was so nervous I was nauseous.

I was right. I knew I was right. And conflict had never been a big thing for me. I'd always thrived on a good argument. But there was something so final about this, like another piece of my old life was being torn away. It was painful, that's what it was. And I'd never been into pain.

I'm counting on you, God, I prayed.

I was sure he answered, *I'm here.*

They were all waiting for me like a bunch of vultures outside Mr. Uhles's room.

"I am not roadkill," I muttered to myself. "It's going to be fine."

"Did you get it?" Deborah hissed to me, in lieu of "hello."

"No," I said.

Gabe swore, and Lance drilled his pointy little eyes into me in that superior way he has. Pavella threw his head back and bonked himself in the forehead with the heel of his hand. Deborah just stared at me coldly.

"Why not? I gave you the codes."

"I didn't use the codes. I didn't even go in his office."

"What, he had an armed guard out there or something?" Lance said. His face had gone so pale he looked more uni-color than ever.

"No," I said. "I just didn't go. I got out of class, and I went down the hall. And then I just couldn't do it."

"You picked a heck of a time to get an attack of conscience," Gabe said.

I didn't tell them it was actually an attack of God. It would have gone right over their heads.

"You wouldn't have gotten caught, Norie," Deborah said. She gave a you-are-so-stupid eye roll. "If somebody had come in, they wouldn't even have questioned you. You're more places than the administrators."

I was somehow aware that I was no longer sick to my stomach. I actually felt calm. It was a good thing somebody was. Gabe looked like he could have eaten the plaster on the walls, and Pavella was clenching and unclenching his fists. He was no longer adorable. As for Deborah—it wouldn't have taken much for her to haul off and slap me, with Lance coolly acting as lookout. I could see it in her eyes.

"It wasn't about being afraid of getting caught," I said. "It was about realizing that this whole thing is wrong."

All four of them looked at me befuddled. "Wrong?" their faces said. Define "wrong."

"It's wrong to try to get good grades?" Lance said, sarcasm dripping.

"It's wrong to cheat to do it, yes," I said.

"Uhles is puttin' it to us with all these pop quizzes and stuff!" Gabe said. "What else are we supposed to do?"

"I haven't figured that part out yet," I said. "But I'm not going to cheat."

"Fine. Whatever," Deborah said with a wave of the long-nailed hand. "The question now is, are you going to tell on us?"

Pavella swore this time. He moved in on me like somebody had just dinged the boxing bell, stopped only by the reluctant arm Lance put across his chest.

"Are you going to quit doing it?" I said.

"What, are you trying to make some kind of deal with us?" Lance said.

Gabe grunted. "Who died and left you in charge of morals?"

"Exactly," Deborah said. "If I don't ace this class, my life is going to be hell."

"Anybody interested in taking a quiz?" said a voice behind us. "Or should I just go ahead and give you all zeroes?"

Mr. Uhles dotted the comment with a smile and went back into the room. Every eye was on me.

"He might as well," Gabe said. "I know zilch about any of this material."

They glared at me as if I were personally responsible for every ounce of ignorance that at that moment permeated the hall. I felt deeply sad.

"I had to do what I thought was right," I said. "That's all I know."

"Fill us in on your final decision, okay?" Lance said. He was yanking on his goatee like it was a lifeline. "I'd like to plan my funeral."

The pop quiz was impossible. People were whining all over the place.

"How come we're having a quiz when you're giving us a test in two days?" Gabe said. He was bordering on pathetic.

"I want to see how close you are to knowing the material," Mr. Uhles said. He glanced at the clock. "Five minutes, people."

Lance muttered a name tightly under his breath. I'd never noticed how much my friends cussed before.

It was a tight, tension-filled five minutes. You could almost touch the anxiety as it pumped through the air. I won't say I didn't have my share.

But even as I turned in my paper, only three-quarters full of answers, I felt a tiny center of calm. I clung to it like the proverbial drowning man. Make that woman.

During trig, Deborah wrote me a two-page note and dropped it on my desk when she passed going to the pencil sharpener. I read about two sentences of it and threw it away on *my* trip to the pencil sharpener.

I can't believe you're acting this way, Norie, it said. *Ever since you got religion, you're like a different person. Frankly, I liked you better before—*

I snorted softly to myself. *You never "liked" me, Deb. I don't think any of the five of us ever liked each other. We don't even like ourselves. How can we like anybody else?*

That was a sad thought. Not depressing, like hopeless. It was just sad. It hung on me even after I got to the journalism room after school and started to work on the layout.

The only thing that snapped me back to something familiar, like "angry" or "disgusted," was reading Pavella's article on study habits.

"I don't believe this," I said out loud.

The only person who heard me was Wyatt. Mark and some other kids were working on the front page in the back of the room. Rhonda was off who-knows-where.

"What?" he said.

"Listen to this. 'There's basically two kinds of students at King High. Those that studies. And those that don't.'"

"Ooh, now that's sparkling prose," Wyatt said.

"You don't know the half of it," I said. "He misspelled 'basically' and 'studies.'"

"How can you misspell 'studies'? Never mind. I don't want to know."

I went back to the piece and immediately groaned. "'Those that study do pretty much the generic thing,'" I read. "'Read the stuff. Do the papers. Go over the stuff that's going to be on the test the night before. Those that don't study don't do any of that. They obviously get worse grades.'" I slapped the paper down on the table. "What is this? I could have written that in second grade!"

"And it wouldn't have been that bad," Wyatt said. "Was that Pavella's piece?'

"Yes!"

"How that guy got to be an honor student, I don't know."

"He cheats," I said.

"He must."

"No, I'm serious." I looked Wyatt full in the face. "He does. A lot of them do."

Wyatt moved over to the chair next to me and lowered his voice. "You mean, like borrowing other people's homework, that kind of stuff?"

"That's small-time for them," I said. "I'm talking stealing answer keys from teachers—that kind of stuff."

Wyatt gave a low whistle. From anybody else it would have sounded geeky. He pulled it off.

"I just found out about it," I said. "Then they tried to rope me into it so I wouldn't tell. Right away they wanted to use me."

"I get ya," Wyatt said. "That whole thing with you hiding the computer disks?"

"You saw that?"

"I don't miss much."

"You are so cocky."

"Well, whatever." He nodded at Pavella's wretched piece of journalism. "Are you going to try to fix that?"

"It would take me half the night. I'd rather write a whole new piece."

"Why don't you?"

I looked up to see his blue eyes sparkling. He was making no effort to disguise a grin.

"On what?" I said.

"Cheating," he said.

I outdid myself snort-wise. "Oh, right. That would blow this whole thing sky high."

"I know," he said.

The grin grew wider. I started to get one of my own.

"Seriously?" I said. "You think I should—what, do a piece revealing there's a cheating ring going on? Only not give the names?" I could feel my backbone starting to tingle. "That really might do it, you know? They would be so freaked out, they would probably stop cold turkey. Plus, teachers would be on the lookout. This could be so cool."

"Yeah," Wyatt said.

I crossed my arms over my chest. "Okay, okay, so it was your idea."

"No, all I said was do a piece on cheating. You just wrote the whole thing yourself."

I dragged my fingers through my bangs. "This is going to take me forever. I can't whip something like this out. I have to be really careful. Plus, I don't have advisor approval."

"Go ask Mrs. Abbey right now," Wyatt said. "I can finish up this layout, and then you can go home and start working on it. If you need any help, you can call me."

"Why don't you just come home with me?" I said, from out of nowhere. "It'll go a lot faster that way."

He gave that light shrug. "Great. I'll call my mom."

Within an hour we were out of there. The layout was done, except for the space where Pavella's article was supposed to go and mine was now going to live. Mrs. Abbey saw us off with a warning: "You're going to make enemies, you two."

"It's about time," Wyatt said to me as we hurried across the parking lot to Iggy. "I never thought I was going to get any enemies here."

"What are you talking about?"

"I figure if nobody hates me, I'm being too wishy-washy. It even says it in the Bible—I mean, not in so many words—"

"You're into the Bible?" I said.

"Yeah. You?"

"I haven't gotten that far yet," I said. "I just discovered God."

"Cool," he said. "When you get ready for the Bible, we have a dozen different versions around the house."

My own house was quiet when we arrived. Dad, Mom told us, was doing an emergency surgery and wouldn't be in until late. She, of course, got up from the chair where she was reading a Danielle Steele novel and hurried into the kitchen.

"What do you kids want to eat?" she said. "You could have supper while you're working."

"Whatever you fix, Mom," I said.

I started out of the room after Wyatt, but she softly called me back. "There's a checkbook on your desk," she said. "I opened a little account for you today so you can work on your room whenever you want. Just sign the signature card."

I could feel a slow grin spreading across my face. "Thanks, Mom," I said. "You don't mind if I don't do ruffles?"

She wrinkled her nose. "I hate ruffles," she said. "It's your father who thinks women should have ruffles."

"Oh," I said.

I would have loved to have sat down at the kitchen table and discussed that concept over coffee. It might have been the first real conversation my mother and I had had since I first figured out she and my father didn't know everything. About age ten.

But the cheating article was upstairs waiting to be written. Mother-daughter bonding was going to have to wait.

"Let's talk about that sometime, Mom," I said.

"Sure," she said.

As I left the kitchen, I could hear her humming.

When I got upstairs, Wyatt was already in my study room, looking around.

"I like what you've done with the place," he said.

"Shut up," I said.

"You know what you need in here?"

"Not yet," I said crisply. "But I'm going to find out, and then I'll let you know."

He shook his head. "Man, what are your rules? I can't go two sentences without ticking you off."

"We were supposed to talk about that Friday night, huh?" I said.

"Yeah. Somewhere between the mugging in the alley and the argument in the parking garage." He screwed up his face. "I'm really sorry about that."

"Me, too—I mean, about being such a jerk to you."

I felt the unfamiliar rise of blushing on my face. I turned to the computer, knocking over a pile of binders as I fumbled for some composure. "We have to get this thing done," I said. "Why don't you look up some quotes on 'honor,' 'honesty,' that kind of thing, in those books there." I waved vaguely at a stack of *Bartlett's* and such. He went right for them, thankfully. I couldn't have covered my flustered state much longer.

We worked feverishly and quietly for an hour, interrupted only by my mother bringing in Chinese. "I'm sorry it isn't home-made," she said to Wyatt. "I didn't plan dinner for just Norie and me."

"Don't worry about it," Wyatt said. "My mom's into TV dinners. She works nights so it's easier."

"Where does she work?" Mom said.

"Flamingo Hilton," he said. "She runs lights for the shows."

"Does your dad like TV dinners?"

"I don't know," Wyatt said. "I haven't seen him since I was ten."

"I'm sorry," she said.

"I'm not," Wyatt said. "But thanks."

Mom smiled at him, told us to holler if we needed seconds, and slipped out.

"I hope she didn't think I was being a smart aleck," Wyatt said.

"Are you kidding?" I said. "You should hear me when I get going."

"I have," Wyatt said.

Which led us back to our much-awaited conversation about "the rules." "When you talk about rules, you're not thinking about that book that was popular for a while, are you?" I said. "The one about how to get a guy?"

"No," Wyatt said. "I could care less about getting a guy."

"This is good news."

"No, seriously, my mom always said the key to getting along with different people is to find out what their rules are and then either follow them, or get out of the way."

"Example," I said, dipping my chopsticks into the moo goo gai pan.

"You mean, my rules?" he said.

"Yeah."

He laid them out between chews. "Be honest. Be who you are. Don't tell me that what I believe is stupid. Take me or leave me, but if you're going to leave me, don't spread a bunch of lies about me. I hate that."

"I've pretty much followed your rules," I said.

"I know," he said. "That's why I like you."

"But you can't figure out my rules."

"Just when I think I do, you change them."

"I don't!"

"Okay, then explain to me why you act like you're this independent, don't-try-to-help-me-or-I'll-rip-your-lips-off type, but then in your eyes there's all this pain and confusion and stuff."

I closed my eyes. He guffawed.

"That isn't going to hide it," he said. "It's etched in my brain."

"What is?"

"How much you're hurting."

He said it softly, huskily. So much so that I could feel myself blushing again. This was not something I was accustomed to. I dug full bore into the fried rice.

"If you can't admit it, then you're not following my rules," he said.

"I admit it," I said into the container. "Everything that used to be important to me is starting to melt down into this whole different vision of the future. It's scary, it's confusing, it's definitely against my father's rules."

"Ouch."

"Right." I fiddled with the chopsticks for a second and then set down the container and looked at Wyatt. "Okay, here's the thing. The rule, if you will."

"Okay."

"I like to be allowed to be exactly who I am. But who I am is changing, so I guess I give off mixed signals."

"I'll buy that."

"But—and I don't think this is ever going to change—I hate

it when people think that just because I'm a girl I can't do certain things and I can't think a certain way and I can't do thus and such by myself." I scooched around on the floor. I was warming to my subject. "The problem with feminism is that most people don't understand what it is."

"What is it?" Wyatt said. "I'm serious. This could save me a lot of slaps in the face."

"True feminism is the belief that every woman should be allowed to be exactly who she really is. It's our responsibility to find out who we are, but men, and not even just men but a lot of other women, too, poke their noses in and say, 'You shouldn't do that,' 'You shouldn't think that,' 'A lady doesn't act that way.'" I narrowed my eyes. "I hate that," I said. "I guess it shows."

"Not so much now as it did when I first came," he said. "That helps though. Now maybe I won't be getting your back up all the time."

I stretched out and leaned on one elbow. "Why are you so determined to get along with me?"

He gave the Wyatt shrug. "I like you. No, it's more than that. I'm, like, drawn to you." He stretched out, too, so that we were face to face, on the same level. "Do you believe in messages from God? Have you gotten that far yet?"

I got a kick out of being able to nod to that.

"Okay," he said, "well, my wanting to be with you and all, it's like God's saying that's what I should do. Not that I don't want to! I'm not making this big sacrifice. When you aren't leading me down dark alleys, I like being around you."

"I didn't 'lead' you down that alley."

"That's one of my rules: I take care of my friends," he said. "And don't tell me you didn't need taking care of because you probably would have gotten your head busted in if I hadn't come along and saved it. I'd expect any friend to do the same for me, man or woman."

"Did I thank you for doing that?" I said.

"No."

"Thank you."

"Don't mention it."

I wanted to bury my eyes—maybe my whole face—in the carpet so he wouldn't see me going crimson. But I refused to take my eyes off of his. Let him be the first one to look away. He didn't. Must have been one of his rules.

One thing was for sure. If I didn't get up and go to the computer, we were going to kiss.

I got up.

We spent the next two hours putting together what I'd written and what he had come up with.

"This is a great quote," I said, pointing to number three on his list. " 'Such is the end of all who go after ill-gotten gain; it takes away the lives of those who get it.' Where's it from?"

"The Bible," he said. "Proverbs 1:19."

"Can we use that?" I said.

"Why not?"

I couldn't think of a single reason. I was going to have to get into that Bible thing. Meanwhile, we cut, pasted, and edited until my eyes were like poached eggs and my brain was like scrambled. When the phone rang at nine, my hands were almost too cramped to pick up the receiver.

"Nor," Tobey said, "what are you up to?"

I told her. I could have predicted that at the end she would say, "Wow." I loved that about her. I guess I pretty much knew her rules.

"How much longer do you guys have to work?" she said.

"About an hour," I said.

"Well, look, Shannon and I just made a batch of peanut butter cookies. Do you want us to bring them over?" She snickered. "Or would you two rather be alone?"

"Knock it off," I said. "And yes. I'd kill for some cookies . . ."

But my voice trailed off. For the first time in several hours, my hackles started to stand up again. All I needed was for my father to come home and find a third of the Flagpole Girls in my room. I'll be truthful: I was having a really hard time not hating him.

"However," I said, "why don't you just bring them to school tomorrow. We could all meet for lunch again."

"Okay," she said. She sounded disappointed. Not half as disappointed as I was and not even close to as angry. I loved those girls. I needed them. This thing with my father, it was going to have to be worked out. Along with a lot of other things that were ugly in my life.

But as I hung up, my focus was on one thing: the masterpiece Wyatt and I had created.

"You're going to shake up some people," he said.

"I hope so," I said. "And you know what's weird?"

"What?"

"I don't want to shake them up like, 'Look what Norie Vandenberger wrote. This is Pulitzer-Prize-winning stuff.' I want to shake them up like, 'Man, I have been messing up. I have to get my act together.'"

"That isn't so weird," Wyatt said. "I think it's just you, changing the rules."

CHAPTER TWELVE

MRS. ABBEY STARTED TO READ THE ARTICLE BEFORE school the next day while standing up, the way she did just about everything because she was always rushing from one place to the next. About halfway through it she sat down, and her eyes got involved on the page. Wyatt and I looked at each other and nodded.

"I like it," she said, more like she was talking to herself than to us. "I like it a lot." She looked up at us and swept the paper toward my hand. "Put it in," she said. "I have to get the layout to printing by this afternoon if we want a paper Friday."

"Right on!" I said.

"One thing though," she said. "It's provocative."

"That's what we want," I said.

"Just be prepared for what comes with that," she said. Then her mind, as always, whipped off to the next thing, leaving Wyatt and me to paste the article in place.

"This is so rad," he said.

For an instant he put his arm around my shoulder. Then he withdrew it like he thought I might bite him. Bummer.

That was all the "rad" I was going to get for that morning. In fourth period, I took Pavella aside and told him I'd pulled his article. He blew a gasket.

"What was wrong with it?" he said.

It stunk, I wanted to say. But I chose my words carefully. I was already asking for it with him, and I didn't trust his cuteness anymore.

"It didn't really say anything, Jerry," I said. "We were hoping for something with a little more meat."

"If you want meat, go to McDonald's," he said. "You give me this lame assignment, and then you expect me to make it sound like *Newsweek*. Excuse me for not being Norie Vandenberger!"

"Well, I'm sorry," I said. It was pointless to argue with him. The sarcasm was so thick it was blocking all signs of intelligence.

"You are not," he said.

I squinted at him. "What?"

"You're not sorry. You kicked out my article because you want to punish me for being a bad boy."

His voice went up into that nah-nah-nah-nah nasal thing we all did in first grade. All I could do was stare at him and watch his face go from kindergarten to the state penitentiary. "I don't know when you decided you were going to teach us all how to be good little do-bees," he said through his teeth, "but it's starting to get to me like a wedgie. I'm going to do what I want, so don't get in my way, Mother Clarissa, or I'll roll right over you."

I couldn't help it. I had to lean into his face and say, "I think you mean Mother Teresa, Pavella."

He yanked himself back from the table and blustered across the room, straight toward Mrs. Abbey's office—after stopping off to gather condolences from Mark and a group of adoring sophomore girls. It would have been funny, if it hadn't been so sad.

"Did he give you a bad time?" Wyatt said at my elbow.

I shook my head. "He just got all sarcastic and cynical and made a fool of himself. The usual."

I pulled my eyes away from Pavella and looked at Wyatt. "Do I sound like that?"

"Like what?"

"Like he does. Acting like everybody else is messed up, and I have to do satire all the time to show I'm the only one who isn't?"

"Uh, no," he said. "Not anymore."

"Good," I said.

Wyatt put his lips close to my ear. "But when you did it, you were a whole lot better at it than he is."

"Thanks," I said. "I think."

Lance, Gabe, and Deborah were still so mad at me they wouldn't even look at me, much less speak to me. Gabe was especially obvious about it. Lance, of course, kept a beige kind of cool.

When Rhonda whispered to me in chemistry, "What's going on between those guys and you?" they all turned with their ears tweaked up.

"I don't know," I said loudly enough for them all to hear. "I think we had a difference of opinion."

She looked at me like I'd just arrived with E.T. "So what else is new?" she said.

I changed the subject to where she had been the day before when she was supposed to be in journalism doing layout.

"Yesterday?" she said vacantly.

No wonder Deborah hadn't asked her to be in on the cheating ring. She would have asked Mr. Uhles if he had the key.

As for Mr. Uhles himself, he was not a happy camper that day. He called the roll in a monotone and then paced in front of us pounding a bunch of rolled-up papers against his palm.

"These are yesterday's quizzes," he said.

Somebody groaned. He squelched it with a look.

"I wouldn't joke," he said. "This may be the worst set of papers I've ever gotten from a class of the caliber of you folks."

I could see Gabe's neck veins bulging.

"I'm glad I gave this quiz though. It told me what I wanted to know."

I felt a sizzle of fear go through me. I could see the same sizzle going through Deborah, Gabe, and Lance. Gabe even widened his eyes at Deborah.

"And what I know," Mr. Uhles went on, "is that you people are not ready for this test tomorrow." He paced a little more, this time toward the trash can. When he reached it, he dropped the quizzes soundly into it. "As a teacher, I use evaluation tools like this to measure how well I'm doing as much as how you're doing. Evidently, I'm not doing too well. So if you'll take out your notebooks, we're going to review this material until I think I'm getting through to you people. As of now, the test is postponed until Friday."

Everybody cheered like we were out in the football stadium. When Gabe whistled, Mr. Uhles drilled his dark eyes at him. "I'd be doing a little less cat-calling and a little more studying, Gabe," he said. "You got the all-time low score."

"What was it?" Rhonda said.

The class did a unanimous eye roll.

"Never mind," Mr. Uhles said. "All right, chemical equations with ammonia . . ."

I tried not to let out a sigh of relief big enough to blow the class into the next county. A reprieve. It was working already. Maybe they would study now instead of digging into Mr. Uhles's computer. And with the paper coming out Friday morning, they would read it before the test.

"Are you all going to sit there like bumps on a pickle," Mr. Uhles said, "or are you going to take this down?"

I jerked myself back to my notebook. There was a folded piece of paper on it. I got a sour stomach just opening it.

Thanks a lot, it said. *Now back off.*

There was only one thing to do at that point, as far as I was concerned. With no layout to do after school, I took my spiral notebook to Rancho San Rafael.

This time I only had to walk around for about five minutes before I could sit still. I picked a bench way up in a secluded juniper area on a hill overlooking Reno and just stared at the city for a while.

It was a dry, windy, neon-lighted town. But where I was, with the sky-so-blue-it-hurts-your-eyes stretching endlessly overhead, the smell of brittle sagebrush scenting the air, and the mountains cuddling the whole city into a bowl, it was like I was in a center of calm.

Like the one in the center of me, I thought with surprise. I really did feel at peace inside myself, protected from the icy stares of my former friends, the heartless demands of my father, the soul-squeezing pressure of King High School.

I closed my eyes and imagined myself in that center, floating freely and peacefully. It felt real there, authentic, genuine, accepting. I wanted to stay, and I did, breathing and listening, and then knowing.

This isn't like the dream, I thought. *I'm not reaching up for something that isn't there. I'm reaching in—and it's there.*

And I knew what it was. It was God.

I stayed much longer than ten minutes. The sky was turning cold-evening-pink when I opened my eyes and picked up my notebook.

Good work, Norie, I wrote in the words of God. *It's only the beginning, though. Do more. Do much more.*

More pressure, God? I wrote. *Pressure from you?*

For a minute there was nothing more to write. But the center of peace grew larger, like an ever widening space of freedom. I started to write again.

Do more about this, Norie. Don't stop until it's done.

I couldn't have been more sure of what I'd heard. And don't stop until it's done? Now that I could do.

It was strange driving home. I expected everything to be different now that I'd had a mountaintop experience.

But it all looked basically the same. People still drove like idiots down Fourth Street. My father's Porsche was still parked in the garage. My mother was still riding her exercise bike when I went by the laundry room.

What happened? I thought. *I had this blinding revelation of clarity, and now it's like somebody put a reality cloud over it.*

But in my room, as I cleared off my desk and threw out half the stuff that was in my drawers, I felt for the circle of peace. It was still there.

The world isn't any different, I thought. *But Wyatt's right. I am.*

It didn't matter what the world said—Deborah, Lance, and Gabe with their threats or even my dad with his.

I knew I'd heard God. I'd never had this feeling, like I'd just been comforted by some awesome truth. And I had to do what He said.

I reached for the phone and called Wyatt.

"You want to help me with another project?" I said.

"Absolutely."

"Meet us for lunch tomorrow in the theater lobby then," I said.

"Who's 'us'?"

"The Flagpole Girls," I said.

"Girl, you're about eatin' up my social calendar," Brianna said to me the next day—with a grin.

"Did something else happen with the cheating thing?" Marissa said. Then she looked at Wyatt and plastered her hand over her mouth.

"It's okay. He knows," I said. "He's going to help me, in fact. But I need you guys to pray."

"That's what we do best," Tobey said. "Go for it. What is it?"

"I want to write an honor code," I said. "Like the one Shannon's sister had to sign at college."

Brianna looked at me with one eyebrow raised. "And you want to do this because . . ."

"Because it needs to be done," I said. "I'm going to take it to Mr. Holden and tell him I think it ought to be part of school policy here. He can do what he wants with it." I shrugged. "I just can't not do it."

"I'm loving this," Ms. Race said. "What's our prayer focus?"

I grinned at Wyatt. "I want to know what the rules are. I can't think of any better place to find out."

"Hmm," Ms. Race said.

"Why don't you just listen for ten minutes and then write it down?" Cheyenne said.

Once more I had an attack of the guilties. I still hadn't sat her down and talked to her, not with everything that had been going on. Still, this was like the perfect opportunity to get the message to her without making her feel like a criminal. Man, I was changing.

"This needs a lot of power," I said. "It needs all your energy and your faith. It's not just about me." I gave her a direct look. She nodded, and I thought I saw a flicker of recognition in her eyes. Maybe that was enough said.

"Hands," Brianna said, holding out her two elegant ones. "You too, Wyatt Earp."

He grinned. "Nobody's called me that since sixth grade."

"Well, that's about the intelligence level I'm on," she said. "Now take my hand."

We prayed for a good while. Brianna asked for God to let me be as smart as he was going to let me get, since this was so important. Tobey prayed for a clear head, one that wasn't full of worries about other stuff. Shannon said "Amen" to that. Marissa spoke up in favor of my writing what Jesus would have me write, and Wyatt asked for just the right words, expressed in just the right way. It occurred to me that I hadn't ever heard Wyatt pray before. That we prayed to the same God was kind of comforting. The ultimate bonding.

The only person who didn't pray out loud was Cheyenne. I took that as a good thing. She was probably thinking about all of this in terms of herself, and that was just what I wanted.

When we lifted our heads, I didn't have a full-blown honor code spelled out in my head. But I knew it would come.

When the meeting broke up, Tobey waited for me, and we walked to our lockers together.

"I want to be there for you, Nor," she said.

"I hope so. I mean, I'm okay. I'm great, in fact, but I want you there."

She looked at me sideways out of her brown eyes. "You do?"

"What does that mean?" I said. Normally I'd have known. People used to be put off by my obnoxiousness all the time. But I thought I'd changed.

"It's just, like when I called about the cookies, you didn't exactly blow me off, but I didn't get it. Did you just want to be alone with Wyatt or something?"

I let out a huge guffaw—too huge probably. "No!" I said. "Don't be getting ideas about him and me, okay?"

"Then what's going on? You can't do this by yourself, you know. That's what the Flagpole Girls are for."

I stopped and leaned heavily against my locker. "It isn't me, L'Orange," I said. "It's my father."

"I don't get it."

"You wouldn't, not with a cool dad like you have. Trust me, my father is nothing like him."

She looked no less baffled than she had before. I shoved a hand through my hair.

"He thinks I should be hanging with kids with my same goals," I said.

"Oh," she said. Her eyes grew wise. "Like Lance, Gabe—that crowd."

I nodded. The bell rang, and she squeezed my arm. "I don't want you to get in trouble with your dad. Just hang in there; we'll think of something."

"It'll come, right?" I said.

"Yeah," she said. "Just like the honor code."

And it did, sooner than I expected. Like after school when I was lying on my bed with my chemistry book on my chest, looking at my room and trying to figure out what I wanted to do with it.

Just let it express your self, your real self, I thought. Or God thought. It was getting hard to tell the difference.

So, go by my rules, I decided. I hated pink, purple—oh, and yellow. Gross. But red. And deep blue. And black and white. Now, those were me. Definite colors. Hues with principle.

I sat up to imagine some kind of tent thing coming down over my bed, but another thought crowded in. *Go by the rules. Your rules. The ones I give you along the way, the ones that fit the real you.*

"That's it!" I said aloud. "That's the honor code!"

I scrambled for a notebook and a pen. "Give it to me, God," I said. "I have pen in hand."

I wrote down everything that came into my head. It covered two pages, front and back. It would definitely need some editing.

I charged through my homework, giving chemistry double time, and then I called Wyatt.

"I have a first draft," I said. "Want to see it tomorrow, and then come over tomorrow night to work on a final?"

"You really want me to help you?" he said.

My heart took a dip. "Don't you want to?"

"Yes, I want to." I could hear him grinning through the phone. "I'm just still feeling out the changes."

By Friday I was tired, but I'd never felt better. I'd just spent two days submerging myself in chemistry, an honor code, and God, and I had this exhausted-but-energized thing going on. I tried to describe it to Wyatt while we were waiting to see Mr. Holden before school, the honor code typed and in its professional-looking folder on my lap.

"Okay, this is going to sound lame," he said. "But it's like when I bowl a good game. I'm totally wiped out, but I'm jazzed, too."

"So are you going to take me bowling?" I said. "Or am I going to continue to be deprived of this exhilaration?"

"Baby, I will take you bowling, out to Denny's, and down to the pool hall. We will have the full white-trash experience."

I was about to question his use of the word "baby"—some things die hard—when Mr. Holden rushed in and shooed us into his office. He really was a pretty decent principal. Tobey had had her problems with him during her exposé of the sexual assault, but he had turned out all right. She warned me that he had to have more proof than a district attorney to convince him of anything though.

So I was ready with a prepared statement, and Wyatt had his part, too. Mr. Holden listened with nods and eye contact. I was encouraged. His verbal response wasn't quite as uplifting.

"I like the idea," he said when we were finished with our presentation. "And I applaud your idealism. We're so busy worrying about who's on drugs and who's cutting class, we don't pay enough attention to the niceties."

"Niceties?" I said. "I don't think personal honor is a 'nicety.' I think it's a necessity. We pointed that out in our introduction."

"I'll read it," Mr. Holden said.

I was beginning to have my doubts already.

"Be that as it may, I'm going to be honest with you—since that's what this is all about." He smiled. Tobey always said he had a nice smile. I thought it was kind of condescending myself. "I'm skeptical about how realistic it is to have an honor code in a high school. I can just hear the teachers at the faculty meeting if I were to present this. Most of them are convinced, by experience, that most students' code of honor consists of 'I won't tell if you won't.' "

"Then don't you think we ought to be teaching people what real honor is?" I said.

He nodded. I could see in his eyes that he thought I was extremely naive. New experience for me.

Amazingly enough, I didn't let it get to me.

"We did it," I said to Wyatt as we rushed off to first period. "I feel good about it."

"Do you think he'll even read it?" Wyatt said.

"God knows," I said. "Literally."

We stopped in front of my first-period class and looked at each other. It was a deliciously awkward moment.

"Thanks for all your help," I said.

"See you fourth," he said.

Then he smiled, and I smiled, and my throat got goopy. As he walked—jauntily—away, I tried to smack myself out of the sort of dream state I found myself in, but I couldn't shake the magic.

Until fourth period.

When the paper came out.

CHAPTER THIRTEEN

TO PUT IT "SUCCINCTLY," AS THEY SAY IN JOURNALISM, everything blew up in my face.

The article itself looked great. Even from its place on the second page, it begged the reader to dig right in with the headline "Cheating Outbreak at King."

It definitely caught Pavella's attention. We didn't have our copies two minutes before he was in my face. I didn't think he could read that fast.

"What's this?" he hissed at me.

"Looks like an article on cheating," I whispered back. "You ought to read it."

"Real funny. Is this what you did instead of my article?"

"Yes."

He called me a name and started to walk away. I went back to reading Deborah's piece on our preparation for Academic Olympics and made a mental note to ask Rhonda why she had let Deb tout us as "the continuing champions" when we hadn't even competed yet. Pavella, I noticed, had stopped and turned back to me.

"What if somebody gets suspicious of us because of this?" he said.

"You mean, somebody like Mr. Uhles?"

"Or Mr. Lowe or Mr. Dixon or Mrs. Bowman."

I stared. He still didn't know what he had just blurted out to me. He shook his head like I was the one who was a complete imbecile.

"That's what you want though, isn't it?" he whispered nastily. "You want us to get caught so the curve goes down and your class standing goes up."

"No," I said, "what I want is for you guys to quit cheating."

"What's it to you?"

"Are you two going to help distribute these?" Mrs. Abbey said. She pointed to the stacks of newspapers on the side table. "Let's get them out before lunch."

I nodded and went for my pile. Pavella was right on my heels.

"So?" he said.

"So what?" I said.

"So what's it to you if we cheat?"

"That isn't the question, Pavella," I said. "The question is, what's it to you? Do you even give a flip what kind of person you are?"

"I'm the kind of person who gets a baseball scholarship," he said. "I'm only doing this to be sure I land one so I can move as far away from here as possible."

"I hear that," I said. "We're all in the same boat."

"Yeah, right." Pavella hoisted his newspaper bundle up onto his shoulder and let his thick lower lip hang down. I think it was supposed to make him look tough. I thought he looked pathetic, and I felt sorry for him.

I didn't hear too much more about the piece until lunch. That was when people sat around with their pizza slices and pudding cups and read past the first page. Wyatt and I just wandered around the eating spots, including the dreaded cafeteria, and listened to the comments. The range was pretty broad, everything from, "How do I get in on that?" to "Man, this bites! Now teachers are going to be all over us during tests!" to "This is cool. I'm sick of people cheating off of me."

The most common comment, however, was "Who's part of the cheating ring?"

Nothing in the article came close to identifying Deborah, Gabe, Lance, and Pavella. It didn't even allude to what class they were cheating in, which I was glad of, since Pavella had spilled that just about every honors and AP teacher was fair game. It only said it was happening on a large and complex scale and that students were literally ripping each other off in the name of achievement. Wyatt's quote from Proverbs fit perfectly right there.

Rhonda and Mark found me as Wyatt and I were crossing the courtyard listening for feedback. Rhonda had her copy of the *King's Herald* folded back to the second page.

"Where did this come from?" she said. Her blonde hair was literally standing on end.

"You weren't there," I said. "Mrs. Abbey approved it. Pavella's piece was awful, and I thought this would be perfect."

She blinked at me. "But I don't get it," she said.

"What is there to get? A bunch of people are running a cheating ring, and everybody is getting the shaft because of it, including them. Especially them."

"I don't believe it," Mark said. He ran a hand across his shaved head.

"It's the truth," I said. "I was approached by them, okay? They asked me if I wanted in. What more proof do you need?"

"Why didn't you tell who they were?"

"Because I'm not out to convict anybody, " I said. "I was just hoping this would stop it."

Rhonda knitted her tiny eyebrows together. "I just don't understand why you would want to print this without using their names. This isn't news; it's your opinion. It should have gone on the editorial page."

"It wasn't my opinion," I said. I rolled my eyes at Wyatt who was listening intently from over my shoulder. "I just chose not to reveal my source. I can do that, you know. First Amendment and all that."

"What's the Bill of Rights got to do with it?"

"That's the Constitution, Rhonda," I said. "You know? Freedom of the press?" I tried really hard to keep the sarcasm out of my voice. Poor baby was making enough of a fool of herself without my help.

"They'll make you tell," she said.

"Who's 'they'?"

"Mr. Holden and all of them. Trust me, they will."

"What are they going to do?" Wyatt said. "Put her on the rack? I hear they have one in a back room in the office."

Her eyes widened briefly before she scowled at him. "Go ahead and make me feel like a dork," she said. "But I'm telling you, be prepared for them to grill you."

"What makes you think they will?" I said.

"I'm the other editor, remember?" she said. Her eyes cut resentfully toward Mark, and her lower lip actually came out in a pout.

"What's that got to do with it?" I said.

"Everything," she said. "Mr. Holden already questioned me."

She and her humongous head of hair made a dramatic exit with Mark trying to match her in stage presence. Wyatt and I stared at each other.

"Whoa," he said. "The man wastes no time."

I shrugged. "Doesn't matter. They can't make me tell, and they know it, period."

Still, I waited all afternoon for one of those little pink slips summoning me to the office. The only pink slip I saw was the one Pavella was carrying in fifth period. It was a large one, with a bunch of signatures on it.

"What's that?" Deborah said to him.

"It's a drop slip," he said. He turned around and gave me a loaded glare. "I'm dropping journalism."

"In the middle of the semester?" Lance said sharply. "You'll lose the credit. They won't give you another class, you know."

"They will if I can prove I was getting a bad deal in this one." He tapped the paper importantly and scowled at me. Gabe nudged his arm roughly and nodded for him to turn around. All four of them positioned their backs against me. It was like having a door slammed in my face.

I tried to put it out of my mind as Mr. Uhles passed out the tests. I wanted to concentrate on all the material I'd worked into my brain in the past few days, not on whether they were speaking to me or whether they were going to cheat on this test.

"Good luck, Norie," Mr. Uhles whispered to me when he put my test paper on my desk.

"Thanks," I whispered back.

"Who needs luck?" I heard Gabe mutter.

He eyed Lance, who ogled him back.

That answered that question.

The test wasn't as hard as the last one, but a couple of problems still wouldn't come out for me. It wasn't that I didn't know the stuff, I realized as I erased an answer for the fiftieth time. It was just that certain concepts didn't make sense to me.

Do what you can and let it go. Wasn't that basically what God had said that first time I'd tried to listen?

I hope you're right, I prayed silently. *And I wish you would whisper that to my father.*

About five minutes before the end of the period, I decided that continuing to stare at the same blank answer slots wasn't going to improve my grade. I turned in my paper and went back to my desk. A note was waiting for me.

Meet me in the bathroom. Deb.

Her seat was already empty. I got a pass from Mr. Uhles and went down the hall toward the rest room. As usual, classroom doors were open, and a lot of teachers seemed to have the end-of-the-class-period-on-a-Friday-afternoon thing going on. Kids were just kind of hanging out. I even caught a glimpse of Brianna in a doorway with Ira.

"Where are you goin', girl?" she said.

"To the bathroom," I said. I was startled at the shaky quality in my voice. I hadn't even realized I was nervous until then. It was pretty obvious Deborah hadn't summoned me to the little girls' room to compare eyeliner.

She was in there, pacing cross-armed. She stopped when she saw me and came at me like a dog does when you step on his property.

"Step off," I said. "I'm not armed, okay?"

She sniffed and flung herself against the post between the potty stalls. The blueberry eyes were too ripe for anything pleasant, and the lanky arms and bony shoulders were doing all kinds of infuriated gyrations. I would always have described her as wholesome-looking before. Right now she looked like La Femme Nikita.

"Very cute move in the newspaper, Vandenberger," she said.

"I liked it," I said.

"What are you trying to prove? We invited you in, for God's sake—"

"Can we do this without swearing?" I said.

She looked momentarily stunned. "What did I say? Forget it. I'm not here for a lecture on my vocabulary, okay?"

"So get to the point," I said. "What are you here for?"

"To tell you that you had better keep your mouth shut about our names, or you're going to be so sorry."

I gave a snort that bounced against the bathroom walls. "Are you threatening me?"

"Sounds that way, doesn't it?"

"With what? Assault with a deadly fingernail? I'm quaking in my Docs, Deb."

"Don't give me any ideas," she said. "I'm so ticked off right now, I feel like slashing you, believe me. Not that it would hurt anything. Your face has never been one of your stronger features."

"Oh, come on!" I said. "If you brought me in here so we can throw insults back and forth, I have better things to do."

She caught me off guard. Hurling herself off the post, she was suddenly in my face, gangly arms stuck out to either side with the fingernails bared. I was too flabbergasted to move.

"You're going to wish insults were all you got when we finish with you," she said.

"Ease it away from the curb, girl," said a voice from the doorway. "'Fore you get yourself hurt."

We both whipped our faces around to see Brianna standing there, looking for all the world like an angel in cargo pants.

"Go on now," she said to Deborah. "Get back, and then get out."

Deborah wasn't going to argue with her. She had turned a few shades paler, and she was pulling her hair back with both hands as she edged toward the door. Brianna stood there until Deborah got right up to her. Staring down Deborah for a second, Brianna then moved aside. Deb bolted like a tagger caught with a spray can.

I turned around and leaned on the sink.

"You are about the last person I'd expect to find 'bout to get in a catfight in the girls' rest room," Brianna said. She came right over to me and took hold of my arm. "You all right?"

"Yeah," I said. My voice sounded wobblier than ever.

"I thought something was goin' down, the way you looked when you went past the classroom a minute ago. But I didn't think you were 'bout to get your tail kicked."

"Neither did I. But don't worry about it. As long as I don't tell who is doing the cheating, I don't think they'll bother me again."

"Huh." Brianna worked her lips intently. "Well, if that girl or anybody else gives you trouble now, you know you have friends. Between Tobey, me, and the rest of them, we have everything covered."

"I know," I said. I felt like somebody had just wrapped me in a warm blanket. "I think it's going to be okay."

And it was. Dad or no Dad, I wanted those girls with me. They were the best thing in my life.

I left school unmolested by either Deborah and Company or Mr. Holden. Even when I went into the office to say good-bye to Ms. Race for the weekend, nobody grabbed me and hauled me in. Ms. Race squeezed my hand and said, "I'm proud of you."

"Thanks," I said. "I don't know how much good it's going to do yet, but I'm still hoping."

"You keep on," she said. "Are you hearing from God?"

"Big time," I said.

She smiled an I-just-won-the-lottery smile. "You go, girl," she said.

I had a great weekend. Wyatt and I went bowling that night. I bowled a twenty-three, which he said was—okay, he said it was horrible, even for a beginner. But I had a blast and treated him to a sundae at Baskin-Robbins afterward. Saturday I took my little checkbook and haunted Mill End Fabrics for hours, coming home with a bolt each of red, blue, white, and black material. I experimented with making a tent out of them over my bed and was talking to Tobey on the phone when my call waiting bleeped. It was the only blot on my weekend.

"Hey," said a gruff female voice. "This is Felise."

It took me a minute.

"Oh, yeah," I said. "How's it going?"

"Okay. Cheyenne can't study with you tomorrow."

"Oh. Okay. Is she sick?"

There was a major hesitation. I could almost hear square-shouldered Felise making a mental choice. Her breathing rasped into the phone. "She just can't study," she said finally. "She told me to call you so I did."

"Okay," I said. "I'll keep it open in case she changes her mind."

"Yeah," she said. And hung up.

"Weird," I told Tobey when I got back to her. "Very weird."

Although I decided to leave it alone, I thought about Cheyenne a lot in the next two days, as I made my tent and cut out big shapes from fabric to mount posters against on the walls. She was even in my mind when I went for my walk at Rancho San Rafael, attended church services, and went to a movie at the Keystone with Wyatt to see a Norwegian film with subtitles.

Will you take care of her, God? I prayed every time. *I don't think she's going to let me do it.*

Obviously, Felise hadn't told me everything. She wasn't lying. I don't think Tassie let them do that, under penalty of starvation or something. But she wasn't giving me the big picture. I'd have to wait until Monday to find out what it was.

I didn't see my father most of the weekend, which was another reason it went so smoothly. In fact, the only time I did see him was when he got home late Saturday night after doing surgery on some guy who ruptured several organs in a motorcycle accident. I'd just gotten in myself, and my mother and I were having decaf cappuccinos in the kitchen. We were right on the edge of talking about my plans for my room.

"Hi," Mom said brightly.

He said "Hi," as if the whole exchange were entirely unnecessary as far as he was concerned.

He looked at me. "Did you have your chemistry test?"

"Yes," I said, trying to be civil. "We had it Friday."

"I thought it was supposed to be Wednesday."

"It was."

I hesitated. How much of this whole mess did he really need do know? I was almost curious enough about what his reaction would be to go ahead and tell him.

Almost.

"So?" he said impatiently. "How did you do?"

I took a breath. "I did my best," I said.

"And how good is that?"

"Quint, honestly."

We both stared at my mother. Her pretty face was splotchy with red, and the soft eyes were right on the verge of sparking.

"What?" Dad said, when his jaw went back on its hinges.

"She said she did her best. What more can we ask for?"

I was in shock. My mother was defending me? To my father, his Wonderfulness?

"It doesn't matter what we ask for, Yo," he said. "It's what Harvard asks for that I'm concerned about."

She didn't quite know what to say to that, which was really okay. She had done enough to jack herself up in my estimation about fifteen points.

"I'm going to bed," I told them. "Thanks for the coffee, Mom."

That whole scene added to the growing sense of peace I was feeling. It was a good thing, too, because I needed all the inner peace I could get Monday morning.

The pink slip I'd expected Friday appeared in my first-period class. When I arrived at the office, Ms. Race directed me into the conference room.

"Am I in trouble?" I whispered to her.

"No," she whispered back. "They are. They're hoping you'll bail them out."

"They" turned out to be an impressive panel: Mr. Lowe, our honors English teacher; Mrs. Bowman, our AP American history teacher; Mr. Dixon from trig; Mr. Uhles; and Mr. Holden himself. They were all tapping their pencils, fooling with paper clips, and otherwise showing signs of suppressed agitation. These were not happy people.

"I think you can guess what we're all meeting about this morning," Mr. Holden said grimly.

"The article I wrote in the paper," I said.

"Right. It's definitely raised some eyebrows."

"How accurate is it?" Mr. Dixon said. Enough with the eyebrow raising. He was ready to tear somebody's cornea out.

"Very," I said. "The four people involved came to me and asked if I wanted to be in on it. You can't get much more accurate than that."

"We're all concerned, Norie," Mr. Lowe said. He was a quiet, balding man I'd always pretty much respected. He called on me more often than most teachers did. "I've suspected for quite some time, as have my colleagues here, that some form of cheating was going on. We just had no idea it was of this magnitude."

"This is definitely serious," Mrs. Bowman said. She was the most nervous of the group. She was fiddling around with every piece of jewelry on her body. "It's one thing to glance over at someone else's paper. I mean, that's still wrong. But this is so . . . premeditated. I'm changing all my computer codes."

"That's all well and good," Mr. Dixon said. "But I want these little hoodlums caught and crucified."

"Let's try to keep this in perspective," Mr. Holden said. "My main concern is that we have enough specific information to proceed."

My hackles reminded me that they were still there, ready to go into operation at any time. "Are you going to ask me to give their names?" I said.

"Now, that is the quandary, isn't it?" Mr. Uhles spoke for the first time. Up to that point, he had been staring sadly at a me-chanical pencil. "As a reporter, you're not required to reveal your source."

"No," I said.

"But as a student at this school," Mr. Dixon said, "I think you have an obligation. You can't just drop a bomb like this and leave us scrambling around looking like a bunch of idiots."

Oh, let's do be careful how we look, I wanted to say.

"It's not your fault you weren't aware of this," I said instead. "These people are sly. All I wanted to do was stop them."

Mrs. Bowman and Mr. Dixon looked at me dubiously, Mrs. Bowman tugging on her earring. Mr. Holden examined his pen. Only Mr. Lowe and Mr. Uhles made eye contact with me.

"It's a definite moral dilemma," Mr. Lowe said. "How do you usually make decisions like this?"

The question surprised me. My answer didn't.

"I pray about it," I said. "Try to listen to what God tells me."

"And what's God telling you this time?" Mr. Uhles said.

"To see it through until it's done," I said.

"Which is how?" Mr. Dixon said. He was making no attempt to hide his feelings. He was contemptuous of the turn this con-versation had taken.

"I'm not sure yet," I said.

Mr. Holden cleared his throat and pulled a folder out from under his copy of the *King's Herald.* It was Wyatt's and my honor code.

"It seems to me," Mr. Holden said, "that if we had an ap-proved, schoolwide honor code, you would know what you were obligated to do in this situation."

"That's true," I said. I couldn't believe this was happening. My first thought was, *Wait till I tell Wyatt and the girls.*

"Honor code?" Mr. Dixon said. "What good is that going to do?"

"Hear me out," Mr. Holden said. He turned to me again as Mr. Dixon clicked the button on his ballpoint pen. "Your code is very well written. I read it over the weekend."

Yikes, miracles did still happen.

"What it doesn't tell us is what should happen if students are caught cheating. If we had a complete code, I think we could attack this problem head-on."

"I agree," I said. "I could add that on."

"I'd like for you to," Mr. Holden said, "in cooperation with a . . . what would we call it? An honor team. Made up of these people here, plus your cohort . . ." He consulted the code. "Wyatt Fox."

"I like it, " I said. The teachers all nodded, except Mr. Dixon, who stroked his beard like some kind of revered sage.

"And I'd like to add one more student," Mr. Holden said. "Any suggestions?"

"What about Tobey L'Orange?" I said.

Mr. Dixon stirred from his prophetic little pose and raised a finger.

"You have somebody you'd like to see on this?" Mr. Holden said.

"Yes," Mr. Dixon said. "Deborah Zorn."

I FELT LIKE SOMEBODY HAD JUST SLAMMED ME IN THE face with a two-by-four.

Apparently no one noticed, because when Mr. Holden asked, "Anyone have a problem with bringing Deborah on?" they shook their heads. No one asked me.

We all went back to class, the teachers chatting importantly among themselves, me moving in a daze. I tried to sort it out as I walked down the hall.

Let me get this straight. The very person who masterminded this scheme is now going to sit on a committee that's designed to stop people from cheating.

Great.

Fabulous.

Absolutely exquisite.

Not only was she going to sit there full of hypocrisy, looking like Rebecca of Sunnybrook Farm and thinking like the Watergate conspirators, but she also was going to get a real charge out of watching me squirm through the whole thing. The very thought of her sitting there in the conference room, smiling smugly while she hoodwinked them into thinking she was the purest thing since the Mother Mary, was more disgusting to me than school lunch.

The worst part of it was, I couldn't vent to anybody. I hadn't told another person, even Wyatt or the Flagpole Girls, who the culprits were. Nobody could tell me what to do about this.

Well, almost nobody.

It was all I could think about when I went to Rancho San Rafael that afternoon, in a driving wind, to listen. I really didn't get much besides the usual, *Don't try so hard. It will come.* I tried to be content with that. At least I didn't feel like I was drowning in a storm anymore.

Yucking it up on the phone with Wyatt that night helped. So did passing notes to Tobey in English class the next day, having my mother help me cover my box spring in cool sheets I found that were printed like a newspaper, and seeing how increasingly miserable Gabe, Lance, and Pavella were becoming.

I wasn't enjoying their discomfort, mind you. I was just glad to see it. I took it as a sign that their consciences were getting to them.

Deborah, on the other hand, was rising above it with remarkable aplomb. Just as I'd suspected, the minute she found out she was invited to be on the honor team, she started to reward me with these self-satisfied smiles that clearly said, "You thought you were so smart. Well, it's backfired on you, hasn't it?"

I never smiled back. And I tried to keep hoping that this was part of some unknown God plan, and not Deborah's exhaust billowing out into my face.

I had a chance to find out on Wednesday. Mr. Holden called a meeting of the committee before school, and he even had breakfast served. Ms. Race looked really cute in an apron as she served up quiche and fruit salad. Really cute and really sleepy.

"Six-thirty A.M.?" she whispered to me as she offered me a bran muffin. "You're all possessed."

Wyatt and I grinned at each other, and then looked suspiciously at the quiche. I wanted to ask if it had been made in the school cafeteria, but I figured that would be inappropriate. Across from us, Deborah beamed wholesomely at Mr. Lowe and complimented him on his tie. I stifled a groan.

But it wasn't until Mr. Holden plunged into reading the honor code for critique that I really got to see Deborah at work. She was impressive.

" 'Because we are all individuals,' " he read from my pages, " 'we do not all agree on standards of honor. Nor should we be expected to on every detail. But the honor code that follows can be agreed on as a community and will establish a minimum standard of honor for everyone to live up to. It reflects who we are called to be as members of a learning community.' "

Mr. Holden looked up. All heads bobbed except Mr. Dixon's, but he didn't say anything. Deborah murmured, "Wow. Incredible." And then Mr. Dixon coaxed himself to smile.

" 'Guideline Number One,' " Mr. Holden read on. " 'It is a violation of the code to cheat on any assignment or test in any way. 'Cheating' is defined as 'dishonestly or deceptively gaining information and thus defrauding the teacher and the other students in the class.' "

I saw Deborah churn restlessly in her seat. Mr. Dixon looked at her in concern.

" 'Guideline Number Two. It is a violation of the code to plagiarize on any assignment, whether the stolen material is copied from a published product, a computer- generated source, or another student's work. Plagiarism is a form of stealing and will be viewed as such. Guideline Number Three. It is a violation of the code to forge a signature—' "

Deborah's hand shot up. Mr. Holden stopped and looked at her through his bifocals. "Yes, Deborah?" he said.

"Can we stop here for a minute? " She cocked her acorn-colored head as if she were extremely distressed. I didn't buy it.

"Sure," Mr. Holden said.

"I have a problem with some of the language that's used in there. I mean, I agree that we shouldn't copy, of course, but . . ." She caught her breath in a frustrated manner that was so fake it was all I could do not to let my eyes roll right up into my brain. "Does she have to make students sound like criminals if they do these things?"

Mr. Holden glanced back at the code. Everyone else studied their copies.

"What specific words did you have in mind?" Mr. Lowe said.

" 'Defrauding.' 'Stolen.' 'Violation.' 'Forgery.' " She put a well-manicured hand to her chest. "Frankly, I just don't think it's that bad around here."

"It's bad," Mr. Uhles said. He toyed with his mechanical pencil, eyes sad the way they had been for days. "If four students are breaking into a teacher's computer and gaining access to answer keys, I think that's bad enough."

"My question isn't whether it's bad enough," Mrs. Bowman said, fingering her pearls. "My question is what are the penalties going to be for infractions? Failure on the assignment? Failure for the semester? Suspension?"

"Suspension? Really?" Deborah said, blue eyes bulging like berries. "Don't you think that's a little drastic?"

"At some colleges they call for expulsion," Mr. Lowe said. "I'm not suggesting we do that. I'm just trying to put it into perspective for you."

Deborah feigned shock. I looked at Wyatt. His eyes were narrowed into disbelieving slits. Yikes. This kid was perceptive.

"So you're saying specific consequences should be spelled out in the code?" Mr. Holden said.

I pulled my gaze away from Wyatt and felt my hackles going up. "Uh, Mr. Holden?" I said. "That wasn't our main reason for writing the code."

"No, it wasn't," Wyatt said.

"Then what's the point?" Mr. Dixon said sharply. "I don't see the sense in telling kids all this stuff is wrong without telling them what's going to happen to them if they do it. Present company excepted, I don't know too many students in this school who are going to let some high-minded code keep them from getting what they want the easy way—unless they know they're going to be nailed big-time if they are caught."

Thanks so much for your faith in human nature, I thought. And then something came to me with ugly clarity. No wonder kids like Gabe, Deborah, and Lance thought it was all right to cheat as long as it was foolproof. Teachers like Mr. Dixon were teaching them that. I couldn't let it pass.

"I need to say something," I said abruptly.

Mr. Holden nodded at me. I could feel Mr. Uhles leaning in to listen, and Mr. Lowe, too.

"Wyatt and I didn't write the code so you all would have one more reason to throw the book at people, all right? Our thinking was that people need to be taught not to cheat, lie, forge, steal, and whatever else it takes to achieve their goals. It's gotten so competitive, cheating is an accepted thing to get where you need to go. We wanted the code to be used like a teaching tool against that."

Mr. Dixon grunted. But Mr. Uhles was nodding intently.

"How so, Norie?" he said. "Do you have any ideas?"

Until that moment, no, I hadn't had any. But I went ahead and opened my mouth, and something amazing came out. "What if—" I began, "—and I'm just saying 'what if' because I haven't thought this all the way through—but what if we had some kind of, I don't know, honor council that was made up of a group like this one? Kids who were caught violating the code would be brought before the council, and we would decide on a case-by-case basis what needed to happen for that student to get straight on what honor is all about."

I had no idea where this was all coming from, but I was liking it. I wriggled in the chair and warmed to the subject.

"We would have creative penalties. Like for instance, maybe we would see that the kid was cheating because he just didn't know how to study, so we would require him to take a study skills class or have a mentor he would have to report to a certain number of times a week. Or if we saw that, like a girl was doing it because she felt trapped, the expectations here and at home were way too much, blah, blah, blah. Maybe there could be counseling so she could figure out how to talk to her parents and rethink her goals. Then she would have to write a letter to everybody involved fully explaining—I don't know; these are just ideas."

"They're excellent," Mr. Uhles said.

"I agree," said Mr. Lowe.

Mr. Holden looked around the table. Mr. Dixon was doing the I'm-Socrates-so-you'll-have-to-wait-until-I've-sufficiently-stroked-my-beard thing. Mrs. Bowman nodded anxiously and twirled her rings.

"It sounds good," she said. "But it would be so much work."

"What else are we here for, Sarah?" Mr. Uhles said. "I'd much rather spend my time doing something like that than filling out attendance forms, averaging grades, worrying about whether somebody's going to break into my computer."

"Have you changed your codes?" Mrs. Bowman said.

I looked quickly at Deborah. She was watching Mr. Uhles like a bird of prey.

Mr. Uhles gave an ironic smile. "I haven't had time," he said.

I really wished he hadn't said that. But I turned my attention to Mr. Holden. He, too, was looking at Deborah. "What's your take on this?" he said.

She acted surprised to be consulted. How modest of her.

"I'm just not sure it'll work," she said. "I think people will find a way to get around it."

"Some will," Wyatt said. "You're always going to lose a few who aren't ready to be helped. But I don't think you should underestimate the integrity of most teenagers. I know I would rather have somebody help me get on the straight and narrow than just kick me out of school for three days. Then I'm in a worse position academically, and I'll probably cheat again."

"Excellent reasoning," Mr. Lowe said.

I wanted to squeeze Wyatt's knee or grin at him or something; I was so proud. But I maintained a modicum of control and watched Mr. Holden for a response.

"I tell you what," he said. "Why don't we do a trial run? We're out for Thanksgiving this afternoon."

I looked up at the calendar in surprise. Where had the month gone?

"Since this is your baby, Norie, yours and Wyatt's, why don't you two work on structuring some kind of honor council? Can you do that over the holiday?"

I looked at Wyatt, who gave me one of his I'd-rather-do-this-than-anything-else-I-can-think-of-except-bowl shrugs.

"Sure," I said.

"Great. Come see me Monday morning, and we'll give it a go. Anybody here not want to be included on the council?"

Mrs. Bowman looked around the table and timidly raised her

hand. I was disappointed that Mr. Dixon didn't raise his. Or Deborah. She was doodling on her notebook and smiling faintly. I had the distinct impression she was pretty pleased with her sweet self.

Nobody else opted out, and Mr. Holden smiled at us all. "I feel good about this," he said. "In the meantime, I want the rest of you to keep your eyes open for possible test cases. Anybody you have any kind of proof is cheating, plagiarizing, whatever, give me their names and we'll try this out on them. Any objections?"

Mr. Dixon grunted. "I'd sure like to do a 'test' on those four in the newspaper article." He looked at me, eyes smoldering. "I think you have just as much of a responsibility as anybody else on this committee to turn people in. I think that ought to be worked into the code, too. If you know somebody's doing any of this stuff you've spelled out here and you don't blow the whistle on them, you're just as guilty as they are."

Mr. Holden looked at the clock. "I'm afraid that's going to have to wait for another meeting. Norie, you and Wyatt think about that while you're working on the honor council over the weekend." He smiled again, and I did think for a second that maybe Tobey was right about him. "I hope we haven't messed up your holiday," he said.

"Don't worry about it," Wyatt said. "What's more important than this?"

In my peripheral vision, I could see his eyes sparkling.

That afternoon in chemistry, we got back our tests. Mine had a B+ and a big old grinning face done in marker by Mr. Uhles with the words, "You're getting there!" printed under it.

I liked it. But I knew my father wasn't going to.

In fact, I almost made up my mind to keep it hidden from him until Sunday night. Chances were good that he would ground me for the whole weekend, and Wyatt and I would have to put together the honor-council plan over the phone.

But I couldn't do it. I didn't even have the idea an hour before it was eating away at me like some kind of vicious termite. *You think Deborah's a hypocrite?* I said to myself. *What are you if you're this champion of virtue, and then you sneak around your own father?*

Nope, I had to take my chances. When he asked me about it, I was going to show it to him. I called Tobey to ask for prayer. She said she would ask Marissa when she saw her, and she would call Brianna. I got on the phone and rang up Cheyenne's house. Tassie answered the phone.

"Cheyenne's not here," she said. "She's been doing so well in school, I let her go to the mall with Ellie and Felise. Thanks to you," she added.

"I don't think it's thanks to me," I said. "We only had that one session." I laughed. "I'm good, but I'm not that good."

"What about last weekend?" she said.

"Last weekend?" I said. I could feel my heart uneasily pick up speed.

"I'm sorry I couldn't be there to cook for you all," she said. "I had the church bazaar all afternoon. We made a lot of money though. We'll get that new roof on the church yet."

"Uh-huh," I said. I squeezed my eyes shut tight. *Please just hang up before you ask me any more questions.*

"Shall I have her call you?"

"Excuse me?"

"Cheyenne. Do you want me to have her call you?"

"Please," I said. *And tell her to have her earplugs ready because she is going to hear it loud and clear from me.*

Dad was on call Wednesday night. My mother was polishing the silver for the next day's feast with half the staff of Washoe Medical Center. Wyatt came over, and we tested her stuffing and worked on the council.

In fact, Thursday was the only day we didn't work on it. At the Thanksgiving dinner, my father presided over the table formally and graciously, like one of the Pilgrim fathers. One of the rich Pilgrim fathers. He was so wrapped up in it, in fact, that he never asked me about my chemistry test. I missed hanging with the girls, but I discovered I couldn't let myself do that either until I talked to him. I was starting to feel like someone else had moved into my skin when I wasn't looking.

Anyway, Friday Wyatt and I were back at it. He was as rabid about the project as I was. I couldn't even talk him into taking a break to go bowling Friday night. He left my house about ten. My father was waiting for me when I came in from taking him home.

"So now you've added a boyfriend to the milieu," he said.

He had me stumped on that one for a second. "I don't think he's my boyfriend," I said. "No, he isn't. We're just working on a project."

"For a class?"

Oh, brother, I thought. *Here it comes. If I could just lie, just this once . . .*

"No," I said, "it's a school project. We wrote an honor code because there's been an outbreak of really serious cheating at King. Now we're structuring an honor council to deal with offenders. Mr. Holden asked us to do it."

"Is Mr. Holden going to take your chemistry tests for you then, since you're using study time for his little philosophical folly?"

"No," I said coldly, "he doesn't have to take my tests for me. I'm doing just fine, thank you. I got a B+ on the last one."

"I know. Ninety-two percent."

I could feel my eyes narrowing. "How did you know?"

"I talked to Chuck Uhles today."

"You saw him at the hospital? Is he sick or something?"

"No, I called him."

"At home?" My voice was incredulously high, and my hackles were higher. I couldn't keep my mouth from falling open. "Why did you do that, Dad? All you had to do was ask me!"

"I had a few other things to say to him."

"Like what?"

"Like suggesting we set up a tutor for you. It's a student at UNR. You'll be meeting with him Monday after school. Here."

I raked both hands through my hair and stuttered myself into my next sentence. "Don't I have any choice in this?"

"What choice?" Dad said. "You either do this or you fail. I guess that's a choice."

"Fail?" I said, voice screeching. "I'm getting a B!"

"That's failing in terms of your goals, and you know it. You will do whatever you have to do."

"Does that include cheat?" I said.

"What?"

"Would you want me to cheat?"

"Don't be ridiculous, Noreen."

"I'm not. All those kids you think are so sharp and such a good example for me, they're all cheating. That's why I'm doing this council thing—because it's gotten so out of control over there that people are doing 'whatever they have to do.'"

"And it's a total waste of your time," he said. He stroked his beard, making me furious because it reminded me of Mr. Dixon. "Give it up. You don't have time to be worrying about other people's morals." He pointed the finger at me. "This is the influence of those little Jesus people you were hanging around with. I told you—"

"Don't call them that," I said. My voice came down from its wiry level and was as hard and stiff as his.

"Watch your tone," he said.

"Then please watch yours, Dad," I said. "Those girls are the only reason I'm not part of the cheating ring. They're helping me become a decent human being—and I think who I become is a lot more important than what my grades are."

"Is everything all right?" Mom said from behind us. She padded across the hallway and stood beside me. I could feel her arm brushing mine, tight with tension.

"Yolanda, were you aware that Norie has been spending all this time on some tribal council?"

"Honor council," I said through my teeth.

"Yes," Mom said. "Wyatt is a very cute, sweet young man, and he and Norie have been working so hard—"

"I don't care if the kid is Mel Gibson. I told you to stay focused."

"I am focused," I said. "On something I really believe in. For about the first time in my life."

"Then you're going soft in the head for the first time in your life. Is this honor council thing going to show up on your college application? "

"I don't care!"

"Then you had better start. Right now! You call this kid and tell him the project is off, and then you spend some time thinking about what's going to get you where you want to go."

I opened my mouth. My mother's voice came out.

"Quint," she said, "could we talk in private, please?"

He raised his eyebrows at her. "About what?"

"Well, if I tell you, it won't be private now, will it?"

It was an attempt at levity. He scowled at it. But he nodded his head from me to the stairs. "Go on up to your room," he said. "We'll finish this later."

When I reached the first landing, I could hear him saying to my mother, "I ought to send you to your room, too. What's going on here?"

I heard her answer stiffly, "I beg your pardon, Dr. Vandenberger. I wish you wouldn't use that tone with me or Norie."

I'd have given a lot to hide behind the ficus and listen to the rest of that conversation. Instead, I hurried into my room and closed the door. The honor code, and what was behind it, was definitely taking over my behavior.

To give myself an excuse to throw things, I started to clean out my closet. Every duffel bag and tennis shoe I hurled was a blast at my father.

Why are you telling me what's supposed to be important to me?

You're running my life like a dictator! You called my favorite teacher, like I'm some kind of lisping little third grader who can't handle her own affairs!

You already told me I can't be with my best friends in the world. Don't even think about telling me I have to give up this honor council project. This is so unfair!

I let fly with an old backpack, nearly hitting my mother right in the face with it. She ducked, grinned, and retidied her already perfect hair.

"Sorry," I said. "I was venting."

"Vent no more," she said.

"Why?"

"Wyatt can come over tomorrow and Sunday, as long as you spend at least two hours on each of those days on chemistry."

I let the ski boot I was holding drop to the carpet with an angry thud. "Why wasn't I involved in these negotiations about my life?" I said.

"I did the best I could," she said.

Her voice caught, and I felt like a brute. After all, in my memory, there was no recollection of my mother ever standing up to my father for any reason, least of all me. She had never had my chutzpah.

"I'm sorry, Mom," I said. "Really. Thanks for sticking up for me."

"He probably won't speak to me for the next three days."

"This is a loss?" I said.

She gave me a look, and I held up both hands in surrender. "Sorry. I know you love the guy."

"And he loves you," she said. "Why else would he be so bull-headed about your schoolwork and your future?"

"I don't get the connection between love and tyranny," I said. "But whatever. Thanks. I really appreciate it."

She turned to go, but I stopped her.

"And Mom," I said. "If you need somebody to talk to, you just come up here. I can always think of something to say."

The smile that spread over her face was like the sun coming up. "I'll bring the coffee," she said.

So Wyatt and I were able to finish our plan for the honor council by Sunday afternoon. We both agreed it was rad.

"We're going to totally straighten some people out with this," Wyatt said.

The next morning, I had more reason than I could have dreamed to hope he was right. I wasn't in the school building two minutes before Ms. Race corralled me at my locker and told me Mr. Holden wanted to see me.

"I hope you have that honor council plan together," he said when I appeared in his doorway.

"We do," I said.

"Good, because we have our first case."

"No way," I said.

He nodded and glanced at the slip of paper in his hand. "Her name," he said, "is Cheyenne Jackson."

CHAPTER FIFTEEN

MR. HOLDEN SET THE "REVIEW," AS WE DECIDED TO call it, for Friday. I left his office with my brain in a mummified state. Ms. Race stuck a cup of coffee in my hand and made me sit beside her desk until the bell rang.

"This is awful," I said.

"Why?" she said. "If this works the way you want it to, then you're helping Cheyenne get her head straight."

"But it didn't have to come to this!" I said. "I suspected she was cheating, but I didn't do anything about it. I thought after our last Flagpole meeting she got the message."

"She probably should have," Ms. Race said. "Look, don't waste time beating yourself up. You have work to do."

"What work?" I said.

She smiled and handed me the sugar. "You're asking the wrong person," she said.

By some miracle, we were doing silent reading first period. I used the time to listen and write. I wasn't so sure I heard right, but I followed the instinct that came out on my page. At the end of class, I poked my head in Mr. Lowe's office, asked if I could be late, and then took off for Cheyenne's PE class. I caught her in her underwear in the locker room and dragged her into one of the showers.

"I can't be late getting dressed out!" she wailed.

"Since when did you become Miss-Follow-the-Rules?" I said into her face.

Her eyes widened.

"I thought I'd made it clear about the cheating thing, Cheyenne. Evidently I didn't. And not only that, but you lied to Tassie, and me, for that matter, about last Sunday. Plus you're avoiding me—the one person who can help you out of this mess."

"What mess?"

"You don't know yet?"

She shook the straggly head of black hair.

"You've been reported for cheating," I said. "You have to go before honor council Friday."

The wonderful lips fell open in an O of terror. I nodded.

"Right," I said. "Heavy-duty."

Cheyenne put a stranglehold on my arm. "What will they do to me?"

"I don't know. See—"

"I can't get suspended! If I get in any trouble, they'll send me back to Wittenberg. They'll take me away from Tassie!"

I thought she was going to cut off the circulation in my arm. I eased her hand away and took her by both shoulders.

"Cheyenne," I said, "chill. Nobody's going to pack you off to jail, okay? You cheated on a couple of tests—"

"Ten," she said.

I stared. "Ten?"

She nodded miserably.

"Why?" I said. "I don't get this!"

"Because you and Tassie and everybody were so excited about my making good grades."

"You can make good grades without cheating!"

"No, I can't. You don't understand. I can't!"

"Try studying," I said. "Or letting me help you."

She just kept shaking her head, the tears tripping over her lower lids, and her hair falling into her face.

"I can't," she said. "I'm too dumb."

"Oh, get over it," I said. "You are not dumb. You don't have a good background, but you aren't stupid."

She wasn't convinced. "I've always been dumb," she said.

"My mother said it, my stepfather said it, all my teachers have said—"

"Then they're dumb!" I said. "I'm not going to let what a bunch of losers have told you about yourself foul you up for the rest of your life."

She smacked her hair away from her cheeks where it was stuck by tears. "Isn't it too late?"

"No," I said. "That's what the honor council is for. It's not to punish you, it's to help you."

"How do you know?"

"I'm on it. I designed it."

For the first time, hope flickered in her eyes. "You won't let them throw me out of school?"

"No," I said.

She started to do some kind of dance, and I grabbed her. "Don't get all hyper," I said. "There are going to be consequences. You're going to have to change. But we'll help you."

She nodded feverishly, a dead giveaway that she hadn't heard a thing I'd said.

"In the meantime," I said firmly, "you cannot cheat anymore—ever again. You got that?"

"Okay."

"No matter how bad your grades are, you earn them honestly. That's the bottom line."

"Okay."

"And this week, we meet every day after school. I don't have to do layout until next week. We'll do your homework together. You can come home with me, if it's okay with Tassie."

"She likes you," Cheyenne said. "It will be okay."

"Well, she's not going to like you if you don't stop lying to her. You even dragged Felise into it, didn't you?"

Cheyenne hitched at her bra. "She wouldn't lie as much as I wanted her to."

"Good for her. So, no more lies. No more cheating. We'll fix this, Cheyenne. I promise you."

She grinned lobe to lobe with those incredible lips and threw her arms around me. I endured it until Coach Gatney stuck her head in the shower room and gave us a very strange look.

"I'm coming," Cheyenne said. "Don't dock my grade."

"You're paranoid, Jackson," she said dryly. "Just get out here."

Between that, enduring the cold stares of Deborah et al, and sitting through an inquisition with Mrs. Abbey, who had it straight from Pavella's mouth that I had "driven" him out of journalism, I forgot one very important thing. I didn't remember it until Cheyenne and I pulled into my driveway and a strange car was there. A beat-up Volkswagen bug with a UNR parking sticker on it. It hit me like a truckload of quarry stone.

"Who's here?" Cheyenne said.

"My chemistry tutor," I said.

"You have a tutor?" she said.

"Not by choice, believe me. Come on. We'll work this out somehow."

Mom was entertaining the dude in our family room, pouring him Earl Grey tea and keeping up the charming chatter while he looked around through thick glasses and assessed our home with I-hope-this-is-what-I-get-out-of-a-college-degree in his eyes.

When we came in, he stood up and pulled the ski cap off his thick, dark brown, curly hair, stuck out his hand and said, "Aaron."

Mom looked curiously at Cheyenne.

"This is going to be a trip," I said. "While you're tutoring me, I have to coach Cheyenne."

"I can do you both," Aaron said. "No extra charge. Is she in chemistry, too?"

"Not hardly," Cheyenne said. "I can barely pass Algebra I."

Aaron shrugged and adjusted the Coke bottle bottoms. "I can do algebra."

"You sure?" I said. "It isn't going to cost more or anything?"

"It would be fine if it did," Mom said. She wafted us toward the dining room. "I have the table set up in here. I'll bring you kids some cream puffs. I got them at Walden's today."

I'm sticking with my theory, I thought as I sank into a dining room chair. *This is going to be a trip.*

As it turned out, it was, but it took a whole different direction than I had suspected. So much for my theory.

Aaron worked out a couple of kinks I was having with binomial equations. While I chewed my pencil over those, he hunkered down with Cheyenne and had her giggling and, to my amazement, giving him the right answers.

"I told you you weren't dumb," I said to her when we took a break to consume cream puffs.

"Who said she was dumb?" Aaron said. He had a little bit of a lisp, which actually got to be cute as the afternoon wore on.

"Everybody," Cheyenne said. "Except Norie."

"Norie was right," Aaron said. "But you know what I think—I mean, I'm no expert, but I know this from my own experience—I think you're dyslexic."

Cheyenne gasped. "Will they send me back to Wittenberg for that?"

"It's not a crime," I said. "It's a learning disability, right?"

"Yeah," Aaron said. "They ought to test her at King."

"I hate tests," Cheyenne said.

Aaron looked at me.

"I'll take care of it," I said.

The next day I did. I went right to Ms. Race before school, and she directed me to the LD lab. They said they would have to call Tassie to obtain permission, but one look at a sample of Cheyenne's writing and the woman told me I was right on.

All right, Aaron.

We got to know Aaron a little better. Unbeknownst to me, he was scheduled for Wednesday, too, which wasn't a problem. But Friday, that I had to wrestle with my father over.

"I'm committed to the honor council after school," I told him Wednesday night. "Aaron says he can meet me Saturday morning at the library at UNR instead. It works for me."

"I see you've taken matters into your own hands," he said dryly.

"Isn't that what we're trying to teach her to do?" Mom said.

He glared at her. The poor thing looked wounded, but she kept her chin up. I was actually feeling pretty proud of that woman. I turned to my father and said, "So, is that okay?"

"I guess it'll have to be," he said.

Friday finally arrived. The Flagpolers met at lunch to pray for Cheyenne, and we had some guests. Wyatt. Ira. Diesel and Felise. They said Avery and Brendan and Ellie wouldn't come, but they sent their "regards."

"God likes regards," Tobey said. "Okay, let's do it."

I felt stronger after prayer. But I was still nervous. Not only was this the first session of honor council; not only was my stomach in knots about whether this was even going to work; not only was I half scared to death that Deborah was going to sabotage the whole thing, but I also wanted more than I'd ever wanted anything for this to work out for Cheyenne.

"It's going to work," Wyatt whispered to me as we came to order. "Just keep the faith."

There wasn't time to pray from that point on. I counted on the Flagpole Girls, who were outside in the hall, for that.

We did some introductory stuff that Wyatt and I had outlined in our plan, and then Wyatt explained the charges to Cheyenne. She sat there with her little hands folded, nodding her head. Brianna had fixed Cheyenne's hair in a ponytail so it wasn't hiding her face. Tobey had instructed her to look people in the eye. She was trying, poor baby.

"Cheyenne," Wyatt said, "your math teacher says he saw you on Friday taking a test and referring to some writing in the palm of your hand. When he asked to see it, you held out your hand, and he saw that you had formulas written there."

I sneaked a glance at Deborah. She was looked blankly at Wyatt, as if she didn't see what the big deal was.

"Do you understand all of that?" Wyatt said.

Cheyenne gave a whispered, "Yes."

"Okay. So now we're going to give you a chance to explain to us what happened from your point of view."

Cheyenne looked at me.

"Tell your side of the story," I said to her. "Just tell the truth."

Cheyenne swallowed visibly. "I did it," she said.

Dixon, Uhles, and Lowe all looked at each other strangely. I didn't know what they had expected, but it obviously wasn't that.

"Okay," Wyatt said slowly. "Do you want to tell us why you did it? Is there some reason we should know about?"

"I can't make good grades," she said, just the way I'd coached her. "They're going to test me for dyslexia, but I didn't even know about that before. I just thought I was stupid."

She started to talk faster, and I knew she was on a roll. That could be good, or it could confuse everybody beyond comprehension. I tried not to look panicked.

"Anyway, I have this really neat foster home now," she went on. "Tassie, that's my foster mom, she's the best. She expects us to get decent grades though, and I tried, I really did, but I couldn't do it. It's a lot harder here than it was at Wittenberg or Lovelock or Parump—"

She started ticking towns off on her fingers. Mr. Uhles cleared his throat. "I think we get the idea," he said gently. "Go on."

"Then Norie started to tutor me so I wouldn't flunk. Only the very first time we studied together I knew I was way stupider than I had thought. But then I heard her talking to some girl about how some people were cheating—"

She looked around the table. In a flash of terror, I knew who she was looking for.

"It doesn't matter," I said quickly.

"Norie asked her what if you get caught," Cheyenne went on. "And the girl said they wouldn't. And then when Norie didn't cheat with them, only she wrote that article and didn't put their names in there, I thought it was okay if you didn't get caught. They got away with it. I thought I could, too." She looked down at her hands, which had been busy wringing themselves out on the tabletop. "I just wanted to be able to stay at Tassie's and make Norie and my other friends think I was smart like them. Please, you guys, don't put me on suspension, or they'll send me back to Wittenberg—"

"Easy," Mr. Uhles said. He looked at Mr. Holden. "I think we've heard what we need to, don't you?"

Mr. Lowe was nodding. Mr. Dixon was staring Cheyenne down like she just had admitted to the Atlanta Olympics bombing. Deborah was doing a slow burn.

"Our job now," Wyatt said, "is to determine how to help you so you can stop cheating and still get the grades you want. Do you have anything that you feel you need, that we should take into consideration?"

Again Cheyenne looked at me. I nodded.

"I want help with my learning disability, if I have one," she said. "I think then I could do the work and not have to cheat."

"Good enough, " Mr. Uhles said. "Now, if you'll step outside, we'll chat about this, and then we'll call you back in to tell you what we've decided. No sense making you suffer until Monday, right?"

She smiled and nodded about a hundred times. Mr. Lowe finally got up and ushered her out of the room. I knew Tobey and Brianna would be out there to take care of her.

When she left, Deborah was the first one to speak up. "I think it's obvious that Norie helped her with all that."

"I did," I said. "Why is that a problem? She was scared, and I helped her find the right words to tell the truth."

"I don't see what's wrong with that," Wyatt said.

"Neither do I," Mr. Holden said. "Any problem with moving on to consequences?"

Deborah crossed her arms huffily. The rest of us dug in.

Mr. Dixon wanted to flunk her for the quarter—teach the little urchin a lesson. Mr. Uhles wanted to let it go at required LD testing and tutoring. Mr. Holden and Mr. Lowe held the line for failure on the test she had been caught cheating on, coming in for extra help during lunch twice a week for the rest of the semester, and one Saturday detention—plus the testing in the LD lab and all the help they could give her. Wyatt and I agreed. Deborah had nothing to say.

I thought it was a really good package for Cheyenne, a little reminder and a lot of help. She, on the other hand, didn't seem to think so. When Mr. Holden read our decision to her, she looked at me in disbelief.

"Is there something wrong, Cheyenne?" Mr. Uhles said.

She shook her head only because she wasn't prepared with an answer, I knew. I sighed. Whatever it was, I was going to have to dig it out of her ASAP.

But when we adjourned, after letting her go, I didn't get two feet out of the conference room before Deborah had me by the arm and was dragging me into the locker hall.

"What?" I said. "I'm getting so sick of you pawing me."

She stuck her nose in my face. "How does that kid know?"

"What are you talking about?"

"How does she know I'm one of the ones? When she went off on that tangent about hearing us talk, about not getting caught, she looked right at me."

"She was standing there that morning you accosted me at the locker," I said.

"No way."

"Yes, way. I don't know how you missed her. She heard the whole thing."

"I didn't even see her," Deborah said.

"Of course you didn't. Anybody who's not in our league is invisible."

"What league?"

"Forget it. What's your point?"

Deborah rolled her eyes in exasperation. "What do you think my point is? If she knows and she's your little protégé, then she's going to open her big mouth to the wrong person somewhere along the line. That's my point."

"So what do you want me to do, threaten her? I'm not sure I can; I don't have as much practice as you do."

"I don't care what you do," Deborah said. "Just make sure she doesn't tell. And if she does, you're history."

"Ooh, ooh, you're scarin' me," I said, voice high-pitched.

"I hope so," Deborah said. Her face wizened down like the tip of a knife. "This is no joke, Norie. We will get you where it can really hurt you—I mean it."

She did. I had never been more sure of anything as she strode away, with her long, gangly arms flapping like a pair of vengeful wings.

"Oh, man," I murmured. "Oh, man."

Still, I was the only one I could talk to about it—myself and God. I did plenty of both, except when I was tutoring with Aaron the next morning. I did a sample test for him, and came out with a 92 percent.

"That's great," he said. "I think we've made progress."

"What progress?" I said. "That's the same grade I got on my last test."

He blinked behind the Coke bottles. "Then why am I tutoring you?"

"Ask my father," I said. "It was his idea. Not that you haven't been great. I think you basically saved Cheyenne's life, academically speaking anyway."

"But I don't get it. I mean, you're not going to be a scientist. You said you're going into journalism, right?"

"Right. I'm telling you, talk to my father."

"I should. You shouldn't be trying to go to Harvard. You would hate it there. Why don't you go for Northwestern? They have an incredible School of Journalism, I hear."

"Best in the country," I said. "I know some people who go there."

"Then what's the problem?"

"You ask my father that," I said, throwing up my hands.

"I might," he said. "He owes me money."

I went from there to King to pick up Cheyenne after her detention. Tassie asked me to when I called. She said I could tutor her over there right after.

Cheyenne was less than overjoyed to see me. She got into the Jeep, slammed the door, and pouted into her lap.

"What's this about?" I said. "I save your neck, and you give me the silent treatment?"

She wouldn't answer. I almost said, "This is stupid" but decided against it. It was starting to snow, and I concentrated on that.

Tassie wasn't quite so patient. She took one look at Cheyenne when she came in the door and pointed to a kitchen chair.

"We're not doing this," she said. "You talk, girl. Nobody can help you if you don't tell us what's going on."

Cheyenne glared at me. "She knows," she said.

"Right," I said. "I have some kind of psychic powers."

"What does she know?" Tassie said. She went after Cheyenne like a drill sergeant. Obviously, she did this a lot.

"She said I wouldn't get in trouble," Cheyenne said. "But I still had to go to detention."

"I said you wouldn't get thrown in jail!" I said. "And I kept my promise. Good grief, Cheyenne, you're getting all this help. . . . What do you want?"

"I don't know," she said. She folded her arms with a jolt and frowned until her eyebrows nearly touched her lips. It would have been funny if I hadn't been so ticked off at her.

"You do so," Tassie said. "Start talkin'. One, two—"

"I don't think it's fair that I have to take punishment when those other kids are getting away with it." Cheyenne leveled her angry eyes at me. "You'll let them punish me, but you won't let them punish that Deborah girl and her friends. I thought you were my friend!"

Tassie and I looked at each other over her head. Tassie gave me the go-ahead with her hand.

"I'm not the one who turned you in, Cheyenne," I said. "I don't know how I feel about that part yet. I'm still trying to figure out if I should narc on them."

"Well, I know how I feel about it," Tassie said. She went to a bookcase under the window and produced a dog-eared Bible. I'd seen it before, actually. Cheyenne had brought it to Tobey's one night in October. The thing looked like it had been read about a thousand times over.

"You ever heard the parable of the weeds, girls?" she said.

I shook my head. Cheyenne kept hers stubbornly still.

"Let me just read here . . ." Tassie licked her thumb and flipped through the onion-skin-thin pages. I sat down on a chair, but Cheyenne wouldn't look at me.

"Here we go," Tassie said. "Okay, there was this man, see, and he sowed his field with good seed, and then while nobody was lookin', some joker came along and threw in a bunch of weeds." She scanned the page. "The wheat sprouted up, but so did the weeds, blah-de-blah. Here it is." She coughed. "'The servants asked the owner, "Do you want us to go and pull them up?" "No," he answered, "because while you are pulling the weeds, you may root up the wheat with them. Let both grow together until the harvest. At that time I will tell the harvesters: First collect the weeds and tie them in bundles to be burned; then gather the wheat and bring it into my barn.'"

"And the point is?" I said.

Tassie chewed on her lower lip with the one front tooth she had. "There's gonna be a separation of the righteous and the wicked in due time. We're not supposed to make that separation now, no sir. That is entirely the Lord's business."

"So you're saying I'm doing right by not turning them in?" I said.

"I think you're doing right by concentrating on the people you can help, not the people you can expose."

"Ooh," I said. "I like that."

She eyed Cheyenne. "I do, too. Now, our job is to get this little missy to see it that way."

Cheyenne shrugged and looked at me. "We should study now," she said.

So we did, there in the kitchen, while Tassie made Christmas cookies and the snow piled up in silvery drifts outside. It was the first hint of Christmas I'd had so far, and it kind of charged me up, even though Cheyenne was still sullen and answered me in as few words as she could get away with.

I talked to Wyatt about it Sunday. He went to church with me, and afterward we walked in the snow along the Truckee and watched the ducks try to navigate around the ice.

"She'll get over it," he told me. "Didn't you resist a lot when you first found out what was right and what wasn't?"

"Yeah," I said. I looked at him sideways and felt the blush

coming up on my face. It had to be the cold, I decided. "Take you, for instance," I said.

"Me?"

"Yeah. At first I stayed away from you like you were some kind of reptile."

"But now you've seen your own stupidity," he said, "and you can't stand to be away from me."

"Oh, uh-huh! Where did you get that piece of information?"

"Wishful thinking," he said.

"Dream on," I said. I grinned at him, and he grinned back and shrugged. I willed myself not to blush, and suddenly he was kissing me. And I was kissing him back. And . . . well, it was nice. Very nice.

I was glad it happened. I thought about it a lot over the next week, whenever I felt myself falling into a black hole. Because that's what started to happen, right after I received the pink slip Monday morning.

This time, Mr. Holden closed his door when I went into his office. His face, his nice face, was absolutely gray.

"We have our next case for honor council," he said.

Oh," I said. "It must be working."

"I don't know," he said. "You might not think so when you hear who it is."

"Who?" I said.

He didn't even consult his little piece of paper. "Norie Vandenberger."

CHAPTER SIXTEEN

"SOMEBODY TURNED ME IN FOR CHEATING?" I SAID.

He nodded.

"Who?"

"Mr. Uhles, Norie."

"But that's impossible! I never cheated in his class." It obviously hadn't sunk in yet because I was starting to laugh. "I'm only getting a B in there. Why wouldn't I cheat myself up to an A?"

He didn't see the humor. He opened a folder on the table and looked at a typewritten list. "Mr. Uhles received an anonymous letter this morning, pointing out several things this person thought he should investigate about you."

I stopped laughing and stared, dumbfounded. "Such as?" I said.

"The source claims you obtained Mr. Uhles's computer codes and have them written on the inside of your binder." He shifted his eyes to my backpack. "I'll have to ask to see your notebook."

I felt like the couch was caving in under me. "I do have the codes," I said. "Someone gave them to me, but I never used them."

It sounded lame, even to me. His expression drooped, and he went back to the sheet. "It says you had access to his computer, to cite only one example, fourth period on November 17 when you were out of journalism for an extended period of time and reported that you were going to the math-science hall. The source points out that because of your familiarity with the computers in this school, you could easily access Mr. Uhles's files with the codes."

"Who doesn't know the computers in this school?" I said. I tried not to sound defensive, but I knew my voice was coming out the way it did when I was arguing with my father. I had the horrible, sinking feeling that I was going to be just about as successful here as I was at home.

"I'm just telling you what it says, Norie," Mr. Holden said. "I'm not accusing you of anything. It goes on to say—and this will answer your point about getting a B in the class—it says you didn't use the stolen answer keys yourself but provided them to other students for money or favors."

"What?" I said. "What favors?"

"They cite here your election to the position of coeditor even though you're only a junior."

"That happened last spring!"

"They say it's been going on at least that long. There are other examples, but it's the money thing I'm most concerned about."

"They say I'm taking cash from people? Why would I do that, Mr. Holden? You know my father draws a six-figure salary. We live in Caughlin Ranch, for Pete's sake!"

I never thought I would be defending myself with my parents' financial statement. But this was unbelievable. So much so, it didn't even feel real. That changed when Mr. Holden stood up.

"Let's go have a look in your locker, then," he said.

"My locker?"

"It says here that you keep your take from the sale of answer keys in an envelope in your locker."

"There is no such envelope," I said.

"Then you won't mind if we take a look?"

"Not at all," I said. "I want you to look. Then maybe you'll see how stupid this is."

I curled my lip at the paper. He put it reverently back in the folder.

"I tend to believe you, Norie," he said. "It does seem a little fantastic to me. But you see why I have to check into it."

"Uh, no," I said as I followed him out of his office. "As a matter of fact, I don't."

He leaned over and whispered something to Ms. Race. She nodded, but even as she leaned across her desk to a small microphone setup, she gave me a disturbed look.

"Let's wait here for the security guard," Mr. Holden said.

"What do we need him for?" I said.

"It's just procedure," he said. "Should we find anything, I have to have an official witness."

"A witness that carries a nightstick?" I said. "This is so ludicrous. Do I get to call my attorney?"

My voice was dripping sarcasm, and he didn't miss it. I longed to make eye contact with Ms. Race, just to be sure I was still sane, but she was talking softly into the microphone. In a few minutes, the guard showed up, curving his arms out from his holster the way they do and looking terribly impressed with himself. My every pore was pumping resentment.

No wonder those little juvenile delinquents that wait outside the discipline office always look like they hate the world, I thought. *I've only been a suspect five minutes, and I already want to kick somebody's tail.*

"What are we looking for?" the officer said.

"Money," Mr. Holden said.

"Drug deal?"

"No, extortion."

Extortion! I almost snorted aloud. *You are going to look like such idiots the minute that locker door is open!*

They continued to talk back and forth in ultraserious, muted tones as if I weren't even there. I marched ahead of them, spun the numbers on my locker, and flung open the door.

"May I?" the security guard said.

He was referring, of course, to the pile of books, papers, spiral notebooks, and jackets I kept forgetting to take home that were crammed in there.

"I'll take stuff out," I said.

But Mr. Holden shook his head. "He'll do it," he said.

"Why?" I said. "Are you thinking I might finger the envelope and hide it up my sleeve? You guys give me a lot more credit than I deserve, believe me."

"It isn't going to help you to pull an attitude," Mr. Holden said. His voice took on a hard glint. I shut up, folded my arms, and watched the security guard defrost my locker. When everything was out on the floor, I started to smile triumphantly. Then he produced a fat, lumpy looking white envelope and handed it to Mr. Holden.

"What is that?" I said.

"I think we're about to find out," Mr. Holden said.

He pulled back the envelope flap and peered in. The look he gave me would have withered a lesser woman. I peered in with him—and then I withered.

"Mr. Holden," I said, with not a trace of sarcasm, "I have no idea where that came from. That money is not mine, and I didn't put it in my locker."

Mr. Holden stuck his hand in the envelope and produced a two-inch thick stack of bills. As he flipped through them for the security guard's inspection, I saw fives, tens, twenties, and even a fifty. There must have been several hundred dollars there.

"That is not my money," I said.

Mr. Holden put it back in the envelope and handed it to the guard. Suddenly it was evidence, and I was a suspect. They didn't cuff me, but Mr. Holden looked at me with unfriendly eyes and said, "Let's go back to my office."

"I was kidding before about calling a lawyer," I said to his back as I trailed him down the hall. "But I'm not now. If you're going to accuse me of something, I'm not going to say anything without somebody here to represent me."

"You can call your parents, if we decide to bring charges," he said. "Let's just talk a little more."

About what? I wanted to scream. *This is a frame-up, can't you see that? Am I the only one left in this place with a brain?*

It was so maddening I started to blow my bangs up with exasperated breaths and to rub my hands up and down on my jeans to get the sweat dried off. It was stupid, for sure. So why did I feel like the Boston Strangler? By the time we reached the office, I was chanting, *I haven't done anything wrong, I haven't done anything wrong* in my head.

Mr. Holden motioned for me to sit down, but he stood over me, which added to the feeling that everyone in the world was now looking down at me. I sat up straight so I wouldn't feel so not-in-control.

"The only thing we don't have," he said, "are the names of the kids who gave you money. You need to know, Norie, that if we had those, we'd have you, and it wouldn't be a case for the council then. It would be a police matter. You see that?"

I breathed a fraction easier. "Who's going to come forward and say they paid me for answers?" I said. "Then they would be in trouble."

"Exactly." He sighed. "I don't know what to do about this, Norie. Ordinarily, I'd come to you for advice on it."

"If that's supposed to make me feel guilty, Mr. Holden, it isn't working," I said. "I don't mean to be disrespectful, but you're making me feel like a criminal, and I haven't done anything. I told you, somebody gave me the codes for the computer. I wrote them down. I never used them. I never cheated. And I certainly never sold anybody any answer keys. Somebody planted that money in my locker."

"Who else has your combination?"

"Nobody that I know of. But people stand there talking to me while I'm opening it all the time. It wouldn't take a brain surgeon to watch me and commit three numbers to memory. And these are bright kids."

I could have bitten my tongue off. Mr. Holden honed right in on it. "Are you suggesting that the same people who you accused of cheating in your article are the ones who are 'framing' you?"

"That's the only thing that makes sense to me," I said.

"Maybe to you, but let's consider the way it looks on the outside."

"Okay," I said.

"What if you wrote that piece to divert suspicion from yourself?"

"I don't follow."

"You have refused to tell us who the cheaters are. Couldn't that reasonably be because, if we had their names, we would call them in, and then they would blow the whistle on you?"

"Then why would I bring it up in the first place? And why write an honor code and spend my entire Thanksgiving vacation creating an honor council with my father breathing down my neck because I'm doing that instead of studying my tail off so I can be number one in this soul-defiling place?"

"All right, calm down—"

"I can't. And I won't. Not until somebody acknowledges that there is a remote possibility I am a decent human being with a solid set of principles who wouldn't do something like this even if it meant never—heaven forbid—going to college at all!"

"All right," he said, holding up his hands and looking at me as if he believed I would hurl myself from the window if he didn't. "All right, I will concede that there are two possible sides to this. But we have to pursue both of them, Norie. If this were anybody else, you would be the first one to point that out." He halfway smiled. "It's ironic, isn't it? Now that you've made honor such an issue around here, you're going to be the first one to walk through fire for it."

Suddenly we're waxing dramatic, I thought. But I met him head-on. "If that's what it takes, then that's what it takes. But I want to go on record right now: I am not guilty."

"Duly noted," he said. "Now I know this is a difficult request I'm about to make, and, granted, I can't put anything behind it. Take it or leave it as you will. But I'm going to ask you, as a personal favor to the council, not to discuss this with anyone until I decide how to proceed. You may tell your parents, of course. And if they have any questions they can call me."

"Questions" would not exactly describe what my father had when I broke the news to the two of them that night. "Hysterical outburst," "psychotic reaction," "insane response out of all proportion to the stimulus," those would be more like it. Mom and I sat on the couch while he wore a two-inch deep path in the family room carpet pacing up and down and throwing his arms around. The tirade went something like this:

"Well, Noreen, your little honor code did you a lot of good, didn't it? I told you that thing was a waste of time. You cannot force morals on other people, I don't care how many come-to-Jesus meetings you go to. If you had minded your own business, this never would have happened. As far as I can see, you've brought it on yourself. What are you going to do about it?"

"Well—"

"I'll tell you what we're going to do about it. Where's the phone book? I'm going to the school board—no, the superintendent. What is that woman's name? No, forget her. I'm calling my Congressman. Yolanda, get Harry's number. These people don't know who they're dealing with. You don't mess with my daughter's reputation and expect to get away with it. This is unconscionable, and heads are going to roll—"

"Dad," I said.

"Don't even talk to me, Noreen. Seems to me you've said enough already and gotten yourself in a pile of trouble you can't even begin to get out from under." He smashed his fist on the bar, unsettling the ice bucket and knocking over a stack of coasters before he took off on another enraged track. "What is the matter with those people? Have they all gone stark, raving mad up there at that school? Holden's obviously walking around with his head up his—"

"Quint!"

"Don't you start in either!" He poked a finger at my mother and then jabbed it at me. "You women have about as much grasp of this situation as the Bobbsey Twins. This is serious. If they find some little stoolie to say he paid you for answers, we're talking juvenile court for you. We'll be in for attorney's fees up to our ears. The whole thing will be smeared all over the *Gazette-Journal*. And for what? Because you had to play Geraldo Rivera. You know what this is going to look like on your college application, don't you? Harvard doesn't take people who have been arrested. You can give up that dream right now . . ."

He went on, I guess. I could see his mouth moving. But my own anger got so loud in my head, I couldn't hear him anymore.

Thanks so much for your support, Dad, I wanted to shout at him. *I really appreciate your standing by me on this. It means a lot to me—*

But those thoughts lurched to a halt like I'd tripped over a rock.

What am I doing? I sound just like him. I could be his clone!

I was deeply sure of one thing: That wasn't what I wanted to be.

"Dad," I said.

"The main thing is to keep this out of the paper. I don't need the publicity. People don't want you opening them up when you're involved in a scandal—"

"Dad," I said again.

He stopped and looked at me, eyes like embers.

"I don't think you have to worry about any of that," I said. My voice was even. I didn't even feel like yelling. "Mr. Holden hasn't decided what they're going to do about it yet, and when they do, I can probably handle it. If I need any help, I'll let you know."

"Oh, you've done a great job so far."

He started off again. I sat there and shut it off. Maybe if I didn't hear it ever again, I wouldn't have to sound like him anymore.

I went to Ms. Race first thing in the morning.

"I don't know anything yet," she said when she saw me. "But you know as soon as I do, I'll tell you what I can."

"That's not why I'm here," I said.

"Okay."

"I think . . ." I blew up my bangs and swallowed and blinked and did everything else I could to keep from crying. "I think I just need a hug," I said.

"Of course," she said.

She wrapped her arms around me and held me while she talked low into my ear. "Listen, Norie," she said, "you have come so far in such a short time."

"I have?" I said.

"Yes, and you hang on to that. Keep praying and listening and writing, and I know the Holy Spirit is going to keep leading you deeper and deeper into the truth."

"How do you know?" I said. "Just tell me how you know."

"I heard it this morning," she said. She pushed me away so she could look in my face. "I have it written down."

That helped. So much so that at the beginning of fifth period, I stood in front of the chemistry room door and waited for Gabe, Lance, Deborah, and Pavella. They arrived en masse, like they were afraid to go anywhere without each other. I couldn't say I blamed them. They had no identity without each other.

"We need to talk," I said to them.

"Maybe you do," Lance said. He tugged his goatee. "We don't."

"I think you owe me that much," I said.

"It isn't a matter of us owing you," Deborah said. She looked at her trio of lackeys. "I think we ought to hear her out. It might be worth our while." To me she said, "Ask Mr. Uhles if we can stay out here for a few minutes."

"You ask him," I said. "I don't think he'll give me the time of day. Right now he thinks I'm the one who stole his computer codes and his answer keys, remember?"

"Oh, does he?" she said.

She smiled slyly at the three boys and disappeared into the room. They glowered at me until she came back out.

"We have five minutes," she said. "And then he wants to see you in his office."

I half expected them all to start rubbing their hands together and licking their chops at that. These couldn't possibly be the people I'd once referred to casually as my friends.

"All right, look," I said, "this thing has gone far enough. Now you're planting money in my locker. Don't you think that's a little drastic?"

Nobody said a word, except Pavella, who said "How did you know—"

Gabe cut him off with a jab in the ribs.

"All I ever wanted was for you guys to stop cheating," I said.

"Maybe I went about it the wrong way, I don't know. But this sure isn't the right way."

"Get to the bottom line," Lance said. "This is getting boring."

"Turn yourselves in to the honor council. It's not about punishment, you know. We'll help you—we'll help all of us do something about this whole pressure thing they have us under."

"I don't think they're going to let us off with counseling for breaking into a computer," Lance said, his voice cold.

Gabe didn't even try to be cool. "Yeah!" he said, face magenta. "Even the little squaw got a Saturday detention and a bunch of other stuff."

"Okay, so you get a detention or even an in-school suspension. Isn't it better than what's going to happen when they find out you framed me?"

"Who's going to prove it—you?" Lance said, smirking.

"Okay, we don't have much time," Deborah said. She swung her hair behind her and put her hands on her hips. "Here's our deal. You confess to the cheating ring thing and you offer to give back the money. I'm on honor council so I'll make sure you get off. Then none of us pays."

"You really think I'm going to do that?" I said. I was so aghast I couldn't even get mad.

"But," Deborah went on, "if you give them our names, we'll take you straight down with us. And there's no way you can get yourself out of it if we all swear we paid you."

That was when the black hole started. I could see myself falling right down into it because she was absolutely right. They had planned this so skillfully there was no way I was going to extricate myself. I'd known all along these were smart people.

Desperately I held on to the top of that hole. "What if I don't confess or tell on you?" I said.

Pavella looked clueless. The other two guys looked at Deborah.

She shrugged. "They'll probably drop it," she said. "But then everybody will always wonder, won't they?"

"About what?" I said.

"About your precious honor. Once this gets out—and it will, believe me—you'll be known as 'that girl who masterminded the cheating ring.' Some people might argue it, but it'll come up every time your name is mentioned. That would be such a drag, wouldn't it?"

"So let's see how much you care about your 'honor,'" Lance said.

He eyed Gabe, and Gabe punched Pavella.

"What, did you just score a touchdown or something?" I said.

"I think we've definitely scored, yes," Lance said. He gave me a beige smile.

"Really?" I said. "I guess that remains to be seen."

I think they were a little surprised that I didn't flip out and start going off. Deborah studied me closely for a second, but I didn't flinch. Even after they went into the room I stood there, still and peaceful. The center of calm was so big I could wrap myself in it.

Yikes, I thought. *I have principles. I wanted something that was so important to me I'd do anything to defend it, and now I've got it.*

"Yikes," I said aloud.

And I went on into the room.

CHAPTER
SEVENTEEN

MR. UHLES HAD EVERYBODY SITTING AT HIS SEAT, WRIT-ing the answers to the questions at the end of the chapter. Not like his let's-get-everybody-jazzed-about-it teaching style at all. When I tapped on the door of his office, he looked up as if he were coming out of a cave. The eyes that settled on me were un-speakably sad.

"Come on in, Norie," he said.

I did and sat stiffly in the chair.

He didn't say anything, as if he were expecting me to go first. I didn't have a problem with that.

"Mr. Uhles," I said, "why did you turn me in to Mr. Holden without talking to me about it first?"

"I can't really explain that," he said.

I felt myself startle. *Wow. An honest person around here.*

"I think I was just so saddened by the whole concept," he said, "that students that I care about and trust could either ac-tually do something like what was described in your article and in that letter—or that they could be so obsessed with their goals that they would attack each other with such guile."

"Then you don't accept that whole thing in the letter as gospel?" I said, hopefully.

"No, of course not. But I guess I just couldn't approach it alone, you know what I mean?"

I closed my eyes for a second. "Yeah, I know exactly what you mean."

"Tell me something, would you?" he said. "Are you kids

really so competitive you would turn on each other like this? I mean, this is no schoolroom spat. You people are trying to draw blood here."

"I hate to say it, but I think it's true. I want you to know something—two things."

"One."

"I'm really working on getting away from that. I was reaching the point where I couldn't even stand myself anymore. I don't know what's going to happen. I may end up having to rent a room from somebody because my father will disown me, but it just isn't worth it to me anymore."

"I'm glad to hear it," Mr. Uhles said. "What's two?"

I leaned against the front of the desk. "I wasn't part of the cheating ring, Mr. Uhles," I said. "Everything I said in that article was true, and not a word of what was in that anonymous letter you received is. I think the only thing I did wrong was that I knew about the operation and I didn't tell you right away. I thought I could stop them. That's what the article was for."

He leaned back in his chair, putting his hands behind his head and looking at the ceiling for what seemed like life-plus-twenty. When he finally lowered his eyes to me, they were damp.

"I want to believe you, Norie, and then again I don't want to believe you. If I take your word, my faith in you is restored, but then I have to live with the fact that four people out there are the worst kind of villains."

I felt a shudder go through me.

"One thing's for sure," he said. "I'm convinced that we have to stop this insanity. Good grief, I sound like Susan Powter!"

He smiled for the first time. I wanted to dissolve into a puddle at the sight of it.

It seemed I had to do one hard thing after another, but if I didn't do them, I knew I was going to slide into the black hole that was yawning at me. The next hard thing was convincing my father that the Flagpole Girls and I needed to have a Plan of Action session at our house that night.

God loves me. When I got home, Mom said he had gone to Vegas overnight for a big consult down there.

"I need to meet with the Girls," I said. "They can really help me with all this. But Dad doesn't want me hanging out with them."

Mom's eyes gleamed. "Then we just won't tell him, will we?"

A month before, I'd probably have given her a high-five and been content with that. But it caught at me like a comb in a hairball.

"I don't want to lie and sneak around him," I said. "That's what this whole thing is about, you know?"

She sank onto one of the counter stools and looked at me. "You make me ashamed of myself, Norie," she said.

"That's not what I was trying to do. You've been great, Mom—"

"No, I'm glad you're making me think. I spend so much time trying to avoid conflict I seldom really think at all." She waved both hands in front of her face like she was chasing off a mosquito. "Anyway, you're right. I'm going to call him and tell him the Girls are meeting here. And then we'll take it from there."

"You would do that?" I said.

"For you, I would," she said. She gave me a misty smile. "Then maybe I'll start doing it for myself, too. I'm going to need some coaching though."

"Just say the word. But, Mom, I don't think you're going to need much."

We smiled at each other, woman to woman. How cheesy does that sound?

I went ahead and put everybody on standby via Tobey. Then I sat in my window seat I'd cleaned off, covered in the cool newspaper fabric, and piled with red, black, and blue pillows, and I listened for ten minutes. God wasn't saying anything specific. I just felt soothed.

I must have dozed off, because the next thing I knew, Mom was kneeling beside me, smiling and holding two brochures.

"We're all set," she said.

I sat up groggily. "Dad said it was okay?"

"I wouldn't exactly say he gave you his blessing," she said. "But he didn't say he was going to ground us both until we were dead." She wrinkled her nose. "It wasn't that bad, actually. He said he was pretty sure he wasn't going to be able to stop you, so go ahead. He told me to listen in and keep you from doing something off-the-wall."

"Like we would."

She smiled proudly. "That's what I told him."

An unexpected thought came to me. *Poor Dad. He doesn't stand a chance now.*

I motioned toward the brochures. "What are those for?" I said.

She held them up. "Do you think you girls will want six-foot sandwiches from Port-of-Subs or Domino's Pizza?"

I put my arms around her and squeezed. "I love you, Mom," I said.

I think I shocked the heck out of her.

Within the hour everybody was assembled in our family room, including Ms. Race. Everybody, that is, except Cheyenne.

"Wouldn't Tassie let her come?" I said. "I know she's really strict about school nights."

"I don't think Cheyenne even asked her," Tobey said. "She just said she couldn't make it."

"She's been acting way weird lately," Marissa said. "I said hi to her in the hall today, and she just blew past me like she was after somebody."

"I thought it was just me she was mad at," I said.

Shannon's blue eyes grew saucer-size. "Why would she be mad at you? Without you she would have probably ended up back at Wittenberg or run away and started doing drugs and a bunch of other stupid stuff—"

She stopped abruptly and gave a violent shrug. We were all staring at her, and with good reason. Her face was kind of a livid purple and her voice had wound up like a spring. It was my guess that it wasn't just Cheyenne she was talking about.

"So let's get started," Brianna said.

"Should we do like we did for Tobey?" Marissa said. "I remember we figured out what needed to be done, and then we all said what part we could do."

"The first thing that has to be decided is whether you're going to turn in the real cheaters or not," Ms. Race said.

"I know we're not supposed to try to solve each other's problems," Brianna said. Her eyes flashed. "But I say hang the suckers."

"That's my first reaction," Tobey said. She looked puzzled. "But I don't think that's right."

"It goes against the whole honor-council concept," I said. "I'd be a hypocrite if I just did it out of revenge."

"I think that's your answer," Ms. Race said. "It isn't so much what you do as why you do it. What's in your heart?"

"Bottom line?" I said.

They all nodded.

"I still want to help them, hokey as that sounds," I said. "And I don't think I can do it by just letting it go. Plus, my honor really is important to me. I want to prove my innocence."

"You are awesome, girl," Brianna said. "I could never be that big about it."

"That's definitely inspiring," Tobey said.

"Oh, man," I said. For a minute, that was all I could say. Believe that, if you can.

"So you turn them in," Brianna said. "No big deal. You just go and do it. But proving that you didn't do it, that's where we come in."

We spread out a big piece of white poster paper on the coffee table and broke out the Magic Markers.

"If my mama had a marble coffee table," I heard Brianna mutter, "she wouldn't let me near it with no markers."

On it, we made an outline of what had to be proven:

(1) Just because I knew how to operate the computer in the journalism room didn't mean I operated Mr. Uhles's.

(2) Although I was given the code, I didn't use it.

(3) The envelope of money found in my locker was planted there.

"They cited Monday, November 17 as one example of a day I did the dirty deed," I said. "That's just one day, and they're suggesting this has been going on since last year. But I remember that day—that's the day we were having the pop quiz and Mr. Uhles's computer codes were given to me." I got a big pang of guilt. "I almost used them, too."

"Almost only counts in horseshoes and hand grenades," Ms. Race said crisply. "Moving on."

It became apparent that none of us knew squat about computers.

"What about that smart little boy you're going out with?" Brianna said, nudging me. "Isn't he Mr. Computer Man?"

"He tinkers," I said.

"Let him tinker with this then," Tobey said. She smiled craftily at the group. "I'm sure he's dying to help."

"Shut up," I said.

"There was no way you could have had time to go into Mr. Uhles's office and get the answer code that day," Shannon said.

"Why not?" I said.

"Because you stood out in the hall with me forever, until Ms. Race came along."

"That's right," Ms. Race said. "I remember that now."

Shannon sat tall on the couch and arranged her pale little face. "If this goes to honor council, I'll testify for you, Norie. Anything I can do to help, I will, if you'll let me."

"Why wouldn't I let you?" I said. "I think it's cool."

"Some people won't let you help them," she said. Her face started to redden again. It was like watching somebody paint themselves with water color. "My little sister, she's so messed up she won't let anybody do anything for her. This kind of makes up for that."

Then she pulled back into herself like a turtle after looking at Ms. Race, who nodded at her and smiled.

Now that was telling, I thought. I made a mental note to be there for Shannon, just as soon as I got through this mess. And with all of them sitting around me, praying and volunteering, I knew I would get through it.

"You know what else might help," Brianna said. "That day I came in the bathroom and that girl was about to go after your face with her fingernails—"

"No way!" Tobey said. "Who was it?"

"One of the people in the cheating ring," I said carefully.

"My testimony on that could be real helpful," Brianna said. "You just say the word."

"Do you need bodyguards?" Marissa said. "Like Tobey had?"

"I don't think so," I said.

Brianna poked Marissa. "She has Mr. Computer Man."

"What about the envelope?" Tobey said. "How are we going to prove that was a plant?"

"I wish we had Cheyenne," I said. "She heard me talking to Deborah right at the beginning. She could at least testify that I didn't ask for money."

"Are you talking about Deborah Zorn?" Tobey said. Her eyes swelled.

I nodded. Okay. It was out of my mouth now. I'd kept it in for so long—as long as I could. But Tassie had been right. I had to help the people I could really help, and this was the only way.

It still felt like a betrayal. But it was a cinch none of the four of them—Deb, Gabe, Lance, or Pavella—had ever thought about it that way when it came to me.

"Aside from the obvious question—Norie Vandenberger has so much money already, why would she need to sell answer keys?—" Tobey said, "I don't think we have much to go on."

But Brianna was shaking her head. "I think some of us should work on Cheyenne," she said. "Marissa, you want to help me find that girl and see what's goin' on with her?"

Marissa nodded enthusiastically. "Yeah, I want to do something," she said.

"Good," Ms. Race said. "And let's pray that something will come to us, okay?"

The next day, it didn't seem to be coming. In fact, it seemed to be going in the other direction. Tobey and Shannon were right outside the door for me when I went to Mr. Holden with the names before school. They said they were praying for all they were worth. But at the end of first period, Deborah and the three guys were at my locker, teeth bared.

"You've made a major mistake, Vandenberger," Lance said.

"You've seen Mr. Holden then," I said.

"Oh yes," Deborah said. She was narrow eyed. "And we told him right there on the spot that we've been paying you through the nose for answer keys. Our lunch money. Our gas money."

"Our church collection plate money," Lance said.

Gabe was punching his fist into his palm. "We'll tell anybody who'll listen."

"And even some who won't listen," Pavella put in.

That, of course, made no sense. Deborah pushed on.

"Mr. Holden says he has to 'pursue' this now, whatever that means."

I decided right then what I wanted it to mean. I left them all standing there and marched to Mr. Holden's office. He was on the phone, but Ms. Race let me wait and rubbed my shoulders until he was free.

"Mr. Holden," I said, "you said the other day that normally you would come to me for advice on this whole cheating fiasco. Well, I'm going to give you some."

"Okay," he said. He was obviously nonplussed.

"I think this thing should go before honor council. That's what it's for—to sort out the facts and give the right consequences. Help people do better."

He studied me for a minute. "You and Deborah obviously can't serve on this case."

"Obviously. We could put at least one other student on. And I trust the teachers on the council. Mr. Dixon is kind of a vigilante, but I think his heart's in the right place."

"I'm sure he'd be glad to know you think that," Mr. Holden said. A faint smile crossed his face. On closer inspection, it was evident he hadn't been sleeping too well. The bags were packed under his eyes. He seemed glad for an excuse to smile.

"I think you're right," he said. "I'd like for the group to handle this. Someone suggested another student that day. Who was it—Tobey L'Orange, maybe?"

I held my breath. If he remembered I'd made the suggestion, it was all over. But he nodded. "I'll call her in." There was a deep sigh. "If it doesn't work on this, we'll know to scrap the whole idea, right?"

"This could definitely make it or break it," I said. "You remember that in the structure of the council, it said we were allowed to provide witnesses and evidence."

"Right."

"Okay. You set the date. I'll be ready."

He glanced at his calendar. "Let's see, this is Wednesday. Let's shoot for Friday."

That gave us two more days to accomplish two more goals. One, to find out why Cheyenne had dropped out of sight and whether she would be willing to testify. Brianna and Marissa told me they had at least cornered her, but she was still dodging the bullet. And, two, we had to come up with proof that until the day the security guard pulled the money envelope out of my locker, I'd never seen it in my life.

God wasn't slapping any of us in the face with the answer to that one, so that afternoon I curled up in my room with my notebook and closed my eyes for much longer than twenty minutes.

What came to me was not at all what I expected. No miraculous finger pointed to the evidence I needed; no still, small voice named the witness who could blow the whole thing to smithereens. But there was this incredible speech that I could use if neither of those miracles occurred.

I wrote it in my notebook. I learned it. I said it over and over in my head for the next two days.

And I waited for Friday.

CHAPTER
EIGHTEEN

IT DIDN'T MATTER THAT I WAS THE ONE WHO HAD SET up the honor council in the first place. It didn't matter that I respected Mr. Lowe, Mr. Uhles, and even Mr. Holden, and that I was pretty sure Mr. Dixon wasn't completely taken in by Deborah's blueberry eyes and undying devotion to mathematics. It didn't matter that Wyatt had told me on the phone Thursday night that Mr. Uhles had let him look at his computer and that because Mr. U. had made some "minor modifications," it would have taken a real hacker, which I am not, to get in without knowing about those—something Deborah probably did know because she was his aide. Nor did it even matter that Wyatt, sitting there at the table, gave me reassuring looks, and that Tobey was right there next to him.

When I walked into that room on Friday after school, none of that mattered. Still no word from Cheyenne. And I still felt like a stranger going on trial in a foreign place where they hanged everybody at sunrise, no matter what they were convicted of.

Except for Wyatt and Tobey, nobody would look at me. Unless you counted Lance, Pavella, Gabe, and Deborah, who were all goring me with their eyes and appeared ready to spit should I look back for too long.

Wyatt got the thing started. We heard the case against us. I had to listen in awe at the intricacies they had worked out with their lies. Pavella shouldn't have been wasting his time on journalism. He was a born fiction writer.

They produced their witnesses first. I gaped when Rhonda

came forward and said all four of them had taken to bumming rides and mooching off of her at lunchtime because they never seemed to have any money.

"Of course they don't," I pointed out when it was my turn. "They stuffed it all in an envelope and put it in my locker!"

Mark Chester, who had been keeping a low profile through this whole thing, sat in the "witness chair" and mumbled that in his opinion Lance, Gabe, Pavella, and Deborah couldn't possibly have made all this up because they were the most honest people he knew.

You don't know that many people, do you, Chester? I thought.

For support, he mentioned that they had been playing Monopoly together for years, and they never cheated.

It was pathetic. But then, so was my "evidence." Shannon and Brianna testified their little hearts out, and Wyatt did his thing about the computers, even going so far as to provide a large drawing as a visual aid. Still, even I knew as I sat there that it was all circumstantial. The question of the envelope full of money hung over me like a guillotine.

Wyatt looked around the table with his eyes pleading. "Is there anything else anybody needs to say before we try to make our decision?" he said.

I raised my hand.

"Go ahead, Norie," Mr. Uhles said. His eyes said, *And please, please make it something we can use.*

I repositioned myself in my seat so I could see my four accusers. None of them even looked like he or she had so much as a butterfly in the stomach. They were going down; they had already "admitted" to taking money for answers. But that didn't seem as important to them as hauling me down with them. They were the ones who needed to hear what I had to say.

Okay, God, I thought hard. *Help me remember what you told me.*

"The only thing that might shed enough light on all this to help everyone see the truth," I said, "is what was behind it in the first place."

"And that is?" Mr. Dixon said, plucking at his beard.

"Gabe, Jerry, Lance, and Deborah have been what I thought were my friends for a long time," I said. "I may not know them as well as I thought I did, but I do know this: Nothing mattered more to any of them, or to me, than being the best at everything we touched. I wish I could say that came from some deep-seated spiritual motivation, but I can't. I think it came from our parents pushing us, the school pushing us, society expecting us to be perfect because we were smart. I think we all bought into what we were being told, which was that if we didn't go to Stanford or Ivy League, we were losers. That if we weren't excellent every minute, we were slackers. And if we didn't win at everything, we were doomed to jobs at McDonald's for the rest of our lives.

"It was the curse of being bright kids. We had no self-esteem. We believed that to be worthwhile human beings, we had to beat everybody else at everything we did. It was like an addiction, because every time we outdid somebody, we needed to do it again and again and again. Rivalry isn't necessarily bad, but it is unhealthy when it makes you think less of yourself when you lose. If you don't dare lose, you'll do whatever it takes to win."

I took a long enough breath to look around the room. They were all listening. That was all I could ask for.

"I've done a lot of thinking and praying about this, and I've learned some things. One is that I am not going to be wonderful at everything. There isn't anything wrong with a B in chemistry because I'm not a scientist, and I never will be. Just because I can't make an A no matter how hard I try doesn't mean I'm stupid or lowly or a failure. Two, I've discovered that in the things I am really good at, like writing, I can't do them well if there is competition. If I'm writing because I want my stuff to be better than Wyatt's or Mark's or Pavella's or Rhonda's, my work basically has no heart. When I'm writing out of passion and a sense of truth, it's right on.

"No amount of cheating could ever give me that. The day I figured that out, I did an about-face in the middle of the hall and left Mr. Uhles's computer codes unused. I told my 'friends' I wanted them to stop stealing answers. I wrote an article that I hoped would wake everybody up to what was going on. And cheesy as it may sound, what I found was my own honor. It absolutely does not matter to me now whether I become valedictorian or get into Harvard or make it into Who's Who. What matters to me is that I can go to bed at night and know that whatever I've accomplished that day, I've done it through hard work and passion and God."

I looked every person in the eye, one by one. I wanted to make sure they were all paying attention. "If that sounds to you like a person who would do what these people claim I've done, then I guess you have reason to doubt me. But whatever you decide, I have something you can't take away from me, and that's my own principles. That's something no envelope of money could ever buy."

There was a full silence in the room. No one moved or made a sound.

Until Gabe stretched his arms above his head and yawned so loudly the Flagpole Girls probably heard it out in the hall. I saw Mr. Holden glare at him.

"Why don't you folks all take a break while we deliberate?" Mr. Uhles said. "We'll call you in when we've come to a decision."

We filed out. I ended up sandwiched between Lance and Gabe.

"Nice speech," Lance hissed at me in reptilian fashion. "Too bad it was all a bunch of bull."

"Come on," Deborah snapped at him.

She pinched his sleeve and took him off who-knows-where with Gabe and Pavella in hot pursuit. I looked for the girls.

Only Shannon was around the corner, waiting with chocolate chip cookies. Ms. Race was there, too. I passed up the cookies and took the latte she pressed into my hand.

They had a jillion questions. I answered some, but I was too drained to even ask where everybody else was. I slid down along the wall and sat on the floor.

"I don't think I can talk about this anymore," I said. "I'm exhausted."

"You look it," Ms. Race said. "But I bet it's a good kind of tired."

I had to cock my head over that one. "It is," I said. "I got to say everything I wanted to. But, you guys . . ." I sighed heavily. "I don't think it's enough to prove anything one way or the other."

"We've been praying," Shannon said.

"Thanks," I said.

"Well, well," Ms. Race said suddenly. "Would you look who's coming down the hall?"

We all leaned in and saw Brianna and Marissa emerging from the shadows of the lockers, looking like bookends to a little waif of a figure with hair straggling in her face. It was unmistakably Cheyenne.

When she got closer, we also saw that her face was about the color of a bowl of oatmeal and her wonderful lips were trembling. She was either being chased by a pack of Nazis or she was demon possessed—that's how scared she looked.

"Cheyenne, what on earth?" Ms. Race said. "What is it, honey?"

Cheyenne just stood there with everything on her shaking, including her feather earrings.

"That isn't tellin' them anything, girl," Brianna said. "You're going to have to start by openin' your mouth."

"Is it over?" she said.

"Norie's review?" Shannon said. "No, they're in there making a decision."

"Is it too late?" Marissa asked.

"For what?" I said.

"For more evidence," Brianna said.

"There is no more evidence, " I said. "What are you talking about?"

Cheyenne plastered her hands over her face. "They wouldn't believe me anyway, would they? They know I was a cheater; why would they believe me?"

She was starting to get hysterical. Marissa rubbed her shoulder, and Shannon shyly edged closer to her. Brianna got right in her face.

"Get ahold of yourself, girl," she said. "You have to go in there now and tell what you saw!"

Ms. Race cut through all of us and took Cheyenne by the shoulders. "Do you really know something that could help Norie?"

Cheyenne nodded, tears and snot pouring from her facial orifices.

"She does," Marissa said. "We kind of saw it, too."

"Don't move," Ms. Race said.

She strode off down the hall, raw silk East Indian print flapping out behind her.

"Can you make them believe me, Norie?" Cheyenne said. She could barely catch her breath.

"I don't know," I said. "I don't even know what you're talking about."

"I think you ought to calm down, Cheyenne," Shannon said. "If you're going to tell anybody anything, you have to be able to talk. Anybody got a Kleenex?"

"What is going on?" I said to Brianna.

"We came in on the tail end," she said. "We been trailin' this girl for days, and I mean to tell you, she has a real future as an escape artist."

Just then Ms. Race reappeared around the corner and waved us all toward her. "The council says they'll hear what you have to say. Now, Cheyenne, I want you to sit up straight and tell them the truth, just like you did at your hearing, you understand?"

Cheyenne nodded numbly. Whatever it was she knew, I had very little faith that she was going to be able to speak a word of it, even with Marissa and Brianna propping her up. But I followed them and Ms. Race into the room and gave Shannon one last bewildered look before they shut the door behind me.

It took a minute for the buzzing to stop, especially from Deborah and her crew. Pavella practically had to be gagged. Tobey looked like she was going out of her mind with curiosity.

When Wyatt finally had our attention, he looked at Cheyenne. "Ms. Race says you have some important information that might help us out." He glanced at his fellow council members. "We all remember that you were truthful with us before; so we think we can count on you to be perfectly honest."

Cheyenne nodded until I thought her head would bounce off. "You can," she said faintly. "I will."

"Could you speak up?" Mr. Dixon barked.

Cheyenne winced, and I wanted to slug him. This guy really needed to attend a sensitivity class.

"Just a little louder, dear," Mr. Lowe said, "So we can all hear you."

"Tell us what you know, Cheyenne," Wyatt said.

Cheyenne looked at him and talked as if he were the only person in the room. It seemed to calm her down.

"When I was caught cheating," she said, "I was really ashamed in front of Norie because I think she's the neatest person I've ever known, except maybe for Tassie, that's my foster mom—"

"We know," Mr. Dixon said. He sat back impatiently in his chair.

"And then when she got accused of stealing and doing all the other stuff you guys said she did, I thought if I could find a way to help her and prove you all were wrong, then I wouldn't look so bad to her. That might sound stupid to you, but—"

"Doesn't sound stupid at all," Wyatt said. "Go on."

I distinctly heard Gabe mutter, "Sounds stupid to me."

"Okay, so I started following . . ." She looked around the room and her eyes fell on Deborah with a thud. "I started following her around."

" 'Her' meaning Deborah Zorn?" Mr. Uhles said.

"Is that her name?"

"Deborah, raise your hand," Mr. Holden said.

Deborah did, for about a half a second. Cheyenne nodded.

"Yeah, that's her. I started following her around."

"Why?" Wyatt said.

"Because I heard her one day trying to get Norie to join in with their cheating thing."

"Really?" Mr. Dixon said. He sat forward again and pierced his little beady eyes through Cheyenne. "And what did Norie say?"

"She was worried about them getting caught."

"Did Norie say anything about money? Did Deborah mention cash?"

Cheyenne shook her head "No. But when Norie got accused, even before she told their names, I knew she—" Cheyenne poked a finger toward Deborah, "had something to do with it. I didn't trust her."

Cheyenne, who was now calmed almost to normal-for-Cheyenne, leveled her eyes at Deborah. She was suddenly no longer our sweet baby Flagpole Girl. I saw a malice on her face that would have given me pause had I seen it in a dark alley.

Just as quickly it disappeared, and she looked back at Wyatt. "I do that thing with the notebook that Norie does."

"What 'thing'?" Mr. Dixon said.

"I listen to God for ten minutes, and then I write down what I heard. That's how I knew to follow Deborah."

Mr. Dixon's beard seemed to come to some kind of incredulous attention. "You're telling us God told you to trail the girl?"

"I don't think it matters where she got the idea," Mr. Uhles said. "Cheyenne, tell us what happened when you did it."

"I've been following her for a couple of days," Cheyenne said. "She didn't do anything suspicious until just now."

" 'Just now,' meaning when?" Mr. Dixon said. He had suddenly turned into the prosecuting attorney here.

"When you let everybody out so you could decide," she said. "I was hanging around outside and I saw them—"

"Them?" Mr. Dixon said.

Cheyenne pointed to Deborah and her group.

"We know who you mean," Mr. Uhles said. He slanted his eyes briefly at Mr. Dixon.

"I saw them running down the hall to the lockers so I followed them and hid behind a trash can."

"You should have hidden in it," Pavella hissed under his breath.

"And what did they do?" Wyatt said.

"They went right to Norie's locker, and Deborah opened it."

"How did you know it was Norie's locker?" Mr. Dixon said.

Cheyenne looked at him as if he were a complete imbecile.

"I've been there a million times," she said. "Norie's my tutor. I hang out with her."

"Good enough," Mr. Lowe said. "Continue, dear."

I was loving it that he was calling her "dear," that Mr. Uhles was giving her his undivided attention, and that even Mr. Dixon was totally into it. I let myself feel a little hope.

"Deborah opened the locker, and that guy—" She poked her finger in Lance's direction. "—handed her a box, and she stuck it inside."

"What was in the box?" Mr. Dixon said.

"I don't know," Cheyenne said impatiently. "That kid—" She pointed to Pavella. "—asked her the same thing."

"What did she tell him?"

Cheyenne sat up straight in the chair. This was the biggie, I could tell. She was steeling herself. "She said, 'It's what Vandenberger needed the money for. Just in case they let her go after that bunch of blank she just fed the council.'"

" 'Bunch of blank'?" Mr. Dixon said. He looked mystified at the other teachers.

"I'm not allowed to use language like that," Cheyenne said. "Tassie won't let us."

"We wouldn't want to cross Tassie now, would we?" Mr. Dixon said.

But he bordered on a smile, and I let that one go.

"Did anybody else see this take place?" Wyatt said.

Marissa nodded timidly. Brianna stuck her hand right up in the air.

"We did," she said. "Well, we got there just as they were all talkin'—those four guys and Deborah." Brianna took a second to curl her lip.

"Was the locker open?" Mr. Dixon said. He actually looked hopeful.

Brianna had to shake her head. My heart sank.

"I heard it slam when we came around the corner," Marissa said. "He still had his hand on it."

Mr. Dixon grunted and sat back. The others looked disappointed. I was about to consume all my fingernails.

"How did they just happen to be there anyway?" Deborah burst out. "You know these girls are all tight. They're all in some kind of religious organization together. They would say anything."

"We were following Cheyenne because we thought she was in some kind of trouble," Brianna spat back at her. "We take care of our friends!"

"Why can't we just go down to the locker, you guys?" Cheyenne cried. "That box is in there!"

"Good idea," Mr. Holden said.

"Mr. Holden, come on!" Deborah stood up, gangly arms gesturing like she was about to have a seizure. "She's making this up. They put her up to this."

"Why don't you just shut up!"

We all jolted in our chairs as Cheyenne came up out of hers.

"My friends are not liars, not like you people who think you're so good."

"Uh, Cheyenne, why don't you back off and take us to Norie's locker, huh?" Mr. Uhles said.

He took her gently by the shoulder and steered her toward the door. I looked at Wyatt, and I almost spewed a laugh all the way across the table. He was still staring at Cheyenne's empty chair with his mouth flopping open. If my entire reputation hadn't been hanging in the air at that moment, I could have gotten a lot of mileage out of that look.

Except for Tobey's holding on tight to my hand, we looked like something out of *Dragnet,* trooping down the hall toward the lockers with our faces all grim and the tension springing out of our pores. We picked up Shannon, Ms. Race, and a couple of afterschool stragglers along the way, so that by the time we reached my locker, I had to elbow my way through a crowd to get to it.

"No, Norie," Mr. Holden said. "Let Deborah open it."

Only after she took a half-step toward it did Deborah stop and snap, "I don't know the combination."

Everyone exchanged significant glances as Mr. Holden nodded to me, and I spun the lock. You could feel the entire hall holding its breath as I pulled open the door.

And then they gave a unanimous gasp.

There really was a box right there in my locker.

"Ever seen this before, Norie?" Mr. Holden said.

"No," I said. "Never."

He turned to Cheyenne. "Is this the box you saw Deborah put in there?"

"Yup," Cheyenne said, beaming. "She stuck it right in there."

"What's in it?" Mr. Dixon said.

Mr. Holden held the box in his palm, removed the lid, and pulled back a layer of tissue paper. His face was already going gray when he looked up at us.

"Marijuana," he said. "And a great deal of it."

"That's what she needed the money for!" Gabe said.

"How did she buy it?" Wyatt said.

"What do you mean?" Mr. Uhles said.

"Didn't you confiscate the money in the envelope?" Wyatt said.

Mr. Holden nodded.

"Then what did she use to buy the dope?"

Lance fiddled with his goatee. "She wouldn't need that much money to make a buy like that," he said. "It isn't that expensive if you know who to go to."

"Really?" Mr. Dixon said. "How would you know?"

"It's common knowledge," Gabe said in his usual bull-in-a-china-shop fashion. "He's not stupid. You make it sound like we're so stupid."

"You are," Mr. Holden said. "Otherwise, why would you have left this in here?"

Heads jerked toward him. He was holding a small slip of paper in his hand.

"What is it?" Mr. Dixon said.

"It's a credit-card receipt," Mr. Holden said gravely. "It was under the tissue paper in the bottom of the box." He held it up so he could see it through his bifocals. " 'Libby Zorn,' " he read. And then he looked at Deborah. "Isn't that your mother, Deborah?"

"DO YOU THINK WE HAVE ENOUGH FOOD, NORIE?" MOM
asked.

"For the entire city of Reno? Yes," I said. "The only thing
missing is duck under glass."

Mom cocked her sleek head at the table. "I didn't think you
kids liked stuff like that."

"We don't, Mom," I said. "I was kidding. This looks incredible, okay?"

She nodded thoughtfully at the spread on the bar in the family room. Every special from Famous Murphy's was represented
there, including my own personal favorite, chicken nachos.

"You sure you don't mind that I ordered out?" she said. "I
know I embarrass you sometimes, but I just wanted this to be
special for your friends. They've done so much. And it was short
notice."

"I'm not embarrassed," I said. And I wasn't. Her throwing
this together between the time I got home from the review and
8:00 P.M. kind of touched me. The minute I'd walked in the door
and told her what had happened, she had insisted on treating
everybody who had "saved" me.

"What about Dad?" I had said.

"I'm sure he'll be appreciative," she said.

I didn't point out that she was being delusional. Instead, I
just phoned the Flagpole Girls.

And now I could hear people stomping through the snow to
the front door.

"I hope nobody had trouble getting up the hill in this storm," Mom said.

"They would walk to get here, Mom," I said. "Any excuse for a party."

They were definitely in a festive mood, all of them. Brianna and Ira were having a snowball fight when I opened the front door, and Diesel was carrying Cheyenne on his back and promising the next ride to Tobey. Marissa was carrying a huge platter of Christmas cookies, and Shannon handed me three loaves of banana bread that her mother had insisted on sending with her. Wyatt brought up the rear singing "Jingle Bells."

Several of us told him not to quit his day job.

With all of them, Ms. Race, and Mom, we filled up even our family room. My mother was grinning like her former beauty queen self as we all jostled elbows to fill our plates.

"This really makes it feel like home," she said to Ms. Race.

"It's obviously always been a great home," Ms. Race said. "Or Norie wouldn't have turned out the way she has."

As I checked to make sure Diesel wasn't taking all the chicken nachos, I heard the sadness in my mother's voice. "I don't know," she said. "I think you and this group might have had a lot to do with it. We should have had more of this in our house."

It gave me a bittersweet pain, right around my heart. I wasn't the only one who had missed out on not having God in the house. I decided to show Mom the notebook thing first chance I could. In fact, a package of spirals might make a great Christmas present.

"What's all this?" The voice bit the air from the direction of the doorway. It definitely chewed right into the party atmosphere. Everybody quieted down—and I felt my hackles starting to wake up.

"Dr. Vandenberger," Wyatt said briskly. "How are you, sir?"

"A little surprised at the moment," Dad said.

He searched the room with his eyes for my mother. He found me first. We clenched gazes for a full fifteen seconds before I could decide what to say.

"We're celebrating," I said.

"Oh?" he said. "You've been exonerated then?"

"In spades," I said.

There was another awkward silence. Even Ms. Race looked squeamish.

"Well," Dad said finally. "Do I get the details?"

"She was awesome," Cheyenne said.

"That certainly tells it all," Wyatt murmured.

But we did tell it all. We settled ourselves on the couches and the floor and pieced it all together for my father. He wasn't the easiest room to work. He never smiled, and he penetrated everybody with his eyes when they talked. But at least he didn't clear the house and tell my mother to start packing.

When we reached the part that happened after the council took us back into the room, everybody leaned in. They still didn't know the outcome.

"There wasn't much they could do but own up," I said. "And, man, were they ticked."

Tobey rolled her eyes. "Oh yeah."

"We're talking smoke coming out of the ears, dagger eyes, the whole bit," Wyatt said. "If looks could have killed, we would be hauling Norie to the funeral home about now."

"All right, boy," Brianna said. "We get the point. You don't have to be so morbid."

"Anyway," I said, "Mr. Holden offered to let me help decide their consequences. Deborah piped right up and said not to bother giving them any rehab. They just wanted to take their punishment and get it over with. They weren't interested in counseling, blah, blah, blah."

Shannon's eyes popped. "I can't believe that."

"What punishment did they get?" Cheyenne said. She looked like she was hoping for the death penalty.

"I didn't say too much after that," I said. "Just meting out punishment was never what I had in mind for honor council."

"What else could you do if they refused help though, Norie?" Ms. Race said.

"I hope you hanged them," my father said.

Wyatt shrugged. "We did what we thought was right. Ten days' suspension, and each teacher they cheated on gets to decide whether to fail them or not. Mr. Uhles is failing them all for the semester unless they want to come in one day during Christmas vacation and take new tests."

"Is he going to do a body-cavity search on them first?" Brianna said.

"And that's just for the cheating infractions," Wyatt said. "The authorities will handle the marijuana thing."

"We're talking about police records then," Dad said. He nodded his approval to that.

"What about what they did to you?" Marissa said. "Is there going to be any punishment for that?"

I blew at my bangs. "I don't think you can make somebody regret something like that," I said. "Do you guys know that weed parable thing?"

Shannon nodded slowly. "You're talking about the one where the farmer says don't pull up the weeds because you might pull up the good stuff, too?"

"That's the one," I said. "I think that applies here. Some things I think we just have to leave to God. You know what I'm saying?"

There was a unanimous nod. Except for my father, who cleared his throat. I started to cringe. "I'd like to say something here," he said.

They all shushed each other as if we were in class. Make that, in court. All rise. The Honorable Judge Quinton Vandenberger presiding—that kind of thing.

He crossed his arms over his chest and used one hand to stroke his beard à la Mr. Dixon. But he surprised me.

"I have to say I'm grateful to you all," he said. "I was ready to go to the school board. I would have if Noreen hadn't been determined to do it her own way. Typical."

There were some nervous snickers. Nobody knew how to take my father. Except perhaps Ms. Race.

"They're a wonderful group," she said. "We appreciate your thanks, but it's entirely unnecessary. We did it because we love Norie."

"She's awesome!" Cheyenne cried. She flung herself across three people to give me a hug. Over her shoulder I saw my father, shall we say, looking askance.

It may or may not have turned into a really mushy, disgusting group slobber thing if suddenly Diesel hadn't said, "Shh! Everybody shh!"

"What?"

Diesel stepped over Ira and Brianna and went to the window, scowling and getting his arms into fight mode.

"What's goin' on?" Ira said.

It was like they had some sixth sense for trouble or something.

Even as Diesel stood there, something smashed against the window. The glass shivered, and a glob of snow ran down the pane.

Another blob hit the other window, and we could hear the same kind of battering in the front of the house. My father took the big foyer area in about three steps with the rest of us squealing and scrambling to our feet.

"Get back," Dad said.

Diesel and Ira really paid attention to that. They were flanking him when he opened the front door. It was snowing like crazy. All we could see were headlights careening like wild laser beams, and all we could hear was the unmistakable whir of a car spinning its wheels on ice.

"Quint, what is going on?" Mom said from the back of the mob that had formed in the doorway.

"Oh, for Pete's sake!" Dad said.

He stooped down and picked up something that he held over his head for us to see. It was the broken half of an eggshell.

"Somebody egged your house?" Brianna said.

Ira broke out the door and called back to us. "Egged. Rocked."

"You got a mess on your hands," Diesel said from beside him.

Dad mowed his way through us as he headed back into the house. The rest of us piled out the door and stared. A good four dozen eggs were plastered all over our walkways, driveway, and the windows.

But our attention was on the car that was still gunning its motor on the road at the bottom of the driveway and going nowhere.

"They're stuck on the ice," Tobey said.

"Who is it?" Brianna said. "Ira, go see who it is."

"I'll help," Wyatt said. He shouldered his way out from between Marissa and me and did this macho stride with the "guys" across the snow.

"You kids be careful!" Ms. Race called out.

"Hey!" I said.

They stopped and turned.

"No revenge thing, okay? They're just being stupid."

Wyatt turned his thumb up, and they trotted on down to the car.

"Well, I'm not going to stand here and miss out on the fun," Brianna said.

She took off after them, and so did the rest of us. I could hear Ms. Race and my mother admonishing us from the porch.

By the time we reached the car, Diesel was tapping on the glass on the passenger side. Whoever was inside was refusing to open the window.

Wyatt brushed the snow off and squinted in. When he straightened up he looked for me and gave me a you-are-not-going-to-believe-this look.

"Who is it?" I said.

Then I saw for myself. There was no mistaking Rhonda's out-of-control head of blonde hair.

I knocked hard on the window, and she finally rolled it down. Beside her, in the driver's seat, was Mark.

"What the Sam Hill are you two doing?" I said.

Neither one of them could answer.

Behind me, Brianna gave a snort. "You call this retaliation?" she said. "Pretty weak."

"Eggs and a couple of rocks?" Tobey said. "It couldn't have meant that much to you, if you ask me."

"Give it up," Shannon said.

I grinned at Wyatt. Shannon acting tough? It was too cute.

"All right, look," Wyatt said. "I'm freezing my tail off. You want some help or what?"

"I can do it," Mark said.

"Uh-huh," Ira said. "You're gonna be here till New Year's doin' it this way. Diesel, you and Wyatt push from the back."

"What about us?" I said. "Girls can do this."

Ira rolled his eyes. "Get on it then. All of you. Let's get this heap out of here."

"Hey, wait," I said. "One more thing."

Rhonda had the window halfway rolled back up when I put my hand on it.

"You two still have a chance to stay straight," I said. "Stay away from this kind of stuff, okay? You're better than this."

Rhonda didn't say anything. She looked at Mark, who looked at me and shrugged.

"Well, at least they didn't tell you where to go," Tobey said to me as we were walking back up to the house arm in arm, with Mark's car slipping and sliding back toward Reno.

"They're gone?" Dad said.

He was standing on the front porch, phone in hand.

"Yeah, we got them unstuck," I said. "They're basically harmless, Dad."

"They need prayer," Cheyenne said.

She sounded like such a little geek saying it, and yet I wanted to hug her. So I did.

My dad looked at us. All of us. And then he clicked off the phone.

"Who were you calling?" I said.

"The cops," he said. "But I guess we don't need them."

"Nope," I said. "We have it handled."

"Yeah," he said. "It looks that way."

It was hard to believe that we only had one more week left before Christmas vacation. We got the paper out and printed by Friday. The wrap-up on the cheating thing was the talk of the school.

"Looks like Pulitzer material," Mrs. Abbey said to me.

"Thanks," I said. "But wait till you see what we have going for the next issue."

Wyatt, Tobey, Shannon, and I were already planning ways to change the pressure-to-excel thing so it wouldn't strip us all of our personalities. Mark actually came up to me in fourth period one day and said he wanted to be in on it. Rhonda didn't. She was still pouting because Mrs. Abbey had demoted her from co-editor and put Wyatt in her place.

"She's overextended," Mrs. Abbey said, as she fumbled around on her desk for her calendar book.

I told Ms. Race she needed to talk to the woman.

By the time we left for vacation, I had a solid B in both chemistry and trig. I looked up the requirements for Northwestern before I went to my father with that news.

"I really don't want to go to Harvard, Dad," I said. "I'd rather apply to some good journalism schools."

"Harvard's going to look a lot better on your resumé when you start applying to graduate schools," he barked at me.

I stared at him. "Dad, I'm sixteen years old. Why do I have to think about graduate school now? I'd like to live this moment first, if that's okay with you."

He rocked back and forth and jingled the change in his pockets. I was about to get told I was a bleeding-heart liberal.

But then he took his hands out and rubbed them together. "Okay," he said. "Do what you want. I guess I can't stop you."

I could have let it go at that and counted it as a victory. But I couldn't. Not after everything that had gone down. "You know, Dad," I said, "I do listen to you. If it weren't for your pushing me, I might not have the high standards I have—and that isn't all bad. I just don't want them to eat me up so I have no soul, okay?"

"Oh, now I have no soul," he said.

"Non sequitur, Dad," I said.

"Touché," he said.

That conversation made it easier when a few days later I decided to quit Academic Olympics. I'd missed a lot of meetings anyway, and I just didn't have a passion for it anymore. Maybe I never had a passion for it.

"Give me one good reason you should quit," Dad said, "Other than you want more time for this boyfriend."

"Right, like I'm going to let some guy stand in the way of something I really want," I said.

"All right. You have me on that. What's your reasoning?"

"I have no desire to be the best at something that is absolutely pointless."

"Being sharp is pointless?"

"No, spitting out a bunch of answers I've memorized is pointless. Now, if I'm going to actually use that information to help somebody, that's a whole other thing."

"You're a bleeding-heart liberal," he said. But he didn't jingle his change or rock on his heels. That was progress.

And you talk about progress, my mother was making it by leaps and bounds. She went to church with me the Sunday after the review, and she got all excited about putting an Advent wreath on our table, going to Christmas Eve services, and making a resolution to go to church every Sunday in the New Year.

"That's great, Mom," I said when we were on the way home through the snow in Iggy. "But there's a little more to it than going to church."

"I know," she said. "I can see it in you. But it's a start."

I glanced at her sideways. "You're really starting to stand up to Dad."

"I am, aren't I?" she said. She glowed like a little girl. "I love your father. I really do. But I'm thinking I deserve to be treated with more respect. I thought I could start with treating myself with more, and I think maybe I can get that from God."

"Yikes, Mom," I said. "You're farther along than I thought."

"I am, aren't I?" she said. "You want to have a cappuccino and talk when we get home?"

That last week of school, I finally started doing some Christmas shopping. Ms. Race and I went to the mall one evening after school. We ended up back at her place wrapping presents and drinking eggnog. Her apartment was decorated to the hilt. She had Christmas tree ornaments from all over the world, and she had the neatest South American nativity scene. It made me feel I was right there at the first Feliz Navidad.

"So what do you want for Christmas, Norie?" she asked me.

"I've already received a major gift," I said. "I don't need anything else right now."

"That's too bad," she said. "Because I have something for you anyway."

She handed me a wrapped present, which I tore into like a five-year-old. I wasn't quite truthful about not wanting anything; I love presents.

When the paper fell away and I opened the box, I could only say, "Wow."

It was a gorgeous pen, hand painted in black, red, and bright blue on a ceramic case.

"You have to have a special pen for the God-writing," she said. "This one's from Thailand."

"I'd love to go there someday," I said.

"What about this coming summer?"

I stared at her.

"That's where I'm going on a mission in June," she said. "There's always room for one more."

"You're serious?"

"Norie, there is no one I would rather take on a spiritual journey."

"Yikes," I said. And then again, I said, "Yikes."

The first thing I wrote in my God-notebook with the new pen—that very night—were the criteria for choosing what I would go after. It has to involve the excitement of learning, God told me. And there has to be satisfaction in the process. And you need to take pleasure in cooperating with other people.

That was why I continued to fine-tune the honor council. And drain the Flagpole Girls for what they thought were significant issues we should feature in the *King's Herald*. It was also why I started a short story, tutored Cheyenne—who was diagnosed with dyslexia and put in a special reading class—three days a week, and saw Wyatt whenever I could.

"Are we, like, a couple?" I said to him a few days before Christmas when we were driving around looking at the lights.

He leaned back in the seat and studied the windshield.

"What are the rules?" he said.

"Rules for romance?" I said. "That sounds like an oxymoron."

"Who are you calling a moron?"

"You if you don't stay on the subject. Come on, I'm trying to be serious."

"I don't know," he said. "I've never actually gone out with somebody before. I've also never liked anybody the way I like you. I want you to laugh at my jokes and think I have a profile like Antonio Banderas. How am I doing so far?'

"You're disgusting," I said. "But I think we're on the right track."

"So let's just make it up as we go along," he said. "God . . . I mean, I think we have to consider He won't let us mess this up."

"Okay," I said. "I like it."

There was one more passion I tapped into. It met all the criteria and besides, it was the most fun I'd had in a long time. Christmas Eve, I delivered a gift to each of the Flagpole Girls. They all received the same thing, only each one was decorated differently.

It was a poster, and it had a message on it that came to me straight from God. I liked it so much, I made one for my own wall.

It goes like this:

> Listen. Listen. Listen.
> Don't criticize. Don't compare. Don't compete.
> Only create.
> And celebrate.

And I do, every chance I make.

I guess the rules have definitely changed.

Join millions of other students in praying for your school! See You at the Pole, a global day of student prayer, is the third Wednesday of September each year. For more information, contact:

See You at the Pole
P.O. Box 60134
Fort Worth, TX 76115
24-hour SYATP Hotline: 619/592-9200
Internet: www.syatp.com
e-mail: pray@syatp.com